SIL

"You'll do as I say." It was a command with no attempt made to soften its authority.

Byrony's head came up with a snap. "Think again. We are not wed yet." She tried unsuccessfully to pull away from him. "Let me go." Her eyes flashed silver fire.

Deveril tightened his grasp on her shoulders. "You want taming," he gritted between clenched teeth.

"Not by you."

Deveril dragged her close. Byrony fought him with all her strength. "Let me go, damn you. You have no right." Trying to kick him in the shins was useless in the thin slippers she wore.

Deveril tightened his hold until her writhing body was pressed against his. He pinned her arms to her side and dipped his head. "Go ahead—fight me. I like spirit and you have plenty."

There was no escaping the lips that crushed down upon hers . . .

THE DUCHESS AND THE DEVIL

SYDNEY ANN CLARY

ZEBRA BOOKS
KENSINGTON PUBLISHING CORP.

ZEBRA BOOKS

are published by

Kensington Publishing Corp.
475 Park Avenue South
New York, NY 10016

Second printing: January, 1991

Printed in the United States of America

Prologue

Byrony crossed the crowded street, barely hearing the noise of the men working on the dock. Disappointment held sway over the bustle of the seaport. A few miles. So close and yet so far. A glance over one shoulder to the open sea beyond the harbor was torture. England lay across the channel beyond reach. No passage either within or without the ships clustered in the bay was to be found at any price. Turning away, Byrony finished the short walk to the gabled inn in weary defeat.

Sadly derelict, the lodge carried the same aroma of defeat and hard times that plagued most of the town. Byrony scarcely noticed for the past was littered with worse places than was wise to remember. But this time was different. The need greater. Mama slept in one of the upper rooms watched over by the slattern the proprietor called wife. There was a door, a great oaken thing that was more warped than beautiful, which opened onto a narrow, uneven flagstone passage. Rickety stairs to another dim hall gained the wayfarers a measure of quiet from the noise of the tap room on the lower floor. Byrony knew the sounds, the smells but minded them not at all.

"So you be back." The pockmarked woman sitting beside the narrow pallet rose when Byrony entered. "Did ya book passage, young sir?"

"It was as you said. There was nothing to be found."

Byrony stared at the figure lying still as death itself on the hard bed. Julia Balmaine, once a beautiful and sought-after heiress, was wasted to a mere shadow. She breathed in shallow gasps but didn't awaken at the sound of voices. It was her wish to die in England that had led them to this dismal inn on the French coast. It was death that dogged her footsteps and had Byrony moving heaven and hell itself to take her home one last time.

"We must get to Dover. Is there no other way?"

"Only the smugglers. But a lad like you with a sick mother wouldn't stand a chance against the likes of them cutthroats. They'd slice your gullet for sport and toss you both over the side for shark bait." The proprietress had developed a liking for the soft-spoken gentleman. He treated her like a lady with his polite madam this and that. She didn't wish him to come to such an end.

"We'll have to chance it. When needs must the devil drives."

The woman laid a dirty hand on the youth's arm. "Perhaps the wait of a day or two would be best for your mother." Personally she didn't think the woman would last the night and then the sprig's journey would've been wasted.

"No. We can't wait. We must go on." Byrony knew what the woman was thinking. But they had to go on. Mama would have her wish. She had asked so little of life and given so much. It was time someone put her comfort first as her husband had never done.

"Then talk to my husband. Mayhap he can aid you."

Byrony turned to her. "How?"

The woman shrugged. "He knows the captains. He plays cards with them most nights."

"Cards?" Excitement coursed through Byrony. This could be providence finally coming to their aid. "Where?"

"The room off the tap room." Now that she had spoken,

she wished she hadn't. If she didn't get a belt for telling the young mister about the private game, her name wasn't Paulette Bouchard.

"Could I join this game?"

Paulette's eyes widened at the idea. "No! No! My husband, he would kill me. And you don't want to be doing that no way. The men cheat and many a time the cards end in a fight. It's no place for a lad like you."

"When needs must the devil drives," Byrony muttered yet again before heading for the door. "Where can I find your husband?"

Paulette wrung her hands. "In the tap room. Don't do it. They'll strip you cleaner than a chicken ready for the stew pot," she pleaded.

Byrony smiled. It wasn't a humorous gesture and the look in the steel gray eyes matched the suddenly mature lines on the beardless face. "I think not, my good woman. I think not."

Paulette shook her head as the door closed gently behind the youth. She had thought him a mere boy. The look he had just given her held too much knowledge for her to believe that any longer. Suddenly she shivered and pulled the tattered shawl more closely about her body. She hoped he did get into the game. The sooner the changeling was out of her house, the better. Sick mother or no, there was something odd about the gentleman.

Byrony neither knew nor cared what the proprietress thought. There was a chance, a slim one, based only on the skill and daring that had been the mainstay of the Balmaine luck. Smooth talking learned at a father's knee won a place in the game for the night. A few coins in a worn pocket and a thin sandwich were all the fortification needed to begin a wager that would gain them the passage so urgently needed.

Smoke was thick in the room, as were the spectators. Byrony surveyed the scene and felt a moment of humor at the way all eyes summed up the newcomer in their midst. So they thought to fleece the green one. A smile hovered but was suppressed. So much the better. The others were so certain of their superior skill. Overconfidence often spawned foolish mistakes. Danger and excitement were familiar companions. The ugliness of the surroundings, the coarse talk were ignored. The gold on the table and the grubby stack of paste board in front of Byrony was all that mattered.

Three hours later the gold was no longer in the center of the table. It was in front of Byrony, as was the deal.

"You have most of our money." The words were thick with anger and threat.

Byrony stopped shuffling the cards and looked up. "So it would seem. Do you make a point?"

The man shifted, glancing around at the others seated at the table. No one spoke as they waited for him to make a move. As the acknowledged leader and the one who had lost the most to this stripling, he had first call on his skin.

"You have had an uncommon run of luck."

Byrony nodded. "It happens that way at times." The acknowledgment was light. The hand that slipped to the hidden pocket deft. Byrony touched the cold metal of the small pistol secreted there, taking comfort in the presence of the weapon. What was lacked in number and weight was made up for by the deadly little gun and the skill of the marksman who carried it.

"One last hand. And this time I deal." The captain reached for the cards.

Byrony moved the deck out of range. "I think not. Winner deals."

Angered, the man slammed his hands on the table and half rose.

Byrony intervened. "But I offer you a chance to get even and, perhaps, to make a bit on the side."

For a long moment greed and pride warred for supremacy. "What kind of deal?" he demanded suspiciously.

"I must leave for England on the tide this day. I'll play you for passage and an inside cabin against all the money that you've lost. If I win, you get half your winnings back and I get the passage for me and my mother. If I lose, you get all I have before me." Byrony ignored the gasp of shock that circled the room. It was a bold move and one guaranteed to appeal to the overweight captain.

"Done!" He sat down with a thump and gestured for Byrony to begin.

No one joined this contest. None were invited and none dared to get between the man with the black temper and the slender boy who seemed to know no fear. The cards whispered across the rough table, loud in the silence of the collectively held breath. A flick of a finger. Another card fell. A muted gasp from the audience. Another card. The slim hands holding the deck never faltered. The last card was raised slowly from the stack, then lay on the table. No one moved. Not the boy. Not the man. Not the audience.

The captain raised his eyes. "You won." Amazement was in every syllable.

Byrony separated his winnings from the rest of the haul and pushed them toward him. "We both did. My mother and I will be at your ship within the hour."

Chapter One

A nervous young man clad in the distinctive burgundy livery of Lord Ravensly paused to survey the imposing structure before him. His disbelieving eyes traveled slowly up the pale gray stone to the top of the four-story domicile and its peaked roof. Even in the opulence of the neighborhood the house stood out as a monument to the wealth and power of the noble owner, the Duke of Castleton.

Remembering his earlier elation at being given the important task of conveying his master's letter to his godson, the duke, Jed felt his courage betray him as he realized who the recipient of his lord's message was. Although newly arrived from the country in his master's service, he had quickly become apprised of all the gossip of Quality which he served. The abundance of the tales poured into his receptive ears had dealt almost exclusively with the duke. His incredible wagers were a constant source of speculation and envy to the gentlemen of the Ton and his address with their ladies had caused more than one peer to wish him in Jericho. But the rumors that intrigued Jed more were the ones about his indifference to the aristocracy, of which he was a leading member. He was, it was said, forever saying or doing something which outraged his peers and set the tabbies' tongues awagging. Jed could not wait to see the man in person.

Clutching the fine paper of his lordship's note resolutely, Jed climbed the wide stone steps to lift the gleaming gold knocker from its resting place. It scarcely had time to fall back before the door swung noiselessly open to reveal the stern-faced visage of the butler.

Swallowing the lump that somehow had lodged in his throat, Jed extended the slightly wrinkled letter and hesitantly explained his errand.

"His lordship requested me to wait for an answer." His voice wobbled in spite of his best attempts to steady it as he shifted uneasily under the older man's impassive stare.

Smithington nodded slightly and motioned for him to enter. "You may wait here while I take this up to his grace," he directed as he indicated the broad, straight-backed bench in the alcove next to the entrance.

Jed sat down quickly with a sigh of relief as the butler, his back ramrod straight, slowly mounted the magnificent marble stairway leading to the upper regions. The young footman took the opportunity to look around him with interest. Alert, curious, he surveyed the impressive proportions of the area and the richness of the paintings that adorned the walls. Even to his untutored eye it was an awe-inspiring sight. He could hardly wait to return to the servants hall to regale friends with his experiences.

Smithington tapped softly on the door of the master suite and waited. In a moment the panel was opened by Meade, his grace's valet. In a whisper, the butler explained his presence and handed over the note into Meade's capable hands.

Deveril St. John, the seventh Duke of Castleton, slept on, unaware of the activity going on around him. As usual he had arrived home just before dawn. It had been a very profitable evening judging from the weight of his pockets.

Contrarily, he had been left feeling restless and dissatisfied and as a result he had imbibed too freely of the excellent brandy offered at his club. Normally a moderate drinker, as of late, he found himself going to extremes to relieve the intolerable boredom of his day-to-day existence. That his excesses gave the tattlemongers fresh gossip bothered him not one wit. The harsher of his critics proclaimed him to be in league with the devil himself, something which amused him greatly when first he heard it.

He continued to be amused when he learned he had been dubbed the Devil Duke. It suited his cynical view of the society in which he lived to pander to the name he was so aptly given. Although by rights, at two and thirty he should have long since ceased to behave so outrageously and settled down to take his place in Parliament, like his noble father, and devote himself to the securing of an heir to inherit his wealth and name. In this endeavor he would have been greatly aided by a wife, had he chosen one.

In his younger days his wealth and title allowed him to look as high as he wished for a bride to grace his table and to share his bed. The matchmaking mamas, after having the best of their crop shunned by his elegant personage, saw the futility of putting their daughters in his way. Not only had Deveril ignored the simpering misses paraded for his inspection but he had a nasty habit of rendering a sharp setdown to anyone foolish enough to try to hold his attention beyond the bounds of a polite greeting. Young schoolroom girls were certainly not his fare. His women, when he chose them, were not only renowned for their flawless beauty but for their experience and intelligence.

Now, however, his reputation made him all but forgotten to all but a few of the peerage. His wicked tongue had earned him many enemies so that he was for all intents and purposes considered a bad wager in the marriage stakes. Of course, he was still a desirable catch for an impoverished title or a family who sought a title to remove the stench of Trade. This state of affairs only increased Deveril's contempt and disdain for most of society. He vowed not to fall prey to any of its hypocrisy or machinations. Deveril St. John lived his life as he chose, answering to no one and laughing at the rules that governed lesser men.

Meade entered the darkened bedroom quietly and approached the raised bed dominating the chamber. With a practiced flick of his hand he pulled the heavy crimson drapes back before he went across to the windows overlooking the side garden and repeated his actions.

Deveril stirred slightly as the bright sunlight streamed into the room banishing the shadows of the night. The duke's face in sleep was wiped clean of its habitual expression of boredom and mocking cynicism. The lips which were usually twisted in a slight sneer were relaxed. He was not a handsome man in the strict sense of the word. In an age when pale, thin, aristocratic features were the vogue, his were dark and rugged with a slightly satanic cast. Even in the vulnerability of slumber he projected an unmistakable magnetism. His raven hair, slightly sprinkled at the temples with gray, sat well with the startling blue of his eyes. Because of his coloring it was rumored there was Irish blood in him, although the Peerage did not show it. As yet, no one had sufficient courage to question the matter openly. When aroused, Deveril had the devil's own temper and the power to give it rein without fear of the consequences. Few men, with the notable exception of His Royal Majesty, dared to say him nay when he desired a favor.

By now the warmth and brightness of the sun penetrated the mists of sleep and wine clouding Deveril's brain. Opening one eye cautiously, he surveyed the thin ferret-like features of the man beside his bed.

"What time is it?" he questioned groggily. "And why the deuce did you wake me? I thought I gave orders I was to sleep undisturbed."

Meade ignored the irate tone, being well acquainted with the duke's unpredictable temper. "It is gone eleven, your grace." He placed a glass filled with a milky liquid within easy reach of his master.

The duke looked over the concoction with a jaundiced eye before, with a shrug of defeat, he picked up the glass and drained its contents with one gulp. "I think you make that witches' brew viler every time. Is it punishment for my sins or a cure for the sinner?" he asked with a quizzical gleam in his eye.

With the familiarity of a valued servant, Meade allowed a small smile to lighten his narrow features. "I wouldn't presume to judge, your grace," he replied.

"Always the perfect valet," he murmured. "I wonder what I would do without your excellent services."

"Well, as to that, I'm sure your grace would do quite well indeed. It is to be hoped, however, you are not required to discover how. I confess I would dislike having to look for a new master. It is unlikely I would be fortunate enough to dress a figure such as yours," he observed blandly.

"So that is the reason you stay. I would have not thought it." As his mind began to clear, he stared pointedly at the paper in the other man's hand. "I suppose you will eventually give me whatever it is you're holding."

Meade handed over the note without a word. The duke accepted the missive and broke the Ravensly seal. A small frown marred his brow as he slowly read the summons it contained.

Your Grace,

It is of the utmost importance I speak to you as soon as is convenient. My day is at your disposal. My servant has been requested to await your answer.

Ravensly

Deveril was silent while he pondered the cryptic words.

Charles rarely asked him for anything and to receive such a summons was unusual to say the least. Clearly, whatever it was that prompted his request was urgent.

"Tell his lordship's messenger to convey my compliments and say I will call upon his master at two this afternoon," he instructed before allowing himself to be shaved and attired for the day.

At precisely two of the clock the duke stepped down from his carriage in front of his godfather's London house. After directing his coachman to wait, he strolled leisurely up the steps and through the door. He was ushered into the book-lined study, where he found Lord Ravensly. With long strides he crossed the room to greet the man who was more like a father to him than his own rigidly cold-blooded sire. Though unspoken, his ties of affection for Charles Ravensly were deeper than he knew with any other living soul. Though richly endowed with wealth, possessions, and power, Deveril had been sadly deprived of love or tenderness of any kind. Only the slender, silver-haired man who rose at his entrance showed him affection untainted by selfish demands.

His lordship's aged features softened in a smile while he surveyed the younger man. The duke's coat of blue superfine cloth and biscuit-colored pantaloons showed not one crease as they molded across his broad shoulders and muscular thighs. Well over six feet in height, he bore himself with easy assurance and unmistakable arrogance.

Once the greetings were dispensed with, the two men seated themselves, the older one behind a massive, heavily carved desk while his visitor settled in a comfortable chair facing him.

"May I offer you some refreshment, your grace?"

Deveril's brows rose at the formality of the address. "Since when have we reverted to titles, Charles?" He paused, a slight smile on his lips. When Charles didn't return his smile, Deveril knew that something untoward was on the horizon. "And no, I don't require anything at present."

Lord Ravensly absently fingered the quill in front of him, trying to find the words needed. His love for Deveril had prompted his summons. His concern for what Deveril was doing to his life had demanded a course Charles feared would put a wedge between him and the man he called son in his heart. He had no choice. He had to make a push to save Deveril from himself. He raised his eyes.

"Actually, Deveril, I am not quite sure how to address you at the moment. Should I use your formal title, your given name, or perhaps your reprehensible nickname by which you are known by everyone from the meanest chimney sweep to his Majesty—Devil Duke! That you should come to this. Kate would weep if she were still alive. I vow I feel the urge myself."

No one since Deveril had come out of short coats, not even Charles, had ever dared to ring peal over his head. Deveril's eyes gleamed with swift and unconcealed anger. Only the affection in which he held Charles stayed the lash of his temper. "I assume I have displeased you in some way, my lord," he observed at his most languid. "I did not realize."

"Don't try that tone with me, my boy. It won't wash and you know it." Charles was well known for his exquisite politeness and control in the most demanding circumstances. But he found his calm deserting him in the face of the waste of a fine mind and the good name of one of the oldest houses in England.

"I think you have said enough, my friend." The warning was unmistakable.

Charles ignored it. "Don't be a fool, Dev. I'm not the one you are hurting with your outrageous conduct. Hell's teeth, man, how could you let yourself be drawn into a duel with a boy, a green boy at that, ten years your junior and the brother of your current flirt as well? I gave you credit for more sense if not propriety," he exploded angrily. He glared across the space that separated them. "This last start is just one in a long list. When will you stop this idiocy?"

As Charles' ire increased, Deveril withdrew more obviously behind the social mask of indifference that he had perfected over the years. Heavy lashes dropped over his blazing eyes, shutting out his expression. "I agree it was careless of me, Charles," he drawled as he reached for his snuff box and flipped it open with a practiced hand. "But what would you have me do? Ignore the young hothead's words or perhaps apologize for permitting him the liberty of slapping my face?"

His lordship was breathing heavily and fast losing what little control he had left. He knew well Deveril's mocking boredom was a shield but that didn't make his behavior any less difficult to swallow. He exhaled slowly, striving for a modicum of calm. To continue as he was surely meant disaster for his plans.

No one knew better than he how deep the pain and bitterness were in the duke. God knew with a mother such as his no one could have emerged unscathed. The duchess was as beautiful as any Circe but her heart was as black as the midnight sky. And when she had turned her cruel eyes on the young son who had worshiped her, the results had been devastating. The ravaged face and the vacant, shocked eyes of the fourteen-year-old marquis still haunted Charles' dreams. He and Kate had taken the boy in that stormy night, had given him the love that they had not been privileged to share with the offspring God had denied them. But their efforts had been in vain. The damage had been done. From that moment on, Deveril had changed. His high-spirited pranks became verbally cruel when he was angered. The eager questing spirit was lost under a heavy layer of worldly cynicism and constant mockery. He cared nothing for Society's opinion and made no effort to hide his contempt for its members and their everyday hypocrisies.

For years Charles had waited in vain for some sign Deveril was recovered from the blow his mother had dealt him. This last episode had finally proven to him that unless something was done, and done quickly, the strong sensitive person who once looked eagerly for tomorrow would be lost forever. Charles had decided then that he would use any means at his disposal to save Deveril from himself.

"Deveril, I ask you to please heed what I am going to say. You are the son of my heart. In the name of that affection I beg it of you."

Deveril stared at him, caught by the plea that he knew Charles had never made to any other man. The very fact that he had lowered himself to do so now was ominous. "Blackmail, Charles?"

"Call it what you will as long as it gains me your attention."

Deveril waved a hand. "You have my complete attention."

"You cannot go on as you are. Even you must see that. What will you do when you are completely shunned by Society? You go out of your way to deliberately antagonize anyone who irritates you. You are so unforgiving. So much the judge. Do you really believe yourself above the rest of us? I cannot think that you do. Can you not see you are becoming just as bad as the ones whom you despise? Whom will you call friend but those disreputable leeches who use your money and care not one whit if you live or die? Can you not see what you do to yourself? By your very actions you allow your mother to hold sway over the man you are. Do you really want this?"

"I have gone too far to turn back now." The truth slipped out before he could stop it. Angered, Deveril drew himself up and prepared to take his leave. But he was denied even that.

"Sit down. I have your promise. Is that, too, no longer of any worth?"

Deveril sat. One did not argue with Charles in this mood or with the truth of his words. Deveril had only one virtue left and that was his word. He would keep it.

"I have a plan as to how to extradite you from the witches'

brew that you and your mother have made between you."

Here he paused to allow his words to penetrate the stillness of the figure across from him. Keeping his eyes firmly on the vivid blue ones studying him so intently, he continued. "You must rid yourself of the notion that anything you can say or do will make the slightest difference to the Dowager Duchess or, indeed, alleviate the pain she so knowingly inflicted that night. Your mother is a woman without conscience or morals. She hurt you in order to vent her hatred of your father. You must turn your back on the past now for your own sake. Forget her and your father. Neither of them ever really cared about you. You are of an age to accept that. You are not like either of them. You must accept that as well and make your own way. You must think of the future and the St. John name."

Deveril laughed harshly, startling them both. "The St. John name means nothing to me. Nor does the future. My sire spent his days in Parliament, where he was safe from his responsibilities at home, and Mother dear spent hers in every bed in England. Rich, poor, young, or old, it mattered not. Neither of them cared about the future of our name. Why should I?"

"You will care because I ask it of you."

A simple request and one that a man of his reputation should have been able to turn away from. Charles knew his opponent too well. He watched Deveril stiffen in shock. He saw the swift anger, the cutting words that only long affection held back from on Deveril's lips.

"You are the son of my heart. When my Kate died you were the only one I could confide in. I loved you and she loved you. It would have hurt her deeply to know what you have become."

Deveril could not hold out against Charles' plea and that angered him further. "Perhaps that is true. But it is too late to mend my fences. You know our world as well as I."

"There is a way," Charles insisted. "You could marry. A

wife whom Society would accept. Someone to grace your homes and to give you an heir or two."

"You belong in Bedlam, Charles." He made no effort to keep the scorn out of his voice. "I want no wife even if you could find one that would have eyes past my title and wealth. I bed no creature for the privilege of handing her pin money, clothes, and all the other trappings of her kind."

"Between us we can find you a mate. Someone you could like."

Deveril had no intention of putting himself in the position of his father and countless others who were cuckolded by the fair charmers they took to wife. He glared at Charles, prepared to tell him so. He could not. The past, memories of all this man and Kate had been to him, stilled his tongue once more.

Charles could almost see the thoughts race through Deveril's mind. He knew there would be a fight when he had chosen this course. But even he could not have expected what came next.

"I accede to your request with one small stipulation. I do not wish to select this female myself nor will I pay my addresses to her. You have conceived this plan on your own so you may choose my bride yourself. Until I appear at the church on the appointed day, I have no desire to lay eyes on the creature."

The duke sat back in his chair, satisfied that he had placed Charles in an untenable position. Crossing one leg over the other he awaited Charles' retreat. But he had underestimated the determination of his opponent.

"I accept."

Not for anything would Charles allow Deveril to see his dismay at how well the duke had spiked his guns. What female in her right mind would accept such treatment. Every decent instinct was offended. Charles studied Deveril for a moment.

"Do you have any special requirements?" Something, he

wasn't sure what, prompted him to see how far Deveril intended to carry out his threat.

Taken aback, Deveril gave a bark of laughter. "I have no desire to spend my life with a vaporous, empty-headed schoolroom miss. Other than that, I bow to your superior judgment." The bargain had been struck. Deveril rose abruptly. "If that is all you require of me now, I will bid you good day."

Charles rose and accompanied Deveril to the door. There was much he wanted to say but the closed look on his godson's face warned against any more conversation. "Thank you, son."

Deveril stopped and faced him fully. "You won't succeed, you know. I have done my work too well. Why not cast me off as my sire did?"

Charles heard something then he had not known existed. There was the faintest hint of regret in the drawling voice. "Dev." He reached out but Deveril stepped back with a lifted brow, habitual cynicism settling into the lines on his face. Charles' hand dropped. "I will send you a message when I have found her."

After Deveril had gone, Charles returned to his study. He opened a drawer and pulled out the list he had compiled of eligible females. The names blended together as he realized not one of the candidates appeared remotely capable of catching Deveril's discerning eye long enough to get with child.

Seeking an inspiration, his eyes sought the portrait of his late wife which hung over the mantel of the fireplace. Her vivid, young face held the joy of living that had lit his life for too few years. She had had such faith in him, such love. No problem ever upset her. "Providence will provide. Just be patient." How many times had she said that? How many times had she been right?

"Kate, my love, I hope you are right this time. I need a very special lady indeed. Someone strong yet loving. Someone intelligent yet fragile. Someone brave enough to take on our son. For he won't be kind. He will hate the trap and will fight to escape. If I didn't love him so much, for his sake and yours I would not consider this plan. But I cannot let that woman's behavior destroy Deveril. It's time one of us stops her. She destroyed Deveril's father but she won't get the son. I swear it."

Chapter Two

Deveril strode purposefully out to his waiting carriage as a footman sprang to open the door and let down the step for him. A frown marred his countenance as he absently told his driver to take him home. While the coach clattered over the uneven cobbled street, his thoughts were occupied with the coil of his godfather's devising.

Having given his word, he could see no immediate way out of the trap Charles had laid so cleverly. Momentarily, he was diverted by the knowledge he had come off second best in the interview, a rare occurrence in his life to be sure. But how to escape the fate Charles had planned? That was the plaguing question.

He was well aware his unsavory reputation would be a protection of sorts. Few families would want an alliance with his despite the monetary advantages the match would undeniably bring to the bride and her family. Charles was right. Between his mother and himself they had certainly dragged the name of St. John and the house of Castleton through the mud. Such an occurrence would have killed his sire had he still lived. His one aim in life had been the guardianship of his noble lineage and the increment of his holdings.

Now that Deveril looked back on his father, he wondered

if the duke had had reasons for burying himself in his estates when Parliament wasn't in session. Surely he had known what his wife was. Half of London knew, for they had probably slept with her. Deveril could well imagine his proud father hiding his feelings behind his many duties and varied interests.

The child he had been then hadn't understood the hell in which the two people he called parents lived. His father hadn't known what to do with a child while his mother had alternately ignored and doted on him. He had been kept in a constant state of trying to please one or the other, never able to please both. School had indirectly catapulted him from innocence to cruel awareness. On a trip home, he had found his mother in bed with the boy he had called friend, a boy moreover a year younger than he was. That had been bad enough. What had come next had nearly destroyed him. She had told him his father was not his father at all, that he was the offspring of a stable hand whose name she couldn't even remember. The lie had been too real. He hadn't questioned it, for it had explained all that he had never been able to understand. He had left home and gone to Charles, the whole story pouring out of him the moment he had arrived. Eventually through Charles' tireless efforts he had learned the truth. His father was the duke. His mother had lied in order to hurt his father.

His carriage pulled to a stop in front of his house, putting an end to the memories. Deveril stepped out and mounted the stairs. After handing over his curly crowned beaver to the butler with a curt word of thanks, he headed for the study. The footman on duty in the hallway opened the door for him. Deveril passed him without a word. The young servant sighed in relief. When his master was in one of his black moods, it was best to remain part of the furniture.

Inside his study, Deveril chafed at Charles' demands.

A wife! The words put pay to every comfort he possessed. A woman in his establishment would mean his freedom was at an end. And brats! What knew he of children? Deveril threw himself down in the chair facing the window. He gazed, unseeing, at the small garden in full bloom. He had an appointment to drive in the park with delectable Olivia this afternoon. He couldn't even bring himself to care whether he put quill to paper and sent his regrets. Trapped! More than a word, a feeling. A need to be free of the City and the convention that surrounded him like sticky tentacles. Rising, he yanked the bell pull. Smithington appeared in seconds.

"Have my coach readied and my bags packed. Send my secretary to me."

In a matter of minutes the entire household was informed of his grace's intent to remove to the country. The staff responded to his commands with brisk efficiency. After issuing final instructions to Meade to follow him to the Castle with his baggage, Deveril mounted his curricle.

Less than two hours after leaving his godfather's steps he was on the road. The pace at which he guided his mettlesome horses through the crowded London streets might have alarmed persons of less iron nerve than the man beside him. But John, who had been with him since boyhood, had a disposition suited to weather his restive master's uncertain temperament. John sat with his arms folded across his solid chest and an expression of complete unconcern on his severe countenance. He betrayed neither alarm at the reckless sway of the vehicle nor pride in the skill of the nonpareil he had taught to ride his first pony. Only in the company of his more discreet cronies did he say, taking his grace in harness and out, no man living handled the ribbons better than the duke.

The curricle Deveril drove was not precisely a racing design but it had been built to his own specifications. It was lightly sprung, capable of covering many miles in an incredibly short time. The new blacks, fresh and decidedly skittish, required all of his lordship's concentration and skill to bring them safely to the open highway without mishap. By the time they were bowling along the wide stretch of road out of town, Deveril had taken the edge off their paces and settled the team into a trot.

"What do you think of them, John?" Deveril asked with a smile of satisfaction at their performance. Pitting himself against the beasts had given him an outlet for his temper. The anger that had driven him was gone for the moment.

"Prime bit o' blood, I must say. Of course, with you picking them, that's about what I would expect," the groom acknowledged with a grin. "I wouldn't be surprised if with a bit o' work they mightin' take a notch or two off the record if we was to give it a go."

The feel of the horses' mouths as they tugged at the bits vibrated through the slender leathers Deveril held. The urge to give them their heads was strong. All thought of Charles and his plan, his prospective nuptials, and the dark memories of his youth fled before the pleasure of the open road and the unpopulated countryside with its vast fields of brilliant green. For now at least he was still free.

Lord Ravensly gracefully seated himself at the breakfast table after having surveyed the heaping platters of food on the sideboard. As he gave his order for the footman to fill his plate, he was conscious of a feeling of eagerness and vigor he had not experienced for many years. Perhaps the deep sleep he had enjoyed the night before accounted for his mood or perhaps the success of his interview with Deveril was the real cause.

Savoring his eggs and the paper-thin slices of ham, Charles considered the challenge that Deveril had set him. His thoughts were interrupted by the arrival of a servant bearing a note on a silver tray. The oddity of receiving a message so early in the morning chased all other considerations out of his head. Ignoring his half-eaten meal, he quickly broke the seal and read the contents. As he scanned the bold script inscribed on the cheap surface, several expressions crossed his features. First and foremost was amazed disbelief, followed swiftly by anger and a terrible urgency.

The bearer stood at his elbow, respectfully waiting to be dismissed. Charles looked up. "Send to the stables and have my traveling coach ready within the hour. We will be making for Dover at all possible speed." It was a measure of his anxiety that he spoke curtly.

The young footman nodded and hurried from the room.

Charles wasted no time in issuing directions and readying himself for the journey, a trip to take him into the past—a past long buried yet never forgotten.

The next hour passed in a flurry of activity as the staff exerted supreme effort to accomplish their orders. Finally, all was in readiness. Lord Ravensly stepped briskly into his coach. As the impressive entourage rolled away, the burgundy-liveried outriders fell back a pace to the correct distance. The four matched dappled gray horses were fresh and eager to be away from the already crowded streets and stepped into the harness with a will.

The miles sped swiftly by. Inside the swaying carriage Charles sat immobile, staring out at the passing scenery as he mentally reviewed the incredible message. His sister, Julia, whom he had not seen since she was eighteen, was in England with her child. At best the details in the hurried letter were cursory. The name of an inn in Dover where she and the child were staying, a request for speed, and a traveling coach.

Julia, the last remaining one of his line except for himself, was coming home. The favorite of his family. What would she be like now? The journey was too long. Eagerness to see her again made him impatient. He called to his coachman asking for more speed. Getting it, he settled back and ignored the increased swaying of the coach.

The child, Byrony. What would he be like. How old? Julia

was twelve years younger than he. Her child could be as much as two and twenty. A frown formed as he realized there had been no mention of the husband, Balmaine. Julia had always been a madcap. Surely she hadn't undertaken a journey from the continent with no one to accompany her but a mere boy. The thought made his blood run cold. So many questions and no answers. The miles were disappearing between them as surely as the day was drawing to a close. Charles felt the slackening of the breakneck pace as the carriage neared the outskirts of the seaport. The air was sweet with the smell of the sea. The muted murmur of the waves breaking on the shore was growing stronger. Almost there. His excitement grew. Julia. How would he find her changed?

Finally the coach stopped. Charles descended stiffly but impatiently. The ostler was already about his business seeing to the jaded horses that had brought him to this place. The door of the inn was open and a light cast a warm glow to welcome wayfarers. As Charles entered, he was struck by the shabbiness of the interior and the dampness of the air. Clearly not an establishment of the first respectability. This impression was further strengthened by the approach of the dirty, overweight proprietor. The man wiped grimy hands ineffectually on a filthy apron while his eyes widened in surprise at the quality of his guest.

Lord Ravensly's nose wrinkled in distaste. Julia must surely have fallen on hard times to be staying in such an establishment. "I understand you have Madam Balmaine staying here?"

The greasy head bobbed nervously. "That we do, your lordship. The lady being real sick an' all. I done the best I—"

Charles held up an immaculate hand and stemmed the flow of words. "Show me to madam's room and have my carriage readied. It is possible we shall be removing from this place immediately."

Again the head bobbed before the figure turned awkwardly around and led the way up the steep, rickety stairs to the second floor. The corridor was as badly lit as the rest of the place—not that more candles could have done anything to dispel the gloomy air of abject poverty and filth emanating from the dingy, peeling walls. The bare floors underfoot creaked with age and rot. The innkeeper shuffled to a halt in front of a narrow door at the end of the hall. With his thumb he indicated that this was the room that Charles had requested.

Charles dismissed him with a curt nod, waiting impatiently for the man's footsteps to fade before he knocked. There was no answer. He tried again. A soft voice replied just as he was about to rap again.

"Who is it?"

Already angered at the deplorable conditions of the situation, Lord Ravensly found his temper sorely tried by the unopened door and the faceless demand. "I am Charles Ravensly. I believe I am expected," he snapped.

Silence. Then the distinct click of the latch being slid back. But instead of the door swinging open as he expected, it remained closed. It took a full second for the implication to dawn on him. Slowly, he turned the handle and pushed. Whatever he had envisioned as a first meeting with his sister, it had certainly not been this.

The tiny room was lit by one tallow candle. Bare of all furnishing except for a narrow bed, a plain wooden table, and a small stool, the space was hardly large enough to accommodate one person let alone two. There were no windows, only a small square vent close to the ceiling to let in light. A meager fire burned weakly in the grate. As he grew accustomed to the darkness, he was able to discern the bed was not empty as he had first thought. A frail figure, barely breathing and showing no movement lay beneath its thin sheets. He took a step toward the light when the same voice that had bid him enter spoke.

"Do not approach too near, your lordship. My mother

sleeps peacefully for the first time in these three days. I will not have her disturbed."

Charles Ravensly was a man accustomed to giving orders, not to receiving them. The surprise of finding himself being so addressed by anyone stopped him in his tracks. He turned around to confront the person foolish enough to command him. His eyes widened in shock. He was staring straight down the barrel of a very deadly-looking pistol. The pale, slender hand holding it was remarkably steady as were the gray eyes, so like his own, studying him. Charles surveyed the tall, thin youth. Without a doubt this must be Byrony.

There was no mistaking the Ravensly heritage even in the dimness of the candlelight. The fine-boned aristocratic features were clearly discernible, although the clothes were decidedly shabby and well worn. None of it mattered against the coolness of the unwavering regard and the ease with which Byrony withstood his silent appraisal.

Reluctant admiration stirred within him. "You are Byrony, I take it?" he remarked calmly.

The pistol lowered slowly to be secreted in the long cape hanging from a hook on the wall. "I am." The youth didn't come closer, only continued to watch Charles steadily.

A muffled moan from the occupant of the bed brought Byrony swiftly to the woman's side. With practiced ease Byrony slipped an arm under the too thin shoulders while coaxing a few drops of the contents of a cup down Julia's throat. Byrony murmured soothingly before settling Julia back on the pillow and smoothing the cover once again.

Charles stood quietly at the foot watching the two of them. There was little remaining of the vibrant beauty that was once his sister. It was apparent even to his untutored eye that Julia was dying. The gray-tinged skin, the shallow uneven breathing, and the weak movements of her hands proclaimed the end was near.

His first inclination had been to go down on his knees beside Julia's wasted body but common sense told him not only would she be unable to recognize him but his presence could do naught but disturb her.

Byrony gestured to the stool nearby. "Won't you sit down. I am afraid it is all I can offer you but at least it is reasonably clean."

He eyed the seat dubiously before lowering himself gingerly. "Perhaps you would be good enough to explain how you and my sister have come to this pass? Why did neither of you send word to me? I would have gladly come to your aid."

Byrony settled on the bare floor, leaning back against the wall. Obviously her uncle saw little beyond his sister's face. As yet he had not tumbled to her disguise. So she concentrated on the truth he had commanded.

"I have no idea how much you know of my mother's marriage so I best start at the beginning. After my mother eloped with Father, they returned to France. The Balmaines were not enamored of the match and made no secret of their dislike of my mother. She felt she could not return to her family as she had brought enough disgrace on everyone's head with her determination to wed Father. So they stayed on the continent. A small allowance was paid but it was never enough to support two who had known nothing but luxury all their lives. Papa had no notion how to go on, you see. Nor did Mama, though she tried.

"Then I was born. Three mouths to feed made a way to get money imperative. Papa turned to gambling. He was as shocking at that as he was at being a husband. We were always moving, most of the time in the dead of night. Mother started to do some fine sewing but that didn't really help much. When I was old enough I tried to do my part but I never was any good with the needle. I was very good with the cards."

Byrony caught the sharp look that Charles leveled on her. He was beginning to understand. "Two years ago Papa was killed in a duel leaving me and Mama alone. Mother's health was gone but we still had to eat. Two women alone were prey to every Captain sharp and every cheat in the land. Needs must when the devil drives. I put off my skirts for good and became her son, a beardless youth with the devil's own luck with the cards and an eye for the target at which I shot. Not admirable qualities for a girl but we survived because of it."

Byrony stirred uneasily, hating to admit even to herself she did not wish to be judged harshly for the shifts she had practiced to survive. Charles said nothing although she expected him to. His silence encouraged her to continue.

"Mama's one wish was to come home to England and see you again, my lord. So great was her agitation I vowed I would bring her. There was no money for the journey because everything we possessed of value had long since been sold. It took a while to raise the blunt at the tables then we started our journey. Being out of my skirts made traveling much easier, as I'm sure you can imagine."

Charles stared. The unemotional way his niece spoke made her exploits seem of no value or danger. He knew better. No woman, and certainly few men, would have been up to the challenge of the task she had undertaken.

"My God!" The oath was drawn from him. His eyes traced her delicate profile, seeing the fragility he had missed on the first look. Suddenly he realized he was sitting on a stool while she had nothing more than the floor for a seat. He started to rise. She stayed him with a hand on his arm.

"No. Please stay there. I am quite comfortable, really."

Charles subsided, having no idea how to deal with the self-possession of this girl-woman who was his niece. "Is there more?"

He was almost afraid to ask. Heaven alone knew what else Byrony had been forced to do to bring them back to England. The recital of how she had secured their passage on the boat across the channel held him speechless.

"You could have been killed. Or worse," he exclaimed when she finished.

Byrony inclined her head. "I know. Don't think I didn't

think on it at the time. But I could do naught else if we were to come here." She spread her hands, absently noting the slender fingers that could deal with equal dexterity from the top or the bottom of the deck. "I think I am hardly a credit to either of our names." There was no self-pity in her words, only truth as she saw it.

"Never think it." Charles caught her hands in his. "You did what you had to do. I could never condemn you, especially since you have brought Julia and yourself home to me."

"I should have come with her sooner." Byrony glanced at the bed. "She's dying. It is not likely she will see the sun rise. Mayhap she won't know she has arrived."

Charles swallowed an unaccustomed lump in his throat. Again there was that quiet acceptance of what could not be changed. The strength to endure impressed him as nothing had in a long time.

"Has a doctor been to see her?" he asked gently.

"Yes, but I did not like him much so I sent him away. He reeked of gin and dirt. I would not have him near her. It is bad enough her last hours must be spent in this awful place," she declared, showing the first hint of strain. "How I wish we dared move her."

The pain in Byrony's voice tore at Charles' heart. "Be at peace, my dear. She is home where she wanted to be. You gave her that. You risked much to bring her home. I honor you for it." Words were inadequate, he knew from his own beloved Katie's death.

The solitary candle burned lower as the minutes crept by. Dawn was near at hand. The man and the girl kept watch over the one they loved. Each held memories bright against the moment when the watch would be done. As the silver-tipped fingers of sunrise drew back the black curtain of night the tiny, frail figure in the bed stirred restlessly.

"Byrony." The thin thread of sound was pathetically weak.

Byrony knelt beside the bed to clasp her mother's hand. "I

am here, Mama."

"I did not see Charles." The words were gasped out at great cost.

Charles went down on one knee on the opposite side and grasped his sister's hand. "I, too, am here, little sister."

Julia's pale, dark circled eyes sought his face. Almost as though she sensed her time was growing short, Julia did not waste her efforts on questioning his presence. "Take care of my child for me, my dear brother." Byrony's startled breath went unheeded as Charles and Julia stared into each other's eyes. The affection they had shared in their youth made words unnecessary between them. It was as if the intervening years had never been.

"She will be safe with me. You have my word."

Julia turned her head slowly to find her daughter's face. Gathering her fast dwindling strength, she spoke carefully. "Can—give—you—nothing—only—love. If—you—love—me—obey Charles." Julia's breath was coming in labored gasps but her eyes remained fixed on her only child's face. "Promise." Her need demanded an answer.

Byrony knew herself well. To give her word would mean her life and the ordering of it would cease to be her own. Charles was a stranger to her and she to him. Yet she could not deny her mother. "I promise, Mama. I will obey my uncle in all things." Byrony stifled the sob that rose in her throat. She would do her grieving in private.

Julia smiled gently and relaxed her pitifully weak hold on Byrony's hand. The smile still remained when the last soft breath echoed in the dingy little room. Julia Ravensly Balmaine had left life as gently as she had lived it. Byrony closed her eyes and knew the future loomed on the horizon with demands and rules she had no knowledge of or training in. The days of choosing her own way were gone.

Chapter Three

Byrony stood at the window, staring out across the mirrored surface of the lake tinted a delicate pink by the early morning sun. Since the death of her mother a month before, it was impossible for her to sleep past sunrise. Here among the beautiful, romantic setting of Ravenscourt she found herself slowly beginning to respond to the serenity of her uncle's home.

Her thoughts turned inward as she examined her feelings for her newfound relative. She sensed in him a kindred spirit that surprised her as well as a deep well of loneliness he strove mightily to hide. His quiet strength and unobtrusive care during the painful days after her mother's passing had fed a spark of empathy, genuine liking, and respect. Giving the ordering of her life into his keeping had lost some of its sting. It had been far less difficult than she would have thought possible for her to face coming to live with him at Ravenscourt.

Now she was surrounded by every luxury. Silk sheets on the softest of beds, perfumed soap and pitchers of warm water whenever she needed them. Lovely clothes, only a few as yet, but soon to be more when the dressmaker was done. All in all she had been offered a life she had never dreamed could be hers. And so far her uncle had asked nothing of her beyond her pleasure and happiness. The sensation of having someone to care and to turn to was new in her life. Byrony wanted to believe and accept all that was being done for her but she kept waiting for the price that the past had taught her always went with gain.

The gentle tap on the door interrupted her thoughts. Tillie, the young maid Charles had bestowed on her, tripped into the room. "Good morning, Miss Byrony." The girl grinned cheerfully. "I brought you a nice fresh cup of tea."

Byrony moved away from the window, pulling the green silk wrapper around her. "You spoil me, Tillie." Tillie's high spirits never failed to lighten her heart. Sitting down in the pale blue velvet chair beside the glowing hearth, Byrony accepted the fragile cup Tillie brought to her.

Byrony watched as the younger girl began setting out the things for her morning toilet. She still found the elaborate ritual not only exhausting but somewhat amusing. It was too easy to remember the times she had dressed in moments so she and her family could flee into the night. Or the times she wore pants instead of hampering skirts. The time of being able to run free was at an end if Tillie had her way. The maid seemed intent on making her into a raving beauty every time she set foot outside her chamber. No curl was left unpinned, no detail too small to escape Tillie's eagle eye. In the stroke of one promise Byrony had gained a guardian and a sweet-natured but stubborn keeper. The idea made her smile. She was a fool to be so suspicious. It was about time her luck took a turn for the better. With that thought in mind Byrony submitted to the daily ritual with enjoyment.

Tillie patted the final curl in place sometime later. She paused to survey her handiwork. "You look a real treat, Miss Byrony," she exclaimed impulsively.

Byrony stood up and studied her reflection in the mirror. In respect to her mother's wishes she had forgone the colors of full mourning. Instead she chose the muted tones of half mourning. Charles had been against her donning the drab shades at all, arguing that there was no reason she should since no one in England was likely to know about her recent bereavement. Plus, he had pointed out, having been deprived of all the pleasures of her youth, she should not be barred from enjoying the entertainments now open to her. Between them they had settled on a compromise. She would wear her half mourning and remain out of society for only six months instead of the usual twelve. It was not the best solution for either of them but it was the only one each would permit given the stubbornness of their natures.

Byrony smiled, liking the pale lavender of the muslin morning dress. Beautiful clothes had always interested her even though she hadn't had many. This gown suited her, highlighting her creamy skin to give it a pearl-like luster that was a vivid contrast to her jet black hair. Her silver eyes appeared tinged with unsuspected hints of purple. For a moment Byrony wished her mother would have lived to see her so gowned. She would have delighted in the prevailing mode of high-waisted styles with their low-cut necklines. She had always said such a cut would flatter Byrony's tall slenderness to perfection and she had been right, Byrony decided without conceit. She had made a passable, if slight, boy. She made a far better-looking woman.

Settling her shawl on her shoulders, Byrony left her room to go downstairs. The portraits that graced the walls of her passage watched her with the same silver eyes she possessed. The effect had been an eerie one at first but now she quite liked the sense of belonging it gave her. She had never really had a family of her own and it was a pleasant sensation to find herself with a heritage that could trace its lineage alongside that of the current king. Finally she was beginning to believe she belonged somewhere to someone.

Charles rose at her entrance into the breakfast room. "How lovely you look, my dear," he murmured with a smile.

On impulse, Byrony went to his side and kissed his cheek. "And why not, uncle. Even the meanest horse improves in looks when groomed properly."

Charles chuckled appreciably. "Only you, my dear, would liken yourself to a horse. Most young ladies in my day would be up in the boughs over such a comparison."

"Well, as to that I know very little about genteel behavior. Mama did her best but there has really been no opportunity for me to see how your world goes on." There was no self-pity in her statement, only fact.

"With a very little polish I think you would do well in Society."

Byrony seated herself in the chair the footman pulled out for her. She thanked him with a smile before replying. "Is that what you have in mind for me?" She lifted a brow as she asked the question. Her curiosity was strong but she disguised it except for that one gesture.

"Does the idea displease you?"

She thought a moment. "Not displease perhaps," she admitted finally. "But I do wonder at the purpose. What little I know of such matters tells me it would be an effort wasted. For one thing I am old enough to be considered on the shelf. For another is my background and the life I have led. If either should come out, you would be embarrassed."

"You could not be an embarrassment to me. Never. I will not have you thinking it. Granted that the gossips' tongues would wag if your past were known. So we must simply contrive to keep it hidden."

Byrony smiled softly at the heat of his anger. "I am curious how."

Charles started to speak, then changed his mind. Now was not the time. "Have you plans for today?" he asked instead.

Byrony looked at him a moment before answering. "No. Was there something you wished me to do?"

Charles waited for the footman to place Byrony's filled plate before her. Then he waved the servants away. When they were gone, he spoke.

"I would like to talk to you about your future. I have

thought the matter over at great length and I have hit on what I believe is the only solution for you."

Byrony's first inclination was to demand the right to order her own life. Her promise to her mother stilled her tongue. The affection she had begun to feel for Charles also muted her anger. He cared for her because she was her mother's daughter. She knew and accepted that. But it was hard to accept his right to rule her life.

"As you wish, uncle."

Charles' face lightened at her acceptance. He had expected questions and possibly resistance. It hadn't taken him long to discover his niece would be lead but not driven. Her unconventional upbringing had much to answer for, yet if his idea was to succeed, her strength of will and her ability to risk what others would not would be the very traits that would see her through.

"Do you remember the promise you made your mother?" He needed the reassurance of her cooperation.

"I do." Wary now, Byrony waited to see where he led.

"Did you mean it? Will you allow me the privilege of knowing what is best for you?"

Byrony saw the trap now. Yet there was no way she could avoid its entanglement. "I have rarely had more than the necessities of life and sometimes not even that. Because I haven't had much to call my own, the things I do have I value. My word I prize above all else. My mother trusted you. She asked for my word. I gave it. I will not break it. I cannot promise that I will like what you wish of me nor can I promise to submit without a word to the future. It is not in my nature to bow to anyone."

Charles heard the warning and oddly honored her for speaking. It would have been easy for her to refuse to remember. Or to meekly accept her fate. She had chosen neither course. He did not fool himself. His time with Byrony had taught him she would hate what he had in mind. For just one moment he wondered if he should follow the plan. But no, he could allow no doubt to creep in. This was best.

"I have decided after long consideration that only marriage will offer you a future and protection if your past should come to light."

Byrony stared at him.

"Marriage! To whom! I don't know anyone in England but you."

"You don't, but I do." So far, she had taken the news better than he could have hoped. "He doesn't know you either."

"Should that make me feel better?" The sting of temper was in her words. "You are jesting, surely. You can't mean for me to marry a stranger."

"Many women have done as much and thrived," he pointed out.

"Well, I am not one of them."

"May I remind you that by your own words you have given me the right and the power to compel your obedience. Do not think that just because you managed a foolish, ill-advised, and totally unplanned trip across the continent that you can survive for long without protection. You are a woman, a damnably pretty one. How long before someone realizes it if you go back to that absurd disguise?"

Hurt at the way Charles had described the trek to bring her mother home, Byrony scarcely heard the rest of his words. Her eyes reflected her painful thoughts.

Charles saw it all and wished he had not hurt her. The truth, however, had to be spoken. "I know what you did was out of love and no one is more grateful than I that you brought Julia home. But you cannot continue to live like this. What would happen to you if I die? You have no family, no accomplishments that Society recognizes, and no money. Where would you go? What could you do? Think, child. The world is a cruel place for one alone, even an heiress, which I could make you. But what good would it do. You would still have no protection, and if your background should come out, many would shun you and then where would you be? I, as the guardian Julia chose for you, could not permit any of that to happen to you." He sat back, weary but determined. "It must be marriage."

"Why now? Could it not wait awhile?" Byrony sensed more stood behind Charles' reasoning than the settling of her future.

"The longer you lack a name behind you, the greater the risk. Our circle is small. Your presence will be noted. Questions asked. I can protect you a little but a husband can do more."

"And what of this husband? What does he get from this arrangement?"

"He will gain an heiress as a wife and the promise of heirs. Surely any man would be proud to have a beautiful woman grace his home and bear his children."

If Charles had gotten her measure, Byrony, too, had learned something of her relative. She saw, now, the stubbornness they shared. He would not tell her more. Later surely. But not now.

"Stop worrying. I promise you there is no cause for you to feel uncertain or anxious. Simply enjoy the pleasures of the countryside and leave the rest to me. I really do have your best interests in mind."

"So you say."

Charles ignored the skeptical comment and said, "I have a surprise for you."

"Another one?" Byrony queried sarcastically and then flushed slightly at her uncle's pained look. "I'm sorry. Forgive me." She might not agree with what Charles had decided but she had to believe he meant it for the best.

"There is a neat little chestnut mare in my stables which I am sure will suit you admirably."

Charles sat back with an air of one well pleased with the favor he so graciously bestowed. The sun streamed in the windows behind him, haloing his thin, aristocratic features.

A treat to sugar the pill, Byrony thought cynically. There was nothing to be gained by calling Charles on the ploy. She was well and truly caught not only by circumstances but by her word. "Thank you." From somewhere she summoned up a smile. "I have missed not being able to ride. I had to leave my horse behind in France. He wasn't a particularly good animal but he served me well. It will be good to be mounted again. Does the mare have a name?"

Charles nodded, relieved that for the moment the storm had passed. "Her name is Sunset."

Byrony finished her breakfast while she and Charles spoke of horses. It pleased him to divert her and for a time she was prepared to allow him to do so. She had learned early on the advantage of playing the waiting game.

Charles laid down his fork on completing his meal. "You will need to wear a riding habit if you are to try Sunset."

Byrony frowned. "I vow I shall never get the hang of having an outfit for every activity. I enjoy my gowns but this constant changing is driving me mad."

Charles laughed. "Bear up, my dear. To steal your comparison: A horse must be properly outfitted for the job."

"Touché, uncle." Byrony rose. "Do you go with me?"

"No. I fear I have some business to attend to. Sam will accompany you. He has been a groom here almost as long as I have been master. You could not be in better hands."

This time there was no kiss as Byrony took her leave but there was a slight smile. She hurried upstairs to change. The chance to blow the cobwebs away and to enjoy a good gallop was heaven-sent.

"Tillie! Oh, there you are," she exclaimed as the younger girl emerged from the dressing room. "Help me change, please. I'm going riding."

The maid deftly began undoing the gown. "But, Miss Byrony, you only have your old riding habit. Your new things have not arrived from London yet," Tillie protested, scandalized. "I would be failing in my duty if I was to let you out of the house in such a rag, begging your pardon."

"Fiddle! As if anyone will see me. I shall be on our own grounds, you know. So none will be the wiser whether I wear a shabby habit or not." Byrony laughed, refusing to be daunted. "Now don't be a slugabed, girl, and hurry up."

Tillie muttered darkly under her breath while she disappeared into the dressing room to return bearing the disputed garment. Nothing could disguise its well-worn fabric or outmoded style. Fashioned in plain, unrelieved black it was almost masculine in cut. With it Tillie carried a white muslin shirt to be worn under the jacket.

In a trice Byrony stood ready in the center of the room. She made an arresting picture. The stark midnight hue was a perfect foil for her milk white skin and wild strawberry lips. The eager sparkle in her eyes and the flush in her cheeks drew attention to her vibrant beauty. One could be forgiven for not noticing her attire.

"I only hope the duke don't see you dressed like this. He will never believe you are my lord's niece," Tillie grumbled.

"Duke? What duke?" Byrony asked, startled.

"Why the Duke of Castleton, of course. He has been home now a week or more. His land marches with Ravenscourt and he and your uncle are thick as thieves. Why, my lord is the duke's godfather."

Tillie was clearly surprised at Byrony's lack of knowledge of her family. Tillie, as was everyone else, had been told only that Byrony's parents had died on the continent. And that Byrony had come to Ravenscourt since Charles was the last of Byrony's relatives.

"You sound like you don't like the duke." Byrony was curious about anyone who was close to her uncle.

"It's not my place to not like the duke."

Byrony raised her eyebrows. Tillie's tone and look held a wealth of meanings and not all of them decipherable.

"He is not like my lord. Not many like him for he gets up to all manner of starts," Tillie admitted after a long pause. "My lord has a soft spot for him nonetheless. Some say he loves the Devil Duke like a son."

"Tillie! The Devil Duke indeed! Are you trying to tell me the man is evil?"

"Not I. It's his mother that gives him a taste for making mischief though he's not cruel like her. Not he." Tillie shook her head. "Course some do say he's in league with the Devil himself. They say when you play cards with him you are bound to lose. And his horses, black as Satan's heart every one. Even that great brute of a stallion he rides is a man killer. None but the duke dare mount him. As for his women, no gently bred female can do aught but fear his cutting tongue and uncaring ways."

"That hardly makes him in league with the devil," Byrony argued. "I've met many worse and they were called gentlemen."

"But they didn't have a witch for a mother. That one is really wicked. The tales of her would curl your hair." Tillie glanced over her shoulder as though expecting to find the woman there. She had shown nothing more than avid interest when speaking of the duke but now there was real fear in her eyes. "That one is dangerous. Truly. She will ruin a person just for crossing her. No man is safe from her toils if she desires him."

Byrony noted the reaction, knowing full well she should not be listening to servants' gossip. But she couldn't help wanting to get a picture of Quality from the inside. If she was to exist in the world that Charles intended to push her into, she had best know the lay of the land. And since the duke was the closest member of Society, what better place to start than with him and his notorious family. A knock at the door silenced any more revelations. It was a footman with a message that the mare was awaiting her pleasure.

Byrony, eager to be in the saddle again, descended the stairs with more speed than grace. Observing Charles' slight frown, she stopped before him. "Don't scold. I know I shouldn't gallop down the stairs. Mama told me often enough but her lessons never really took, you know."

Charles tucked her arm in his. "You mistake my intent. It was your habit that earned my look. I had forgotten that the clothes I had commissioned for you have not all arrived as yet." He led her out the door to the drive. "As to the other. You may always behave as you wish here with me." He was counting on time and a few gentle hints to smooth the rough edges of her haphazard upbringing. But he did not tell her that. She had had enough to adjust to thus far.

Byrony smiled gratefully at him. Much as she enjoyed Ravenscourt and the change in her circumstances, she could not help but miss her old freedom. For a second she wondered if the husband she was to have would be so easy-natured about her shortcomings. She hoped so but feared not.

"Don't worry, my dear. I promise you the future is not as black as you think." Charles patted her arm. Byrony had his pride and knew herself well, her faults and her virtues. "It is too beautiful a day and there is the ride I promised you." He gestured to the dancing horse that stood a few feet away.

At that moment Sunset lifted her head and stared straight at Byrony. The sun glinted off her coat in a red gold glaze. She was all sleek lines and barely controlled temperament. Byrony had little experience with a horse of the mare's breeding but she knew quality when she saw it.

"She's beautiful," Byrony whispered in awe. Disengaging her arm, she extended her hand and crooned softly. So engrossed was she in making friends she did not notice the arrival of a wizened little man and a rawboned hack.

"She'll do, my lord," Sam murmured. "She has a way with horses, she does."

Lord Ravensly nodded in agreement, not taking his eyes from his niece as he watched her being thrown lightly into the saddle. He turned to the man beside him as Byrony walked

Sunset a few paces down the drive. "See that she takes a gallop around the long course and over the jumps if you think she has the nerve and the seat for it."

Sam said nothing for a moment. "The duke. He practices there at this time."

Charles nodded, his eyes steady. "Yes."

Sam glanced at the girl who handled one of the hottest-tempered horses in the Ravensly stable with ease. Now he understood the choice of mount. "As you wish, my lord."

Chapter Four

Byrony guided Sunset down the path away from Ravenscourt. It was impossible not to relax and enjoy the beauty of the grounds and the feel of the horse beneath her. The only thing that would have enhanced her pleasure would have been being astride rather than perched on the sidesaddle. Of course, her old riding habit, the only garment that remained of her life before she had donned her breeches, was unfit for such a practice. It was only by some unlucky chance she had the thing at all. Somehow she had mixed it up with her mother's few clothes and tucked it into her valise.

On second thought, perhaps it was just as well. Byrony didn't think Charles, for all his kindness about her lack of polish, would have allowed her out without the proper attire. The presence of the groom dogging her heels was ample proof of his careful guardianship.

"His lordship suggested you might like to take a look at the long course," Sam called, bringing his horse alongside of Sunset.

Byrony drew to a standstill at the fork of two paths. "The long course?" she queried with interest.

Sam indicated the path on the right that seemed to lead deeper into the forest. "Aye. My lord set it up some years ago to train his hunters for the season. Not that he uses it much himself these days. The duke says it is one of the best fields in this part of the country."

For a second time that morning the mysterious duke cropped up in conversation. However, this time, the promise of a challenging ride held more interest than finding out about her uncle's friends and the life they led.

"Is it far?"

"No, miss. It is not far. We have only to go through here. Sunset knows the way. And would enjoy the work if you wish to give it a go," he assured her.

Byrony nodded and turned the mare to the right. Here the sun barely filtered through the dense branches overhead. The thick carpet of dead leaves muffled the steady thud of the horses' hooves as they trotted slowly down the well-worn trail. All at once, the narrow, dark tunnel opened out into a lovely green meadow. Byrony reined to a stop. They were on a little knoll that gave a bird's-eye view of the whole course. Each obstacle blended in with the land around it and yet each presented a unique test to both horse and rider.

Byrony ached to try Sunset but not in the damnable habit she was wearing. She stared down at the trailing skirt wishing for her threadbare breeches. She looked back at the course. Her uncle had invited her to try it. He wouldn't want to see either her or the horse injured. Turning to Sam, she said. "I want your saddle. Get down please."

Sam stared at her, shocked. "My saddle, miss?"

"Of course. You don't think I am going to try those jumps in this rig, do you?" she demanded, waving a slender hand at the offending tack.

Sam settled more firmly on his horse. "I can't let you do that, miss. Think what his lordship would say if he knew, not to mention if someone was to see you. He would have my hide, he would."

"Fiddle! You and Tillie must be kin. Never have I heard such goings-on about what I do or what I wear. No one is going to see me, and even if they did, surely it is permissible on our own land. Besides my uncle said I could try the course and you must admit to give it a fair trial is more than I could do at present," she argued relentlessly.

Without giving him a chance to help her, Byrony leapt lightly out of the saddle and began unbuckling the girth. She looked over her shoulder to find Sam staring at her in dismay. "Well, don't just sit there watching me, lend a hand. The sooner I ride the sooner we leave, and I warn you, I will not jump the smallest log on this contraption," she said, tossing the sidesaddle to the ground.

Sam dismounted reluctantly and transferred his tack to the back of the mare. Byrony frowned thoughtfully at the heavy, trailing skirt of the habit. "Do you have a knife?"

The older man turned around sharply. "What would you be wantin' a knife for?"

"For this skirt. If Sunset steps on this she will come down, bringing me with her."

Sam glared at his young mistress. First the sidesaddle, and now this. Surely his lordship did not foresee his niece careening about the countryside like a hoyden.

"No need to look daggers at me. You wouldn't want to see us come a cropper, now would you?"

Defeated, Sam reached in his pocket and produced a small penknife without a word.

Byrony took the blade and bent down to hack at the dragging material. The edge was sharp but the fingers that wielded it were more interested in speed than neatness. The result was a jagged cut around the back of the skirt that showed an unseemly length of leg. "Done," she announced in satisfaction as she threw the remainder of the fabric away. "Now if you'll toss me up, I shall be set."

Glumly, Sam bent over and cupped his hands. That Ravensly stubbornness had much to answer for. Her uncle had it too. It was enough to turn a man gray when they had the bit between their teeth.

Byrony placed a foot in his hands and vaulted into the

saddle. Her skirt rode higher, exposing a good deal of stocking-clad leg. She hardly noticed, being more interested in the adjustment of the stirrups to the proper length. When Sam finished she touched the mare's flanks lightly with her heels and they were off.

Byrony allowed Sunset to choose her own pace as she gloried in the surge of power under her knees. Ears pitched forward eagerly, Sunset gathered herself at the first obstacle and soared into the air like a bird in flight. They cleared the brush and timber barrier with ease, inches to spare. Murmuring soft words of praise and encouragement, Byrony set the horse at the next fence. Again Sunset responded effortlessly. Barrier after barrier rose and fell before them. They were three quarters of the way around the course when Byrony sensed a subtle change in Sunset's gait. The mare was tiring. Hating to leave the course but knowing it was foolish to take a risk with the gallant horse, she decided the next jump would be the last.

Suddenly, she was aware of the steady drumming of hooves behind her. She turned to look over her shoulder. The flaring nostrils of a great black stallion were only inches away from Sunset's sweating flanks. The mare, without any encouragement from Byrony, increased her pace to shake off the relentless pursuer. But he would not be denied. In a few strides he drew alongside. Instead of sweeping past the now laboring smaller horse, his rider thrust out a hand and grabbed the flying reins near the bit.

Byrony tried to turn Sunset away but the man beside her hung on with an iron grip while the weight of the larger horse forced them off the path toward the center of the field. In seconds the mare stood trembling, her head hanging in an exhausted droop.

Byrony was not so meek. Eyes flashing silver darts of rage, she blazed, "How dare you sir? What right do you have?"

The man was just as angry. "Why the right of any horseman to stop a woman from attempting a feat beyond her power," he returned. "You would ruin a good mare with your stupidity. I wonder that the man who owns this beauty would allow you to abuse her so."

Byrony's back stiffened at the insult to both herself and her uncle. "Blast!" she swore, ignoring his start of surprise at the oath from a lady's lips. "I don't know who you are but no gentleman would dare to speak so to a lady."

Deveril's eyes ran over the bedraggled habit, the bared legs, and masculine seat on the horse. "What lady? All I see is an impetuous brat with no sense or decorum," he drawled.

"I will have your heart for that," Byrony vowed. His laugh was a goad she didn't need.

"You'd better bring help, my dear."

"I need none but if I did, rest assured, my uncle would see to it," she shot back.

"And who pray tell is your uncle?" Damn but the woman was beautiful despite the temper. Deveril's glance traveled the length of her body, noticing for the first time the soft curves encased in the worn habit. Hot! Fiery! A woman a man could enjoy taming. Who was she?

"That . . ." Byrony began through gritted teeth, ". . . is my lord, Charles Ravensly."

Deveril's brows drew together in a frown. "The devil you say."

"If you don't believe me, ask my groom over there." Byrony gestured abruptly to the knoll where Sam waited.

"Charles has no kin."

"Then who am I and how did I come by this horse and the escort of his groom?"

"I don't know but I mean to find out," Deveril decided angrily. No one would batten on Charles if he had anything to say to the matter. Everyone in England knew Charles had no kin left. His sister might be still alive but since no one, including Charles, had heard from her in years he doubted it. And anyway, this woman was too young to be anything but an adventuress.

"Let go of my reins." Byrony tried once more to jerk away but could not.

"Not until I find out what's going on here." Deveril nudged his stallion into a trot, forcing Sunset to keep pace.

Byrony swallowed the more visible aspects of her temper. Pulling on the reins had proved less than useless. She would not disgrace herself further with more wasted efforts. Revenge was within her grasp. This creature would soon know she spoke the truth. Sam would set him straight.

To her amazement the groom greeted the other man like a favored friend, calling him his grace. This ill-tempered, arrogant male was none other than the Devil Duke himself.

"So you are Charles' sister's child?" Deveril cocked a brow at the woman whose horse he still held. Now that Sam had confirmed her identity, it was easy to see the Ravensly stamp on her face and those distinctive eyes. She had a look of Charles as well, the arrogant tilt to her chin and the I-am-who-I-am expression that had made Charles so different from most of the sycophants that peopled his world. But she was a woman and a damnably stupid one at that for risking a horse of the mare's caliber over that course. He scowled, remembering the sharp lash of her tongue. She had no manners either.

"I think you'd best dismount and allow Sam to resaddle your horse."

"I won't. There is no need."

"There is every need. A lady—" the emphasis he placed on the term wasn't lost on Byrony "—would not appear in public dressed as you are."

"And what do you know of ladies?" Byrony was so angry she let the guard on her too-blunt tongue slip beyond her control. She nearly quailed at the look leveled on her. She didn't need Sam's indrawn hiss of shock to tell her she had erred badly. She opened her lips to tender an apology but Deveril didn't give her the chance to take back the unwise words.

"Ladies are outside my realm. Certainly, I have had only one example of that extinct species, Charles' wife, Kate. But I do know the demimonde. And let me tell you, my girl, you ape them well."

Byrony flushed at the insult. Her words had been impetuous. His were deliberate. Tillie had said he seemed to deliberately set out to antagonize. She had not believed it. She did now.

"If I had a sword, I would run you through," she said through gritted teeth.

He laughed. "You could try, my pretty, but I doubt you would succeed." With one smooth motion he dismounted and was at her side.

Before Byrony could deduce what he was about, he lifted her from the saddle and set her on her feet without even the pretense of gentleness. "How dare you?"

He flicked her nose with an impudent finger. "You repeat yourself."

Byrony stepped back with a glare. Damn him for laughing at her. She preferred his anger to his amusement. Scarcely noticing that Sam was changing the tack, she focused on his wickedly rugged face. "You are no gentleman," she declared roundly.

"And you are no lady."

"And have no wish to be. But I am no tart either. I'll thank you not to treat me as one."

Deveril's eyes raked over her. This time he saw more than the Ravensly stamp and more than the beauty which she had in abundance even in the deplorable habit. No woman of his acquaintance would have stood up to him the way she had. She showed plenty of spirit but not an ounce of fear. A tiny measure of respect was born, surprising him. Until now he respected no woman but Kate. His mother and all like her had taught their lessons well.

"Sunset is ready, your grace. Shall I mount Miss Byrony?"

Deveril turned to find Sam watching him without expression. "I'll do it."

Byrony wished the sidesaddle to Jericho. If it had not been for the awkward saddle, she could have mounted herself. All she wanted was the ride to be done. She devoutly hoped she never laid eyes on the Devil Duke again. The idea of having to be pleasant to him for Charles' sake galled her.

"My lady." Deveril bent down and cupped his hands.

Despite his almost bowing position he didn't look the least diminished. Byrony stared at him, wishing she dared refuse his help. But caution and an instinct for survival made her heed the warning in his eyes. And the challenge. Words never learned at her mother's knee sizzled through her mind. She gave voice to none of them. She had had enough insults to last her a lifetime. If it killed her, she would act the lady until she was safely out of his reach.

"Thank you, your grace." Gritted teeth did not make for sweet speech, she found. It also didn't protect her from the insufferable man's silent laughter. A second later she was settled in the saddle and was able to look down on him from a superior position. She couldn't resist making use of it. "You do that well. I had no idea that dukes were trained in the arts of a groom."

There was no hint of anything beyond humor in his voice as he replied, "But then you know little about dukes, I think."

"Cochon!" she muttered, feeling safe in venting her vexation in French.

But she was not safe, for he took up the gauntlet in excellent French. Though he spoke softly, this time there was no amusement in him. Byrony flushed hotly and kicked her horse to a trot, refusing to look at the duke.

On the ride to Ravenscourt, Deveril wasn't certain what he felt. There was no artifice in this hoydenish niece of Charles', no attempt to bewitch, no lies, certainly no missishness. He was even beginning to wonder if he had misjudged the situation on the jump course. Before he had stopped her, she had been handling the barriers and the mare with consummate ease. He had been so intent on watching her he hadn't even identified the horse she was riding. Not surprising despite his familiarity with Charles' stables. Sunset was the new acquisition that Charles had touted the last time they had been together, before the summons that had prompted him to head for the country. Odd that Charles had purchased the mare when he usually preferred geldings. Had he known Byrony was coming?

The pink-tinted walls of Ravenscourt rose majestically before them as the three riders broke out of the trees. The lush lawns of the surrounding area lay like rich emerald skirts around its stone feet. The large fountain gurgling in the cobbled courtyard provided diamond-like jewels to adorn its splendor. Ravenscourt was one of the showplaces of the area, second only to his own home, Castleton.

But Ravenscourt had a quality that his home lacked, or at least it had always seemed so to Deveril. There was a peace here that he had never known within his walls. Built by Lord Charles' grandfather as a home for his beloved wife, it began a tradition of serenity and love for all the future generations. Each descendant had been blessed with a love match which endured until death. Somehow coming to Ravenscourt never ceased to promote a tiny feeling of envy in Deveril's breast, an emotion with which he had little familiarity.

For a moment he thought back to his childhood. There had been no love in his family, not for himself, his father, or his mother. Hate, barely controlled from his mother, and cold logic and a demand for perfection from his father had colored his later years after he had learned the truth of his mother. Before that, there had been the adoration he had held for the beautiful, deceitful woman that had given him birth.

Byrony looked neither right nor left when she halted in front of the main entrance. The duke's hands spanned her waist to aid her down. She suffered his touch in silence, conscious of her surroundings and her unmannered behavior. She couldn't bring herself to apologize. But at least she could avoid adding any more tinder to the fire.

Deveril stepped away from Byrony, no more eager to bandy words with her than she was with him. Fortunately for both, Charles came down the stairs at that moment to greet them.

"I see you two have met," he observed, inadequately hiding his satisfaction. "Did you enjoy the ride, my dear? Was Sunset all that I promised?"

"Yes, the mare is a delight." She attempted to infuse warmth into her voice but only partially succeeded.

"And you Deveril? How was she? Was she all that I told you?"

Deveril's eyes narrowed.

"She is a sweet goer," he replied carefully.

Charles came as close to beaming as a man of his dignity could. "Good." He turned to Byrony. "I shall take Deveril into the study while we wait for you to change and join us."

Byrony searched his face, sensing some hidden motive. A month had given her a measure of her uncle but certainly not a deep enough knowledge to ferret out all his thoughts. The duke was watching Charles, a look on his face, she suspected, that was similar to her own.

"As you wish, uncle," she agreed finally, not reassured by the delight her acquiescence spawned. She turned to Deveril determined to behave with decorum. She would not risk embarrassing her relative with rag manners. "Thank you for your escort, your grace." The stilted phrase lacked warmth but at least it was civil.

Deveril's blue eyes flashed at the patent insincerity. He preferred her honest insult to the lip service she now offered. "The pleasure was mine," he drawled, equally insincere. He observed the flare of angry color in her cheeks.

Byrony swung away quickly and hurried up the steps. Charles saw the way his godson's eyes followed Byrony's angry exit. And she was angry. As was Deveril, if he was any judge.

"So you have crossed swords with my niece, have you?" Charles waited for Deveril to face him. He hadn't missed the stiffening of the duke's body when he had spoken.

"Let's just say she takes after you in all but manners."

"I'll wager it was an even draw who came off second best." His words were a goad meant to stir Deveril to betray himself. It didn't succeed.

"I had no idea you had any kin, Charles."

"She is Julia's daughter. Surely you guessed." Sadness, controlled but distinct, darkened his voice for a moment.

"And Julia?"

"Dead. Byrony brought her home to me just in time."

"Byrony?"

Charles gestured him up the steps. "Come in and have a drink and I shall tell you. You, of all people, will appreciate my niece and what she went through to come to England."

Deveril wasn't certain that he wanted to appreciate anything about Byrony. But if Charles wanted to talk he would just listen. It was the least he could do after all the times the younger man had poured his troubles into Charles' ears.

Chapter Five

"She held a pistol on you?" Deveril exclaimed. "I can believe the part about the breeches. I found the chit astride a horse not an hour ago. She rides like a man." And spits like a cat when she's angry, he added silently. "But a pistol?"

Charles frowned at the disapproval in Deveril's voice. "She wouldn't have lasted long in her world if she had not learned how to protect herself," he pointed out.

"Why didn't she write you? She obviously knew who you were and where to find you."

Charles couldn't say he had not wondered the same thing himself. "Pride perhaps."

"Misguided then, surely." Deveril took a drink and sat back in a languid sprawl. If Charles wanted to believe that rough-and-tumble female even knew the meaning of the word, then far be it from him to enlighten him.

Charles studied the man across the desk from him. He had hoped Deveril would receive the bizarre tale with more appreciation. "I would have thought my niece's unconventional behavior would appeal to you of all people."

Deveril's brows rose. "Why should it matter what I think of the girl?" Despite his outward control, Deveril felt his insides tense. Only a fool would miss the look in Charles' eyes. Damn my promise, he thought savagely.

"You have never wanted for sense, Dev. I hope you remember to whom and of whom you speak."

"I remember too well." Bitterness slipped out as Deveril slammed his glass on the table beside his chair. "Get to the point. I have no doubt there is one."

Charles inclined his head. "You gave me the right to choose your bride. I choose Byrony."

"The devil!" Deveril shot to his feet. "The whole purpose of my getting leg-shackled was to redeem myself with Society." The sneer in his words made the name almost a curse. "What can that hoyden possibly contribute to my position? Her past allied with mine only compounds the problem."

"Her heritage is unexceptional," Charles fired back, surging to his feet. "And I'll thank you to remember that. Byrony can be taught the social graces before the season begins. We can put it about that she has been living on the continent until now. None will gainsay us."

"I am no tutor. And I'll be damned if I'll act as cover for your ewe lamb."

Damn! He could feel the noose closing about his neck. And worse still was the knowledge he had put the rope there himself. And for what? To satisfy the hypocrites like his mother that ruled his world. The thought galled him. To have his future held in the hands of a hoyden was beyond anything. If he had any sense, he would go back on his word.

Charles took a deep breath and tried to control his temper. Nothing had ever been gained with Deveril when his back was up. "You need not do anything. I shall see to Byrony's education. If you give her a chance, she will make you an admirable wife. Certainly, she will be able to understand you better than those milk and water creatures that await you at Almack's or the like. Think on it, Dev," he advised quietly.

"Perhaps I don't wish to be understood." Deveril stared out the window for a moment. "Release me from my word."

He turned to Charles. "Leave me to pay my own way to Hades."

Charles shook his head. "I cannot. My Kate loved you as the son we never had. For her, if not for myself, I cannot."

"And what of your niece? Have you thought of her?"

Charles smiled grimly. "Do not pretend you care about her. It is yourself that concerns you."

Deveril jerked away to pace to the window. "I am selfish. I admit it. But in this case you must see this is insane. It cannot work."

"It will work. Byrony needs a protector. I cannot be that for her. You can. You will know how to control her strength and she will match you in ways you don't know."

"You're dreaming." Deveril swung around and stalked back to the chair. He flung himself against the cushions with a scowl. "We shall tear each other to shreds. She's a hellcat."

"And you are a devil." Charles resumed his seat. "A perfect match.

"A fool's errand."

A knock sounded at the door. A moment later Byrony stepped into the room. Arrayed in a soft gray muslin gown of severely straight lines, she appeared tall and elegantly serene. Her back against the door, Byrony surveyed the occupants of the study. Deveril looked furious. Charles' face held lines of strain. An argument. Tension was in the air. Hiding her apprehension, she came forward and took the chair Charles held for her.

Deveril studied her as she moved across the room. The hoyden was gone and a lady stood in her place. Beautiful! She had a grace of movement. A maturity that most women would envy. With her hair drawn away from her face, he could see the strength and the spirit Charles spoke of. The combination was unusual and intriguing. The instant Deveril realized he actually liked the look of her, he scowled. He would not be caught in her toils. No woman was what she seemed and this one was no exception. He had seen her act the termagant. She had a temper beneath that serene exterior. And she used it.

Byrony stayed silent. She braced herself as her uncle began to speak. Nothing prepared her for the words that filled the silence.

"I have just been telling Deveril about you, my dear, and between us we have come to an agreement. Deveril is to be your husband."

Appalled, Byrony stared at Charles. Her worst fears were more than realized. She and that detestable man were to coexist peaceably without resorting to murder. It was impossible! It was insanity!

"I refuse." She could do naught else. She had agreed to allow her uncle to settle her future and her marriage but this she could not tolerate. Fingers linked tightly in her lap, she stared at him, willing Charles to understand.

"Are you retracting your word?"

"You cannot expect me to keep it in these circumstances."

"I told you it would not work." Deveril added his voice to the discussion. Part of him was relieved the chit was backing out of the arrangement. Another side wondered at her refusal. Despite his reputation, he was not considered completely unmarriageable.

Byrony turned on Deveril with a fierce look. "You may want this match but I assure you, sir, *I* do not."

"One does not address a duke as sir," Deveril observed scathingly.

"And one does not address a tyrant as husband!"

Charles frowned at the open antagonism both showed. They looked ready to go at each other tooth and nail. "Enough. You sound like children throwing tantrums. I won't have it. You have each given me your word."

"I cannot marry him," Byrony said angrily. "Choose any other and I will gladly do as you say."

"And who else would take you?" Deveril taunted. "You

need the protection of my title just to pull you out of the muck of your background."

Byrony swelled with rage at the slur on her past. "Don't talk to me of background. I, at least, had an excuse for my behavior. What's yours?"

"She has a point," Charles murmured, earning a murderous glare from both Deveril and Byrony.

"Shut up, Charles," Deveril growled. "I will not be chastised by some chit with more hair than wit."

"And I won't be branded by a rake as unfit to wife," she snapped, jumping to her feet. "You and the society whose opinion you so value can go straight to Hades."

Byrony couldn't have said anything more idiotic in Deveril's eyes. He surged to his feet, ready to shake some sense into the brazen girl.

Charles instantly had him by the arm and waved Byrony from the room.

"Calm yourself," Charles commanded.

"I congratulate you, Charles. She's a shrew."

Charles pushed Deveril back in his chair. "You provoked her."

"I did—" He stopped on seeing the look in Charles' eyes. "Not that much." He changed his statement to fit the truth.

"She has a temper. You knew it."

"She's a shrew." He wasn't going to back down on that point.

Charles shrugged. "Perhaps. Give her time to cool down and then go after her."

Deveril glared at the older man. "This was your idea. You go after her."

Charles sat down again, wondering if his Kate could have handled the two stubborn people any better. Somehow, he thought so. If they had been two cats trapped in a bag and shaken and then dumped in a mud puddle, they couldn't have been angrier or more ready to spit and claw. Yet, the moment he had interfered, both had turned on him.

Odd, that.

Deveril took a deep breath. He wasn't given to shouting. His temper might be legendary but it was usually ice cold, not white hot. That woman had a lot to answer for. "Suppose you tell me what else you have planned for my nuptials. Since you have chosen the bride, what of the wedding?"

"Since Byrony is in half-mourning, the ceremony will be private and held here at Ravenscourt. Then I will send the proper notices to the *Gazette*. Naturally I will attend to the outfitting of the bride. Even as we speak, her dress is being readied in London. It should arrive within the week."

"Rushing it a bit, are you not?" Deveril drawled.

Charles shrugged. "There is nothing to lose."

"Except my freedom."

Charles ignored the mutter, wanting to get through the business part as soon as possible. "Now for the settlements."

"Settlements? I thought you said the chit was penniless."

"Her name is Byrony. I would thank you to use it. It will avail you nothing to continue in this vein." Charles glared at Deveril, making no secret of his displeasure at Deveril's disrespect. "I will not have you treating Byrony as one of your lightskirts. She is my niece and a lady. You would do well to remember that."

Deveril gave him back look for look. "Apparently she will soon be my wife."

"You will treat her as she deserves as my relative. For me and for my Kate if not for yourself and Byrony."

"You use that debt well." The moment he said it, Deveril wished the remark unspoken. All others might be prey for his tongue and his black temper, but not Charles.

Charles rose, looking older than Deveril had ever seen him. "Perhaps you are right. I withdraw my offer. You may choose your own way to Hades."

Deveril was before him in an instant. "I spoke too hastily."

Charles watched him for a moment. He knew what his

words had cost. To his knowledge Deveril had never apologized to anyone for anything. Charles touched his arm. "Can you not believe I have only your best interests at heart?"

Deveril could, but he just could not see that Byrony was the one to do all that Charles hoped. The chit was impossible. Argumentative, unladylike, a shrew, and more boy than girl in her behavior. "Any other but her."

Charles shook his head. "None other but her. Now shall we speak of settlements?"

Byrony fled the walls of Ravenscourt as though chased by the hounds of hell. How could she bear it? Her mother could not have known what her promise would mean. The man was impossible! A rake! An unprincipled creature that few called friend! To live with him, to give her life and her person into his keeping was a fate not to be borne. Yet what else could she do? Charles' summation of her future was too accurate to ignore. And her word. The chain by which she was bound. She, who had lived a life of freedom so unlike that of other women, was soon to be caged.

Only luck guided Byrony's footsteps to the path leading to the heart of the woods. With one furtive glance over her shoulder she quickly lost herself in the dense undergrowth and trees that guarded the back of the mansion. As soon as Byrony knew she was safe from being seen from the house, she slowed her pace. The narrow trail twisted deeper into the forest until the sun dimmed to a soft duskiness. Suddenly, she stepped into a small clearing, an isolated haven in the midst of the green world of silence.

Her feet kicked up tiny showers of dead leaves when she crossed the open area to sink down on a fallen tree trunk which was lightly covered with dark moss. Muted sounds of birds from the less dense part of the thicket filtered through the trees but she scarcely heard them. At any other time she would have found pleasure in the beauty of the glen. But at the moment she was blind to everything but the problem looming on the horizon. The minutes passed as she sat alone and unmoving. No matter which way her brain turned, she could find no way out of doing as her uncle asked. So deep were her thoughts she was unaware of being observed.

Deveril stood on the edge of the clearing studying the still figure. To see her now was to be deceived by her silence. With a stray shaft of sunlight glinting on her raven wing hair, she had the power to stir a man's blood. But not his, he decided angrily on feeling the heat in his loins. They may be bound together in this farce but he would not succumb to her allure. No woman would ever hold him in thrall.

Determined to prod Byrony out of her preoccupation, Deveril stalked closer, making no attempt to muffle his approach. Her eyes kindled when she saw who had followed her. He was glad at the show of temper. This was the real Byrony.

"What are you doing here?" she demanded irritably.

Deveril's lips twisted as he sat down. "I came to find you."

Byrony glared at him. "Why?"

"I thought to get to know my betrothed better."

"I have no desire to further our acquaintance," Byrony managed icily. "The less I know of you, the better."

Deveril grinned, this time amused. "I had thought such a course would prove onerous for you when it comes time for us to share the marriage bed." He gave an elaborate shrug. "However, I suppose you know your own mind best."

Incensed was not the word for the emotion that filled Byrony's mind at his indelicate comment. This was plain speaking indeed and clearly designed to offend.

"We will not be sharing a bed!"

Deveril managed to look surprised. "Do married people not do that any longer? I am surprised. I thought that was the whole purpose of getting shackled."

Byrony surged to her feet. "You arrogant . . ." Words

failed her. "I am no brood mare!"

Deveril looked her up and down as though making a mental list of her good points. "I can see that."

Byrony clenched her hands into fists. If she had had the strength, she would have planted him a facer. He was baiting her and they both knew it. And fool that she was, she was rising to the lure at every cast. Frustration rode her temper with sharp spurs. "Please leave me. I don't want you here."

Deveril rose to his feet, his humor falling away in an instant. "That's too bad, my girl, because I intend to stay. You and I have some things to discuss. And I wish to do so away from the house where we cannot be disturbed."

"I'm not interested in anything you wish to discuss." Byrony started to turn away. Deveril caught her by the shoulders.

"You'll do as I say." It was a command with no attempt made to soften its authority.

Byrony's head came up with a snap. "Think again. We are not wed yet." She tried unsuccessfully to pull away from him. "Let me go." Her eyes flashed silver fire at the continued imprisonment.

Deveril tightened his grasp on her shoulders. "You want taming," he gritted between clenched teeth.

"Not by you." The challenge was out before she could stop it. The answering challenge in Deveril's eyes warned Byrony of her mistake.

Deveril dragged her close. Byrony fought him then. He laughed at her struggles. This he understood.

"Let me go, damn you. You have no right." Trying to kick him in the shins was worse than useless in the thin slippers she wore.

Deveril tightened his hold until her writhing body was pressed against his. He pinned her arms to her sides and dipped his head. "Fight me. I like spirit and you have plenty."

There was no escape. His lips captured hers with no

pretense at gentleness. His will against hers. His strength matched against hers. Byrony twisted, turned, and kicked. Nothing worked. The kiss went on and on. Drawing the breath from her body. Darkness swirled about her head. With one last effort she gathered her strength and pushed up and away from his chest. His grunt of pain was thick in her ear as one arm came free. Swinging out without thought she tried to hit him. Deveril must have seen the clenched hand coming. His arm came up to block but not soon enough to keep her from connecting. The jar from her wrist hitting his forced her hand open so that the blow was a heavy slap that snapped his head back. Byrony backed up, her breasts heaving with the exertions. Deveril rubbed his aching jaw and glared at her. She glared back.

"You meant that."

"Should I have let you paw me?" Byrony tossed her head angrily.

"I did not paw you." Deveril was furious but wary. She had put quite a bit of power in that slap. His thigh where she had caught him with her knee was throbbing painfully. He felt as if he had been in a battle and come out the loser. His eyes narrowed on her face, seeing the results of his own handiwork. Byrony's lips were swollen and she was rubbing one shoulder as though it hurt.

"I hope, madam, I won't be treated to this kind of behavior on our wedding night."

"You are unspeakable! You attack me and you say that! Do you think if I had a choice that I would ally myself with an unprincipled, overdressed dandy? An arrogant coxcomb?"

"My part of the deal is no better. A shrew! A woman who fights like a man! Don't you know what a slap is?"

"No but I'm certain you do," she returned triumphantly.

He started to take a step toward her then changed his mind. She looked ready to take another swing at him if he touched her. For the moment he wasn't prepared to give her the chance.

Byrony braced herself, knowing even as she did so her strength wasn't up to much more.

"I am going back."

"I will escort you."

"I can take care of myself."

Deveril inclined his head. "But who will take care of the ones you attack?"

Without a word she turned toward the path, ignoring the fact that Deveril followed. A pace separated them as they headed back for Ravenscourt. Byrony counted the steps, with each one taking more out of her than it should. She was never more grateful for the sight of the pink-tinted walls of Charles' home. The need to escape Deveril's silent presence was almost overwhelming.

Charles waited at his library window, watching the couple stroll toward the house. He frowned at the distance separating them. He had hoped that they would have found a way to be comfortable with one another if they were away from the house. Charles sighed and glanced at the portrait of his wife above the mantel.

"It seems, my Kate, that neither will give way. Two stubborn ones, my love. I almost wish I had not thought of this scheme. I care for both. What if I have chosen wrongly? Deveril has had enough trouble in his life. And Byrony too."

He turned back to the window in time to see Deveril take his leave with little more than a nod in Byrony's direction.

"Fool! He has more address than that," Charles muttered. "Would it choke him to smile? And she is no better. So rigid! No hint of softness in her manner. I have truly set us all a task."

Byrony entered the house angrier than when she had left it. The first person she saw was her uncle coming out of the library. "I must speak with you," she said on impulse.

Charles inclined his head. "If you wish but it will change nothing."

Byrony followed him into the study. "You must see we cannot like each other."

"You have not tried."

"Tried! If you could have been with me a few moments ago, you would know differently." Charles' raised brows told her of the need to lower her voice and to control her temper. She swallowed and took a deep breath. "There must be another way." To be reduced to pleading went against the grain but she would do anything to avoid the alliance looming in her future.

Charles took her hand in his. "It will not be as bad as you fear. Deveril is a good man. Given half a chance he will make you a fine husband, perhaps even one that you could love."

Byrony stared at him, stifling a desire to laugh. "Never."

Charles ignored her as if she had not spoken. "But you must do your part."

Byrony pulled her hand free. "You ask too much."

"And you, my dear, are a very stubborn young lady," Charles returned, losing his temper.

Byrony headed for the door. "I came by the trait honestly," she threw over her shoulder.

A moment later she gained the relative quiet of her chamber. And there she stayed, sending her regrets to her uncle for dinner and refusing the services of her maid. She stood at the window, barely aware of the passage of time as evening became night. No moon lit the landscape just as no thought provided a way out of the coil in which she was entangled. Restless, worried, she paced back and forth, each stride more determined. The angry swirl of her skirts punctuated every turn. From the window then back to the bed then to the window once more. The breeze drifting in through the open casement was a tantalizing whisper. To be away if only for a little while! The thought grew into a desire that had to be fulfilled.

Unable to stand her gilded cage a moment longer, Byrony stripped out of her skirts and dug into the huge closet, praying that Tillie had not thrown away her breeches. She emerged triumphant an instant later, the rough garment held aloft like a trophy.

Stealth born out of a need to escape undetected got her dressed in record time and down the back stairs to the stables. Sunset, being a prize mount, was housed too deep in the stable to be reached easily but Sam's hack was near. Saddling the gelding took a few precious moments then she was astride. Urging the horse out of the yard at a controlled walk, she guided him toward the path she had taken earlier that day. In no time they were far enough away for her to increase the pace to a trot.

Byrony knew little of the countryside so she counted more on the hack's sense of direction than her own. No one marked their shadows as they crossed country lanes and passed small darkened cottages. Occasionally a dog barked but Byrony scarcely noticed. For the first time in many days Byrony allowed herself to relax, to breathe in the night air without wondering if she had broken this rule or that, if she had been too honest or too quiet. The duke and the plans for her future receded with every mile that passed beneath the gelding's feet. For now it was enough to be unfettered.

Suddenly shots rang out. The gelding bucked then settled beneath Byrony's expert handling. Curiosity had always been Byrony's besetting sin. She could not pass this opportunity by without at least seeing what was amiss. Ahead loomed a small thicket of trees beside the road on which she rode. Pulling the pistol her father had given her from her pocket, Byrony cocked it.

Curious she might be but foolish she was not. Moving as quietly as she was able, she approached the grove carefully. Voices . . . two of them. A woman's scream. A man's curse. A robbery. Even as the idea was born, Byrony was pushing through the trees to go to the aid of the hapless travelers.

The gelding neighed in protest. The robbers, warned, turned and fired on her. Another horse screamed to her right as the shots whizzed by her head. A deep voice shouted a command just as a huge black stallion broke through the trees. Byrony, her hands full with the now bucking hack, could do little to help as Deveril thundered after the ruffians when they took flight. By the time she got her mount under control, Deveril had returned and the young couple she had thought to help were climbing back in their carriage.

"You little fool!" Deveril roared the moment they were alone. "You could have been killed!"

Byrony glared at Deveril, her hands tight on the reins. "I almost was, thanks to you. I had everything under control until you came charging in here."

"I saved your life," he snapped.

"It didn't need saving," she snapped back, yanking the hack's head around to return home.

Deveril caught her bridle, thwarting her attempt to escape. Byrony pulled on the reins, suddenly conscious of a searing pain in her left arm. She groaned as her mount threw up his head and put further pressure on her arm.

"What's amiss?" Deveril demanded, peering at her in the darkness.

"Nothing. Just let me pass." Byrony tried once more to dislodge his hold on the bridle.

Deveril crowded closer until his stirrup touched hers. "Stop struggling. I'm not letting you go until I see if you are hurt."

"I told you I am fine." Byrony gritted her teeth against the lie. Her shoulder felt on fire and her balance was none too steady. One of the bullets had entered her shoulder. Her hand was wet with her own blood from where she had instinctively touched it.

Deveril ignored her words. "Get down before you fall off," he commanded.

"I never fall."

"Stop arguing and do as I say before someone comes along. If you cannot have care for your own reputation, then think of Charles'." With those blunt words he reached across and curled an arm about Byrony's waist, pulling her in front of him onto his stallion.

Byrony made one ill-advised attempt to escape, but succeeded only in hurting her arm. Her head swam for an instant with pain and she groaned again. Before she could protest, Deveril slid from his horse and lifted her to the ground.

"I should leave you here to face the consequences of your actions but I won't," he muttered, tearing at the vest and shirt she wore until her shoulder was bare to his touch. Cursing the lack of light to allow him to assess the damage, he gently probed the wound on her upper arm.

Byrony stiffened against his hand, not only because of the discomfort his blind search created but because no man had handled her thus in her life. Deveril's fingers against her bare skin were not to be borne and she told him so.

"Quiet. If you think I'm interested in more than your health at the moment, you're an even bigger fool than I thought." Yanking a handkerchief from his pocket, he pressed it against the graze then tucked her torn shirt closed. "We shall make for the Castle. Ravenscourt is too far."

"No!"

Deveril rose, his mouth tight at her continued stubbornness. "That was not a question. We are going and you will be still. Every time you move, you bleed more."

"I know that. I have been shot before," she snapped as he lifted her carefully in his arms.

She did not see the flicker of surprise in his dark eyes. "How the devil—" He bit off his question. This unfeminine creature had probably been dueling or something equally unsuited to her gender and breeding.

Byrony held herself stiff as Deveril lifted her onto Orion's back. Much as she hated to admit it, Deveril was right. She hadn't the strength to fight him at present. His words about Charles and his position in the neighborhood held too much truth as well. Whether she wanted it or not, she had to accept Deveril's help.

"I shall go with you out of regard for my uncle but you do not have the right to take me to task."

Deveril mounted behind Byrony and pulled her snugly against his chest. "We have had this discussion before. I take whatever rights I deem necessary for my comfort. And if I feel like turning you over my knee, I shall. I shall not be a complacent husband who lets you roam at will. It is past time someone taught you some manners and some discretion."

"You—teach me discretion?" Byrony laughed shortly.

Deveril guided the stallion through the trees to a back lane where there was little chance of their being spotted. "Who better than I?"

Byrony was caught once more in the stinging banter that colored all their exchanges. For once she was glad of the sharp replies. To stay abreast of Deveril as her pride demanded, she had to concentrate on his every word. That left precious little time to be concerned with the pain in her shoulder and her need to lay her head somewhere to rest. She could almost find it in her heart to be grateful to Deveril for finding her. That feeling lasted for the first two minutes of his tirade on her behavior. By the time they reached the Castle, she was back to hating the sight, sound, and touch of the man.

Chapter Six

"I can walk," Byrony protested as Deveril started up the stairs with her in his arms.

"And I said you won't." He shifted her carefully, glaring down at her when she groaned. "Lie back and pretend you're an ordinary woman for a change."

Byrony grimaced but subsided. Truth to tell she was glad she didn't have to climb the winding stairs. Her shoulder hurt. She was tired and discouraged. The idea of having to be in Deveril's debt was more than she could bear. The thought of what her uncle would say if he found out what she had involved herself in plagued her. Until Deveril had so callously pointed out the possible consequences of her behavior, she hadn't considered beyond the need to be free for a while. Now, she realized how selfishly she had acted and that rankled almost as much as her arm pained her.

Deveril pushed open the door to his chamber and strode to the bed. He laid Byrony down and then lit the lamp. Pausing only long enough to shed the light coat he wore, he rolled up his sleeves. "Now let's get you out of your vest and shirt."

Byrony looked at him suspiciously. "That is unnecessary, surely?"

"'Tis the only way and well you know it, my girl. So

dispense with the act of maidenly modesty and let's have done. Unless, of course, you wish me to call my manservant to dress the wound for you?" One brow rose as he awaited her reply.

"All right but turn your back and give me something to cover myself with." On this she would not budge or so she thought.

Deveril stalked to the dressing room and returned with a small towel. "Use this." He flung it at her before turning his back.

Moving gingerly, Byrony managed to get free of the vest without betraying the discomfort her maneuvering cost her. But when she tried to remove her shirt, she could not hold back a gasp of pain. Deveril was beside her in an instant, muttering a curse even as he gently eased her out of the bloodstained garment.

"Only a woman would risk further injury to herself to protect her virtue."

Byrony lay back against the pillows, trying not to notice how Deveril's eyes were tracing the shape of her breasts before he tossed the towel over her. "A moment ago you implied I was less than a woman. Now you say the opposite. Are men always so contrary?" Baiting him kept her mind off the pain as he probed the wound.

Frowning, Deveril rose and disappeared into the dressing room without answering. When he returned he had a bottle of something that smelled vile and stung like the very devil. Byrony bit her lip to keep back a cry as he cleaned the long gash thoroughly.

"You are a woman. There can be no doubt." He grinned as he said it although he didn't so much as look at Byrony's face.

Deveril lifted her to his chest with one arm while he began winding a bandage around her back to pin her shoulder to her side. "I am going to strap you up so that you cannot move this until we get you back to Ravenscourt and your own bed. The bleeding has slowed but the jarring of the ride is bound to start it up again." He pulled the towel away as he spoke. His fingers glided over the pearl smooth fullness of her breasts, lingering for a moment on their softness. He raised his eyes to hers.

Byrony stared back at him, the newness of his touch a shock to momentarily overshadow her temper.

He glanced down, wanting to do more than just trace the silky flesh. The impulse surprised him, making him draw back. She was no different from the rest of her kind. "You would do well to remember that you are indeed a woman."

Byrony jerked away as if scalded. "Seducer!" she accused.

He grinned. "You flatter me."

Byrony maintained a stony silence, speaking again only when Deveril thrust a glass of brandy under her nose and demanded she drink it.

"I will not." She had had nothing to eat since breakfast. Spirits on an empty stomach were demons that hardened drinkers had trouble handling.

Deveril wasted no time with an argument. He simply sat down on the bed beside her and held the glass to her lips. "You will drink or I shall pour it down your throat. The ride will pain you a lot less with this inside you."

Byrony looked at him, seeing the grim set to his mouth. He really meant to make her swallow the vile-tasting liquor. She lifted her head without replying. The brandy burned hot in her throat, making her cough a little. One sip, two. Surely it was enough but no. The glass was still there. By the time Byrony finished the drink, her tongue was numb and her head was starting to spin. She flopped back on the pillows, jarring her shoulder. A groan escaped her lips before she could stop it. Closing her eyes against the pain and the effects of the liquor, she missed the concern on Deveril's face. She scarcely felt the hand he touched to her forehead.

"Rest for a moment while I clean up and then we shall be off."

Byrony heard the words but found it more difficult with each passing second to concentrate on their meaning. The brandy combined with her injury had rendered her too dizzy to lift her head. Or to protest when a few moments later Deveril cradled her in his arms and drew one of his own shirts and a cloak around her. Then, without a word, he carried her down the back stairs to where he had left their horses tied.

"Wrap your fingers in the mane, Byrony," Deveril commanded in a harsh whisper as he settled her onto Orion's saddle.

Byrony obeyed, swaying when he had to let her go long enough to mount behind her. She was glad to lean against his chest and know that his arms would keep her from falling. "I hate brandy," she muttered irritably. "I never could hold it."

His soft chuckle was warm against her ear. "Does it give you a head?"

"Yes," she admitted with a groan. "I promise I will hate you in the morning for making me drink that devil's brew."

Deveril was relieved to hear her talking with even a bit of her spirit. The sight of her pale face when he had returned to his chamber after disposing of the bloody evidence had been a shock. While he wouldn't have minded having her in his bed at his mercy, he found he did not wish her to be laid so low. She was a damnably unfeminine woman but she had pluck to the backbone. Other than a groan or two she had shown more courage than many men he knew would have in the same situation.

His arm tightened on Byrony's waist as Orion stumbled on the dark path. He swore as he felt her tense. "Are you all right?"

"I shall be as soon as we reach Ravenscourt," Byrony managed carefully. If she spoke slowly she could make sense, she discovered.

"It's just ahead. Look."

Byrony peered into the darkness, barely making out the

looming shadow of Ravenscourt. The windows were dark so it would seem her absence was still undetected.

"I shall get you to your chamber and rebind your arm. Will you tell Charles or shall I?"

Deveril's question cut through the mist of pain and liquor. "Neither. There is no reason to worry him."

Deveril frowned over her head. "You cannot mean to hide the wound. How can you? If no one else, your maid will see it."

"Not if I take care." She definitely was not up to arguing with Deveril now.

"A doctor should see it."

"No. There is no need."

"I say there is." He stopped the horses beneath the trees near the rear entrance. After being certain Byrony had a good hold on Orion's mane, he slid to the ground and reached up to lift her down.

"You have no right to demand anything in this." Her head swam with the downward movement. Leaning against him, she muttered into his chest. "Don't think to rule me just because you have helped me tonight. Remember it is your fault that I was shot in the first place."

Deveril gathered her in his arms, glaring down at her pale face. "My fault. Your attic's to let. I rescued you from getting yourself killed," he hissed. He should have known she wouldn't see the truth of the situation. "As I recall, you were occupied with handling a horse that was out of control."

"A horse you caused to bolt with your stupid knight errant charge," she shot back, barely remembering to keep her voice down. Now that they were inside Ravenscourt, it would be too easy to arouse the household.

Deveril countered her charge with an oath he never would have spoken in front of a lady. A fact that Byrony was quick to point out to him. The second oath was no less colorful than the first and coincided with their arrival at her chamber.

"You may put me down here. Even I know a lady does not

entertain men in her bedroom at this hour of the night."

"Don't provoke me, madam." Deveril pushed open the door with muted violence. He held her even tighter, staring down at her with equal measures of anger and a sudden desire in his eyes. "By God, I wish you were up to entertaining me." The words escaped him before he realized it.

Byrony's eyes spit sparks of silver as she uncurled her arm from about his neck and decided not to grace his comment with a response.

Deveril deposited her on the bed, being careful of her sore arm. He sat down beside her and began to slip the shirt he had loaned her off her shoulders.

"I can do it," Byrony protested.

"We have already discovered once this night that you cannot," Deveril replied, taking no notice of her protests. "And we don't have time for any of your maidenly shyness either. Soon the whole household will awake. I must be gone before then and you must be abed as innocently as may be." The shirt came away, leaving Byrony no protection from his eyes. Once again Deveril allowed himself to view the woman he would take to wife.

Byrony crossed her arms over her bare breasts, the movement pulling at her wound. Tears of pain and anger started in her eyes. Deveril saw them before she could turn her face away.

"Little fool," he rasped as he tucked the shirt about her. "I'm not about to ravish you."

"You were staring indecently at me."

"I can't help looking at a beautiful woman," he said after a moment.

Byrony blinked, gazing at him in surprise. This was the first compliment she had had from her future husband and a distinctly uncomfortable one it was, too, she realized. Better his anger than the desire she could see kindling in his eyes.

"I am not beautiful. Nor by your words am I much of a

woman. Remember, I prefer my freedom to marriage to you and my breeches to skirts."

Byrony burned at the way his eyes slipped over her curves until there was no secret of her body unknown to him. She tried to draw the counterpane across her body. He stopped her easily enough.

"I can change your mind," he breathed, lowering his head to take her lips. If the first kiss had been rough, this one was not. It was pure seduction, meant to touch the deepest inner needs of a woman. Byrony had no defense against Deveril's expertise even had she had the strength to resist him. With one hand he held her free arm above her head. The stretch gave him access to her body and he took it, stroking her in a way she had never known. She groaned against his lips. Hating him even as she responded to the caress of his fingers.

When he lifted his head, her lips throbbed with new sensations and her body felt as though it belonged to someone else. "If I had the strength, you'd pay for that," she gasped when she could talk.

Deveril laughed. "So I would, hellcat. But for now save your energy. You don't have time to do a good job of it. Let's cover you up so I won't be distracted while I rebandage your arm."

Byrony wanted to refuse the safety of the nightgown he brought from the dressing room and helped her into. She wanted to order him from her sight. She could do neither. Instead she submitted to his ministrations and in the end suffered yet another kiss. Only this time it was placed on her forehead with all the power of a nanny's salute to a hurt child.

Deveril rose and strolled to the door. On the way he collected Byrony's breeches, his shirt, and cloak. "I shall dispose of these for you, have no fear, my lady."

Byrony lifted herself enough on her one good arm to glare at him. "I'll never marry you. You're nothing but a libertine." It wasn't much of a parting shot but it was the best she could do in the circumstances.

Deveril touched his fingers to his forehead. "More compliments? You'll spoil me if you're not careful." One brow kicked up at the hiss of rage that swelled her breasts beneath the thin lawn of her gown.

Byrony could see only one thing within reach of her hand to throw, a small enameled box. Deveril caught it easily.

"A gift as well. I don't think I have ever had a woman give me presents before," he remarked, staring at the trinket before tucking it in his pocket.

Byrony flopped back on the pillows. "Oh, go away," she muttered. "My head hurts, you abominable man."

After he had left, tears filled Byrony's eyes as she looked into her future. Until Deveril had touched her she hadn't really thought of the marriage bed. It was enough that she had to relinquish her freedom but to be possessed by a man. The idea violated her in ways she was just beginning to realize. But more than all of these was the knowledge that she had responded to a man she professed to hate. How could that be? Was she like those women who sold themselves? The ones her mother had warned her about? Had she moved in a man's world for so long she had truly lost her need to give herself to only one?

She had no answers and no one to ask. Charles would not know even could she bring herself to confide in him. Touching her lips, she wondered how she would survive her life at Deveril's hands.

"*Maman,*" she whispered in the darkness. "How I wish for your counsel in this marriage my promise has brought me. I know little of ladies. And less of husbands."

No soft voice replied to her plea for help, the first she had ever made in her life. Only silence, as deep as the night itself answered her. Byrony was on her own.

Sunlight streamed in the windows, bathing Byrony's

slumbering form in a golden glow. She turned fretfully in her sleep as Tillie opened the remaining blue velvet drapes. Blinking drowsily, Byrony tried to awake but found it difficult. That brandy had done its work too well. Now her head throbbed worse than her shoulder.

"I'm sorry, Miss Byrony, but his lordship asked me to wake you. It has gone past eleven and his grace has been downstairs waiting this hour or more." Tillie came to her side, frowning when Byrony groaned as she struggled upright. "Is something amiss?"

Byrony bit her lip to hold back a gasp of pain. She had moved too quickly. "No, nothing," she replied as soon as she could trust her voice. Inhaling slowly and carefully, she sat up and swung her legs over the side of the bed. "Please tell my uncle I shall be as quick as I can."

Tillie headed for the door. "I shall have the footman deliver the message then I shall help you with your toilet." It wasn't the first time her young mistress had tried to send her on an errand and taken on the task of readying herself for the day.

"I really would prefer to be alone this morning."

Tillie turned around and peered at her. "Are you certain you are all right? You look pale."

"A touch of a headache," Byrony admitted as though reluctant to part with the information.

"Shall I prepare you a draught?"

Byrony managed a smile. "You could but I shall not drink it. If you wish to do something for me, let me be alone for a while." When Tillie still hesitated, she added, "Good as you are, sometimes I need to do for myself."

It took a moment but finally Tillie nodded her understanding. "But I will do your hair."

Byrony was perfectly willing to make that concession since styling her hair would require the use of both her arms. And even if it had not, she would have given way for she knew her tresses were Tillie's pride and joy.

"A bargain."

With a nod Tillie was gone. Byrony didn't hesitate. The maid would not be long and she had much to do before she returned. It was imperative she have her dress on to cover her injured shoulder. But more than that she had to get downstairs as soon as possible to find out what Deveril had told her uncle. Since the doctor was not at her door, she could assume nothing. Charles might know everything or Deveril may have kept silent.

A little over an hour later she had her answer. Deveril, for whatever reason, had kept his own counsel. Charles greeted her just as he had every morning for the past five weeks. Deveril's manner was also the same. Nothing of what had happened the night before showed in those vivid eyes; no hint of anything familiar lurked in the bored drawl with which he said her name.

"You are almost in time for luncheon, my wife to be."

Byrony ignored the provocation of his remark. "I am sorry to keep you waiting."

Charles waved her concern aside with a smile. "It is nothing, my dear. You must sleep as long as you like. The only reason I had Tillie awaken you this day was because I thought you would prefer to know what is afoot for your upcoming nuptials."

Byrony paused as she started to take a seat beside the fire burning in the grate. "What are you speaking of, uncle?"

"The banns will be posted this week. Your clothes shall be arriving shortly and the ceremony is scheduled to be held here in our own chapel. I trust that meets with your approval." He spoke to Byrony but he included Deveril with a look.

"So soon?" she queried faintly, sitting down with more speed than grace.

"There is no need to delay," Charles pointed out. He was on shaky-enough ground as it was. If he gave these two stubborn people any time, one of their fertile minds might devise a way to escape his plan.

Byrony looked at Deveril and wished she had not. If anything, he appeared more bored than ever. Why didn't he do something? He had to want this match even less than she.

Charles rose to his feet. "I must leave you alone for a few moments now. There is a small matter I must attend before we dine."

Before either Byrony or Deveril could say a word, he was gone.

"How do we escape this coil?" Byrony exclaimed. "Have you not thought of something yet? Surely you cannot wish this marriage. I will not be a good wife for you."

"Of that I have no doubt, my girl." Deveril got to his feet and stalked to the window, his hands clasped behind his back. "But . . . I have given my word." He turned around to spear her with a look. "I would not take it amiss, however, if you refused to have me."

"And why should I be the one to break my word?" Byrony said sharply. "I, too, have a sense of honor."

"Then it seems we are at an impasse." Deveril observed her pale face. "How is your arm?"

"Sore."

"Worse than last night?"

"It is not infected if that is the information that you seek." The abrupt switch in topic had to be a ruse. Deveril was up to something. He had to be. The question was what?

"The maid is in your confidence? She knows what happened?"

"No." What was he asking? She looked at him more carefully but could see no clue to his thoughts.

"And your head?"

"Hurts."

His lips twitched slightly at the snap in her answer. Byrony was not amused by the tiny betrayal of amusement. "I told you I did not want it."

He inclined his head. "So you did. I, however, deemed it

necessary. Will you tell me now it did not make the trip less taxing?" His steady glance defied her to lie.

"It dulled the edges," she admitted grudgingly. "But I could have done without it."

"Perhaps. But you would have been a fool to torture yourself needlessly." The sounds of voices in the hall warned that Charles was on his way back. Deveril rose and came to stand before her. "I wish your word on something."

"What right—"

"For my silence I want your promise you will inform me if your wound does not heal as soon as may be. For your sake, we will forgo the doctor but I want no corpse for a bride."

"Blackmail?" Byrony's brows raised as she stared up at him.

"Common sense. If you cannot think of yourself, consider you uncle. You owe him loyalty if nothing else for the way he has taken you in."

"I am well aware of that and need no reminder from you."

"By all that is holy, woman. You would try the patience of a saint."

"And we both know you are not that."

"Your tongue will be the death of you yet," he muttered, stifling the urge to shake her until her teeth rattled.

Byrony put a hand to her head and closed her eyes.

Deveril watched her for a moment, skeptical of the wilted droop of her pose. When one minute became two, he realized this was no ploy for sympathy. With a quick glance at the door he wondered why Charles was lingering outside. Another look at Byrony's pale face sent him from his chair to the tray on the sideboard. Pouring a glass of ratafia, he carried it to her.

"Drink this."

"I don't want any more brandy," Byrony muttered without opening her eyes.

"It is not brandy. It is that concoction your gender deems refreshing." Bending over her, he tipped her head up slightly and held the glass to her lips.

Byrony opened her eyes and looked straight into his. The deep color was even more startling than it had been the night before. "I don—"

"Drink," he commanded. "I promise it will make you feel much more the thing."

Byrony grimaced. "You know it won't do any such thing," she replied before taking a sip.

Charles chose that moment to enter. Both Byrony and Deveril looked toward the door in time to see the wide smile he bestowed on them. Her brows arched as she glanced at Deveril. His grin was faint and more cynical than she liked but at least it held a measure of amusement.

"Now that is what I like to see. I knew you both would come to your senses soon."

Chapter Seven

Byrony stood at her bedroom window watching the dawn inch its way across the sky. One more day gone. Her wedding drew closer and still she could not reconcile herself to the settlement of her future. Her uncle wore a perpetual smile, clearly considering his attempts at matchmaking a success. The reason—one arrogant duke. Glaring at the beauty stretched before her eyes, she reviewed his behavior of the last days. When anyone was near, he pretended to grow increasingly attracted to her. When they were alone he baited her, reverting back to the cynical personality that was no ruse.

At first, the change in him had disconcerted her until she realized it was his way of kicking at the traces and better still, she was certain in her mind, a way to irritate her. He made plans without consulting her. And that rankled. He knew it and his every look told her so. The constant state of silent war ate at her control and her peace. She slept badly, ate little in his presence, and in general heartily wished she could do something that would even the scales. A stupid wish, as it turned out, for her petty attempts to balance the power had failed abysmally. Finally, in desperation she had taken to acting the foil to his lover-like attitude. As yet her strategy had done nothing more than make her uncle smile with greater frequency and much anticipation and Deveril watch her with amusement lurking in those vivid eyes.

The sound of Tillie's footsteps in the corridor brought Byrony to the center of the room. She had been standing at the window for more than an hour. Wrapping her robe around her, she stretched out on the chaise just as the door opened.

Tillie hesitated slightly on seeing that she was awake. "Miss Byrony, could you not sleep again?" She set the tray she carried down on the table beside the chaise. Steam rose delicately from the elegant teapot and the aroma of pastry drifted from beneath the silver-domed cover next to it.

Byrony glanced at the tray then at Tillie. "No," she admitted with a sigh.

Tillie shook her head while staring at her. She started to speak, changed her mind, then changed it yet again. "I would do anything for you," she said slowly at last. "Servants talk among themselves, it is true, but some of us know how to keep a secret. You can trust me."

The offer was given with more seriousness than Byrony had ever heard from the woman. The maid looked worried, she decided as she tried to frame an answer that would not offend and still show her appreciation of the offer. Just for a moment Byrony surprised herself by wishing she could confide in the country woman.

"If I had need of help, I know I could count on you. It's just that I am not used to this life. It is strange and confusing. Too many things have happened in too short a time." Tillie appeared skeptical but Byrony pretended not to notice. "What have you brought me today? Suddenly I feel like eating something." She wasn't really hungry but the tray and its contents provided a diversion.

"Cook made those biscuits you enjoy so much. And tea." She lifted the dome to display the rounded mound of delicate pastry bursting with fresh berries. The aroma alone should have been enough to tempt Byrony's appetite. "She said I was to see that you ate at least half of these or not to come back to the kitchen," Tillie added with a meaningful look.

Byrony had to smile. The cook was a tiny woman with a soft voice who somehow ruled the lower floor with an iron hand. Even the austere butler bowed before her when she was in one of her moods. "Then I suppose I must get busy." She waved a hand and Tillie poured her a cup of tea. She wondered aloud at the prepared tray at so early an hour.

"Have you forgotten your engagement? His grace said you might," Tillie murmured, handing Byrony a small plate with a biscuit.

"Forgotten?" Damn him! What had he concocted now behind her back.

"Your ride this morning to the Castle so that you may see your new home." Tillie frowned, sensing something was amiss but unsure what. She had begun to wonder if the tales of the duke had not been exaggerated by the London tabbies. He was not nearly as bad as he had been painted. He was unfailingly polite to those beneath him, a trait any servant admired. He never forgot to inform her of Byrony's plans though her mistress often did herself.

"Today? I had no knowledge . . ." She stopped herself, realizing how much of her situation she betrayed. "Well, I daresay Deveril neglected to mention the matter to me or I did not remember if he did."

The lie stuck in her throat, spoiling her appetite. Not that she could allow that to show or Tillie would have grounds for her obvious suspicions. For two days her betrothed had seen fit to ignore her very existence. It wasn't that she wanted his irritating presence but she was fully aware of the appearance he was creating. Already she was subject to the smiles when he seemed to dance attendance on her and the pitying whispers when he did not. Only pride kept her head high and her expression serene while she went about preparing for this marriage she detested. Anger and humiliation were sharp spurs. If Deveril had set out deliberately to irritate her, he could not have done a better job.

Sipping at her tea, Byrony watched silently as Tillie laid out her new riding habit and boots. The clothes from London had arrived and proved to be an excellent fit. The colors were beautiful and the fabrics richer than she had ever seen. But they brought her no pleasure, not this morning. The sight of the long trailing skirt on the habit made her wish for her breeches. She hated having to ride sidesaddle. But at least she would be mounted as she hadn't been for the days it had taken for her arm to heal. Slow carriage rides down country lanes were not and never had been a favorite and that was all that detestable man had allowed her until he deemed her fit to ride. The thought that he had refused to take her word on her well-being still rankled. As did the fact he had insisted on seeing for himself, over her very strenuous objections, the wound in question. She could still remember the feel of his fingers on her bare skin after he had held her tightly against him and pulled open the collar of her gown. The helplessness she had felt pinned against him beneath the trees where they had stopped had driven her past the point of controlling her temper. She had struck out at him. He had blocked the blow easily, laughing as she swore. Byrony touched her lips, remembering the kiss that had followed. A punishment. There was no other way to describe what he had done. When it was over, she hadn't protested as he had refastened her gown and carried her to the carriage without a word. That was the last she had seen of him until this morning.

Setting her empty cup on the tray, Byrony rose. She could not escape. Deveril had laid his plans well. She suffered her toilet in near silence, doing as Tillie suggested without any real thought to the end result. She scarcely looked in the mirror that the maid held.

"You are a real treat," Tillie said with a smile, visibly pleased with her handiwork.

"And you are a treasure." Byrony returned the compliment as she took the gloves Tillie handed her.

The walk along the gallery gave her a moment to compose herself for what she was certain would be an ordeal. Charles could be waiting downstairs as would Deveril if he had arrived. Pinning a smile to her face, she started down the steps just as the butler opened the door to admit Deveril. Of Charles there was no sign.

Byrony was a vision of charming elegance. Her deep lavender habit was cut in the fashionable military manner, setting off her lithe figure to fine advantage. A frothy white jabot tied at her throat lent a frilly touch of femininity to her ensemble. A riding hat was perched at a rakish angle atop her smoothly coiled hair. One single plume curled bewitchingly around the brim to the soft line of her cheek. It fluttered to a halt at the corner of her lips. The effect invited the viewer to focus on the kissable mouth. Deveril appreciated the picture, his eyes gleaming with masculine approval. The weeks with Charles had enhanced Byrony's looks. With each passing day she became more the lady. If he had not known her from the beginning, even he might have been taken in. As it was, he was having a difficult time remembering she was the bait for the trap.

While Deveril was studying her, Byrony had been taking in his appearance. She was obliged to admit he carried himself with the grace of an athlete. In a dark green coat cut by a master hand, buckskins, and topboots, he was a superb figure of quiet, restrained fashion. When he took her fingers in his and drew her to him, she noted the amusement in his flashing eyes and the mocking knowledge at her attempt at poise. He lowered his head and brushed his lips across hers.

"Well done, my girl," he whispered, his breath stirring the slender tendrils of hair in front of her pleasurably. "You learn fast."

Deveril straightened with reluctance when he glimpsed

Charles emerging from the study. When Byrony didn't fight him, she was a pleasure to behold. Trailing a finger down her cheek, he added, "We are about to have company. Try to appear as if you enjoy my touch."

Byrony bit back a retort as she turned to face her uncle.

"Prompt as usual, Dev," Charles welcomed him with an outstretched hand. He glanced at Byrony, taking in the attractiveness of her attire. "You look lovely, my dear. Don't let me keep you from enjoying your ride." Signaling for the duke's hat, he linked arms with his two relatives and shepherded them out the door to the waiting horses.

Deveril's lips twisted in a cynical smile at Charles' blatant tactics. He never missed an opportunity to push them together. Byrony was less than pleased with the rush, he knew. And that made bearable the prospect of the coming expedition. She was still not tamed to hand despite the seeming docility. The flash of temper in those gray eyes heralded a storm ahead. Exhilaration coursed through him at the battle they would surely start as soon as they were out of earshot.

"But uncle, his grace, I mean Deveril has just arrived. Surely there is no need for such haste," Byrony protested desperately as the duke assisted her to mount. The last thing she wanted was to be alone with the son of Satan.

"Nonsense, Byrony, Charles is right. We have much to do and it grows late," Deveril replied firmly while he settled her foot securely in the stirrup. He grinned at her as he arranged her skirt over Sunset's gleaming flank. It didn't take much guessing to know she detested the heavy cloth draped about her and the sidesaddle that she now sat.

Byrony controlled the urge to glare at him, especially when she caught the rueful exchange of glances between the two men. Deveril had no need to stretch his imagination to know what disquieting thoughts were occupying his bride to be. The militant sparkle in her eye told its own story even when her expression remained calm. He wondered briefly if her temper would hold until they were away from the house. Casting a knowledgeable eye over her as he swung into the saddle, he decided that it would. With an unconcerned wave to his host he urged his stallion into a trot down the drive, forcing Byrony to follow suit.

It was a glorious day, one made for enjoyment. The clear blue sky was dotted with puffs of snowy clouds which floated gently overhead. A slight breeze stirred the leaves on the trees, whispering a melody on the morning air. At the end of the drive Deveril guided Orion across the road to the open field. Here the lush green pastures grew in wild abandon to the delight of the sheep that browsed there. Deveril did not ease his pace, knowing Byrony could easily keep abreast. She had been caged for too long. He could feel her need to break free and sympathized with her though he would not tell her so.

Byrony pushed Sunset to match the brisk pace, forgetting Deveril in the enjoyment of being active. She had no intention of allowing Deveril to see how much she needed the fast gait. He was sure to slow to a walk immediately if he knew. So she kept her face free of the pleasure she found in the countryside and the day. So engrossed was she in controlling her expression she was unaware that Orion had dropped back to match Sunset's stride until Deveril's hand shot out to grip the mare's bridle, bringing the horses to an abrupt halt. "I was surprised to find you in such a bad temper this morning. We both agreed days ago that there was no way we could honorably cry off. For you there will be money, security, my title, a home that many envy, and eventually children. All a woman dreams of or so I am told." His eyes were dark with the knowledge of the world and its values. "I shall be gaining a wife of impeccable lineage though not of a comfortable disposition. You will grace my table and my home, provide me with heirs, and a way, according to Charles, to win back my tarnished reputation. We both gain. Once we are safely riveted, we need see each other as little as possible. The best course, I'm sure you will agree. My holdings are vast. There should be no difficulty in avoiding one another. So you would be well advised to put a good face on this business. You have no other choice."

"I have never been one to go tamely to my fate," she snapped.

"Only a fool fights when he cannot hope to win," Deveril replied softly. He urged the horses forward. "Charles and I have thought it is only fitting that you should see where you will remove to after our wedding. In the normal course of events there would be a chaperon to accompany us but as you are alone and Charles has no relations close by, we decided to dispense with the formality."

That decision raised Byrony's brows. "I thought the whole purpose of our marriage was to quiet the tabbies. This hardly seems the best course."

"Perhaps not but certainly it is in keeping with Charles' hope that we shall form an attachment to each other," he responded cynically.

At that moment they topped the rise and Deveril pulled to a stop. Before them in a tree-shadowed valley lay sprawled the Castle. She had seen it before only at night. Now Byrony stared at the huge structure momentarily at a loss for words.

Built two centuries before as a fortress and a haven in the times of war, it was home for the ruling family of the countryside. There was no attempt at beauty in its construction, only strength and a sort of enduring timelessness. The solid walls were of gray stone dotted here and there with vast, velvet green expanses of clinging ivy. The surrounding grounds were laid out with military precision from the flower-filled bowers near the walls to the lush green parkland where slender-legged deer grazed undistrubed in the shade of the massive oak trees.

Byrony had given little thought to her future home. In her most farfetched dreams she would not have envisioned this daunting establishment. She did not have the least idea how to run a small manor house, much less a place of this grandeur. Realizing her horror must be visible on her face, Byrony made an attempt to control her feelings. Turning to Deveril, she prayed he had not noticed. Lady Luck was not so kind. His eyes held the knowledge of all she would have hidden. She started to make some trivial remark but the look in those eyes demanded the truth.

"I did not realize . . ." She gestured helplessly.

"Is this the Byrony who greeted Charles with a pistol, who brought her mother single-handedly across the channel now being imtimidated by a pile of stones?"

"A pile of stones? You can say that only because you have lived there all your life."

Deveril smiled. "We'd better move on. Luncheon will be waiting. The servants will probably want to greet us." He glanced at her then at his home. "Don't worry about them. You will be fine."

His words were oddly kind. "I am relieved to hear it," she said.

Deveril's lips twitched at the mumbled comment, his humor restored. Suddenly he was looking forward to watching her contrive in an unfamiliar environment.

Together they started up the drive. Deveril had not mistaken the matter. There was a formidable welcome prepared for her arrival. The house steward, flanked by the butler and the underbutler, were the first out of the wide double doors to greet them. Two grooms moved on silent feet to grasp the bridles of their horses as they dismounted. From where Byrony stood, she could see what appeared to be an unending line of servants assembled in the entrance hall.

"Good morning, your grace," the house steward said as he bowed low. "I hope you had a pleasant ride. On behalf of all the household, I should like to convey our congratulations on your betrothal and our wishes for your happiness on your marriage."

"Thank you, Dawson." Deveril turned to present Byrony to him. "This is my fiancée, Miss Byrony Balmaine," he said formally, drawing her forward to stand at his side.

With another bow, this one not quite as low as the first, the steward repeated his best wishes before leading the way indoors. In the hall the servants were gathered in order of precedence. Each bowed or curtsyed to Byrony as the steward called each one by name. As well as the three she had already met, there was a groom of chambers, a valet, ten footmen, a steward's footman, two oddmen, two pantry boys, and a lamp boy. On the female side of the staff there were eight housemaids, two sewing maids, two stillroom maids, six laundry maids, two kitchen maids, a vegetable maid, a scullery maid, and a nursery maid. The monarch of the kitchen was a formidable French chef named André. At the very end of the line, slightly apart from the rank and file, stood a tall, thin woman with graying hair dressed somberly in black. Around her waist dangled an enormous bunch of keys. The steward identified her as Mrs. Tippet, the housekeeper.

Byrony smiled at the older woman, liking her on sight. Unless she mistook the matter, this was the person she would need to know better if she was to survive in comfort as Deveril's wife. When the housekeeper smiled back, Byrony allowed herself to know relief. Perhaps it would not be so bad after all, she thought, if everyone was as ready to accept her as it appeared.

"I shall be showing Miss Balmaine over the house and then we shall have luncheon in the small dining room," Deveril instructed before signaling the dismisssal of the staff.

With an impersonal hand under her elbow, Deveril escorted Byrony up the wide marble stairway. "Normally I would leave this task to Mrs. Tippet but I thought you would prefer the freedom of being able to ask whatever question that occurred without having to concern yourself with appearances."

Once again Byrony was surprised at the consideration he was showing her and said so.

Deveril shrugged and then drawled, "I have no desire to expose your ignorance. It would not reflect well on me."

Byrony halted abruptly, pulling away from his light touch. "Believe me, I shall do my best not to disgrace either of us," she managed in a cool tone.

"I will not have my name made more notorious than it is. You are to help repair the damage, not create more.

For a long moment they faced each other in the narrow gallery that was hung with portraits of many of the Castleton ancestors. Pride and stubbornness of almost equal strength warred in a battle that, in that instant, neither had the power to win.

"Will you abide by the same rules?" Byrony dared to ask.

"That, my dear, is not your concern." Deveril took her elbow again, ignoring her attempt to pull away. "We shall continue. Luncheon waits."

Conscious of the footmen on duty, Byrony held her tongue when every instinct was offended. So she would be Caesar's wife, would she?

Deveril started speaking again, only this time his conversation was a running commentary on the Castle. It was difficult to concentrate on the architecture when she was in a temper but Byrony made the attempt, knowing she would be sorry if she did not.

She could not help being impressed by the sheer size of the ducal seat. Vast, high ceilings decorated with elaborate moldings and large gilt-framed, formal portraits along unending hallways seemed created for a race of giants. Even the windows draped in lush velvet were huge panes to spill in the sunlight. Yet, despite the darkness of the exterior, the interior was all light colors and uncluttered rooms. The contrast was pleasing to the eye and certainly gentle on the moods of the inhabitants. Deveril did not hurry her along, allowing her ample time to stop and enjoy whatever struck her fancy. So it was a long two hours later before they repaired to the small dining room

Small was quite definitely a misnomer as far as Byrony was concerned. The gleaming oak table was the focal point of the chamber and sat at the very least twenty guests. The paneled walls were lightened by the sun streaming in through the floor-to-ceiling windows which opened onto a broad stone terrace. The half wall which surrounded the patio still allowed an excellent view of the well-cared-for flower garden. The heady mixture of scents perfumed the air, bringing the outdoors in. Byrony inhaled, enjoying the fragrance.

"It is truly lovely here," she murmured, taking a seat.

"Well, at least something pleases you," Deveril remarked, signaling for the meal to begin.

"Must we fight now?" she asked before she could stop herself. "As you pointed out, neither of us can change anything by scratching at each other."

"So the rank of wife to the duke holds more appeal for you now, does it?" He lifted a glass and saluted her before he tossed off the contents.

She understood immediately. He thought the evidence of his wealth had swayed her. "You are a fool!" She started to rise. He caught her hand in one swift movement.

"Do not try me," he warned, the temper that was never far from the surface blazing to life.

Byrony hated the feeling that trickled down her spine. Deveril had the power that no man had ever had, the power to touch her with fear. Slowly. she obeyed the downward pressure on her arm.

"I am no fortune hunter! If anything, I wish we were not so far apart in our positions."

"Do you?"

"It would make the future far easier if I did not have to learn how to be a duchess. All I see ahead are mistakes and they are all mine."

Deveril studied her closely. Was she lying, hoping to impress him? Did she think to fool him? Those eyes were steady enough but he had seen women look at a man and tell him the worst kind of untruths. That face. So innocent. No woman who had done all that she had could still be innocent. That, at least, had to be a lie.

"It won't be the first time this house has been let down by its caretakers," he said finally.

Byrony chose to give a harmless interpretation to his words.

"Some of the caretakers obviously did do right by the Castle. Certainly the proof is in the difference from the inside and the out."

"My father was responsible for the most part although his father actually began the remodeling. The renovations were completed shortly before I turned one and twenty." Memories that he rarely allowed surfaced in his mind. The bleakness of his life at home during that time was in his eyes.

Byrony started to speak, intending to draw him out. The look on his face stopped her. The pain and the reflected misery were startling in one who habitually kept his feelings buried deep beneath temper and mocking cynicism. She watched as his hands clenched the delicate stem of his wineglass until she was certain it would break under the pressure.

The footman coming to remove the empty plates broke the spell of tension. "I thought if you are not tired we could take a turn around the grounds. They are reputed to be something of a showplace," he suggested coolly.

"I would be delighted, your grace," she replied as she, too, got to her feet. His scowl stopped her from moving away from her chair.

"I thought it was decided that you would call me Deveril."

Byrony lifted her chin at his sharp tone. "I had forgotten . . . Deveril."

The momentary softness Byrony had felt vanished. He

did not need her compassion and would scorn it if offered, she suspected.

They walked through the open windows onto the terrace without speaking. Before her eyes stretched a clearly marked path of short green grass wide enough for them to walk side by side. They strolled leisurely along, stopping occasionally to admire the riot of flowers blooming in profusion among the borders of emerald shrubs. Finally they came upon a small lake, its mirrored surface still as a sheet of blue glass. A group of weeping willows trailed supple tendrils in the shallows along the bank. Deveril guided Byrony to a white bench in the shade of the gently swaying trees.

The Castle was the one place Deveril owned that he truly loved. His worst and his best memories were here. Neither his mother nor his father had ever really valued this country setting. But he did despite the fact he spent little time here. Deveril watched Byrony as she sat absorbing the beauty of the setting. Despite himself, he had to acknowledge that she seemed to fit his home.

"If you are finished admiring the view perhaps we could go," he suggested abruptly, suddenly unaccountably irritated.

They rose together and cut across the gardens to the stables where the horses waited. Beyond the necessary exchanges about the route they would take to Ravenscourt, they spoke little on the way back. Byrony sensed Deveril was once again plagued by his temper. The ruthless way he urged the horses on was proof enough of his mood and how much he wished to be free of her presence. For her part, Byrony, too, was glad to see an end to the day. Deveril made her feel things she had never known and that she could not like.

Chapter Eight

The few remaining days before the wedding passed in a blur of activity. The gowns Charles deemed necessary for the bride of a duke were finally complete and hanging in a glorious array in the enormous depths of Byrony's closets. The white confection Charles had commissioned especially for the big event billowed in clouds of silk and lace beneath its protective covering. The chapel was cleaned, and the vicar had come and spoken to her about the duties of a wife of a peer, as had Charles. Everyone and everything was ready. Except Byrony.

Since the day Deveril had taken her to the Castle, Byrony had seen little of Deveril and then never alone. At first, she had believed it was the press of the preparations that kept him elsewhere. Finally she had realized he was avoiding her. But she couldn't discover why. They did not get on, it was true, but there was still no reason for him to pretend she did not exist. Or worse yet, treat her as if she were a villain. It wasn't that she wanted him to fawn on her or dangle after her but the least he could do was to drop the icy detachment that characterized his dealing with her of late. She preferred his temper.

Byrony stared down at the heavy gold ring encrusted with flawless diamonds from which, in the center, rose a single magnificent emerald. The green stone glowed with life in the light of the single candle beside her bed. Just for a moment she allowed herself to dream of how different her life would be if the circlet she wore had been placed there by a man who loved her and whom she could love. Tomorrow was her wedding day and she was marrying a stranger, a cold, aloof nobleman who would hold supreme power over her. Though not normally given to vapors and weeping, she felt a strong desire to cry. She had no knowledge of the marriage bed, no experience in the upper levels of the society which her uncle and Deveril were born to, and no support beyond her husband's once she left her uncle's house. Surely her mother, who had married the love of her heart, would not have wanted this for her only child. How could Charles, who had loved his own wife so dearly, sacrifice her to his rakehell godson? She clenched her hands together tightly as she felt panic dig into her. Escape—she wanted desperately to escape. Pacing to the window, she stared out. It would be easy. Sunset was in the stable. She could steal the clothes she needed from one of the stable hands or the servants. Then she could be away.

For a moment the temptation was honey sweet. Then cold logic washed away the sweet and left behind the bitterness of reality. A child could hide her head beneath the covers. A woman grown had to face the truth. Her uncle had said it, Deveril too, and even herself. There was no other way. Even if she did not marry Deveril, she would have to wed someone or batten on her uncle for the rest of his days. And that she would not do.

Resigned, she turned away from the window and blew out the candle. One thing was for certain—Deveril was getting no bargain for a wife. But perhaps in that they were even, she decided as she slid into bed. She would be marrying an ill-tempered rogue with a reputation for wildness. An equal match, some would say.

* * *

Byrony paused in the open doorway of the Ravenscourt family chapel and took a deep breath to calm her nerves. Robed in white silk, she appeared as virginal and as untouched as the first snow of winter. Her gown with its high neck fell softly from her slender shoulders in nunlike simplicity. The long flowing sleeves were heavily encrusted with tiny seed pearls and silver threads in an intricate pattern which intertwined the crests of the House of Ravensly and the House of Castleton. Three delicate silver chains linking fragile diamonds and pearls were clasped around her waist. Her veil of fine imported Venetian lace was so transparent it resembled miniature interlocking spider webs. Charles presented it to her as part of his gift to the bride, explaining it had been his Kate's own.

The organ softly struck the solemn notes, heralding the beginning of her last walk as mistress of her own fate. At the end of the aisle stood the man to whom she would give the sole control of her life. Raising her eyes to stare straight ahead, Byrony saw for the first time the interior of the chapel. A sea of empty pews gave mute evidence to the mockery of the ceremony to take place within the ancient walls. Beside her, Charles stepped forward to escort her to the altar. His arm was warm and reassuring beneath her icy fingers as her slippered feet whispered over the stone floor worn smooth with age and long usage. His steadying presence kept her from faltering as she drew nearer to the tall, forbidding stranger who was to be her husband.

Deveril's midnight blue attire stood out vividly against the lushness of the banks of flowers behind him. He watched her approach with cold, detached eyes in a face wiped clean of emotion.

Byrony's fingers tightened on Charles' arm as for an instant the panic of the night before returned. Charles stepped back to relinquish his place by her side to Deveril. For Byrony the ceremony was a nightmare seen through eyes clouded by a veil of white mist. She shivered in spite of the warmth of the room. Blindly, she stared at the soft velvety petals of hundreds of blossoms and their intertwined green leaves, the ferns that decorated the dais on which they stood. The altar was adorned with snow white linen and ornate gold vessels. The candlelight cast a warm glow over the nearly deserted room but it did nothing to dispel the chill in Byrony's body as the vicar began the service.

Silence reigned except for the slow sonorous drone of the solemn vows. Byrony responded without thought at the appropriate places in a near whisper. Deveril, apparently immune to the unusual nature of the situation, made his avowals in his normal drawling manner. Finally, the ordeal was over and Deveril turned to her. He lifted the delicate veil to reveal her face. For a long moment he stared at her dispassionately. The emptiness Byrony saw in his brilliant blue eyes was chilling.

His arm slipped around her waist, causing the slender chains to nip at her flesh beneath the thin silk of her gown. His lips took hers in a harsh kiss that held too much anger for Byrony's liking or comfort. But before she could fight his touch, she was free. Grasping her hand, he drew her down the aisle toward the anteroom where they were to sign their marriage lines.

Charles was there, waiting with a smile to congratulate them both. Byrony stood at Deveril's side, leaving the speaking to him. She could not bring herself to utter a word. The deed was done. Now there truly was no escape.

"Shall we repair to the dining room?" Charles suggested with a grin. "Although Ravenscourt's chef cannot hope to compare with your own, Dev. I feel you will be pleased with his efforts."

Charles reflected that their life would be stormy in the beginning but he believed that both would soon come to know how well they suited. For now he would try to mitigate Deveril's anger if he could. He did not wish Byrony to start her marriage with Deveril's black temper as a companion.

"You do me too much honor, Charles," Deveril replied. "I

am sure that you underrate your man."

Charles sent him a sharp look which was met with a deceptively bland expression. "I know my man's worth." Two could play the same game. He had spent too many years around politicians not to recognize a subtle thrust when he heard one.

Lunch was an elaborate affair with each succeeding course more delicious than the last. Byrony had little appetite to appreciate the cook's skill. Charles made an effort to include her in the conversation, unlike her husband, who ignored her as much as possible. At first his attitude was a relief but as the meal wore on it became a burden. Charles, too, was aware of the way Deveril pretended Byrony was not there. His smiles grew strained and finally disappeared altogether as his voice took on an edge.

Byrony watched the scene, removed from the tension in a way that would have frightened her had she thought about it. Food stuck in her throat but the chilled wine did not. She never noticed her glass being kept full by the footman. Just as she never realized that the lethargy creeping over her was due to its potent effects.

Detached, Byrony studied her husband as he parried a remark from Charles. He was an exceedingly attractive man, she decided, wondering why she had not noticed that before. His eyes were alight with intelligence and a knowledge that any woman would find beguiling. No wonder he had such a reputation with the ladies of the Ton. What female in her right mind could hope to resist him if he truly meant to possess her?

At that moment, Deveril turned his head to catch Byrony staring at him. His twisted smile derided her attempt to hide her scrutiny and she flushed furiously. Angrily, she reflected that she bore his name but she would not belong to him, ever. Her chin raised, her spirit reasserted itself. It was a measure of her strength that she could stare back at him.

Charles read the storm signs and intervened quickly.

"Why don't you go upstairs and change, my dear? I am certain you would be more comfortable and you two will want to get started for your own home soon."

"I would prefer something cooler," she agreed slowly, rising with grace. "If you will excuse me?"

The moment they were alone, both men resumed their seats. Charles waved the footman from the room and confronted his godson. "Dev, I wish to speak with you a moment without my niece's presence."

"I think you have done enough, my dear Charles. I am safely riveted as you wished. Your relative is now a titled lady of such station that few if any would dare to impugn her honor. What more do you wish?"

"I have no wish other than to see you take your rightful place in our world. And I have grown to love Byrony and wish the same for her. But know this, Deveril." Charles paused, his eyes steady on the younger man. "Byrony is your wife. She is also an innocent. Do not play your games with her. She will be hurt and that I will not tolerate."

"Innocent!" Deveril laughed harshly. "How came you by that odd notion?"

Charles frowned, not liking the tone. "'Tis the simple truth."

"How do you know?"

"It is as plain as a pikestaff."

Deveril was shaking his head even as Charles spoke. "She is not Kate. She is but a woman and a damn shrewd one at that. She is no innocent, I promise you."

Anger and dismay coursed through Charles. It had never occurred to him that Deveril saw Byrony in this light. Suddenly he feared for the marriage he had promoted so strongly. Byrony could be seriously hurt if Deveril believed her to be no better than a lightskirt or, worse yet, a title-seeking adventuress.

"You are wrong, I tell you," he grated.

Deveril's brows rose in surprise at his vehemence. "And

you are too trusting. Kate was an exception in the world of women. You were a lucky man to have had her. Byrony is not of her mold."

Byrony stood just outside the door, frozen at the words coming from the dining room. She had rushed through her toilet, wishing only to be away from the need to pretend everything was as it should be. She had come downstairs expecting to find Deveril waiting for her in the hall. When she had found the entrance deserted, she had come to look for Charles and her husband. She hadn't meant to eavesdrop, thinking only to spare both men the embarrassment of hearing their discussion. She should have known better. She had suspected Deveril mistook her character but she had not been certain. Now she was.

"Don't let your mother's behavior and that of your lightskirts blind you to the worth of your wife. She is a fine girl and with your help she will make a very special woman. I believe she has a great capacity to give love to the right man. With gentle handling you could be that man. Take her home with you and stay with her. Put away your anger and bitterness and let yourself know her. Maybe you can find it in your heart to love her. There is no greater gift you can have, I assure you. I had my Kate and I miss her every day of my life. I still treasure every second that I was privileged to spend with her."

Byrony clenched her hands as she listened to her uncle's words. That he should plead so eloquently for her future by exposing his own deepest feelings warmed her even as Deveril's words chilled her.

"Love! A fool's dream!" Deveril declared contemptuously. "Oh, I'll grant you Kate loved you. But do you truly think Byrony knows such an emotion? She thinks like the boy she acts. As for me? Why should I desire any part of love? I have seen strong men brought to their knees on the whim of a woman. No skirt will ever lead me around by the nose."

Charles suddenly felt very tired and old.

"Do not crucify Byrony for another's faults."

Deveril rose with a shrug. "If she behaves herself she will have nothing to fear from me, I promise you."

With that Charles had to be content.

Byrony burned with humiliation. If she behaved! Ha! It took every ounce of control she possessed to pretend she had just arrived as Charles and Deveril came out of the dining room and to hold her tongue when Deveril's eyes skimmed boldly over her figure.

"You look charming, my dear," Charles murmured.

"It seems I have acquired a most attractive wife," Deveril drawled.

Byrony needed no one to tell her she was in looks. The rich blue satin of her gown with its lavishly ruffled hem was one of her favorite creations. The imported lace of her native France around her neck not only was a striking addition but also made her feel less a stranger in this new land. She would not be subdued by this English peer. His equal in rank and strength she may not be, but she had yet a few tricks to surprise him.

Deveril signaled for his hat and coat. "I think it is time we were leaving, Charles."

Charles embraced Byrony warmly, praying that he had not erred in this marriage. To Deveril, he gave his hand. "Take care of her."

"I have given you my word. And all of us know I shall abide by it."

Charles could not relax even as he watched Deveril take Byrony's elbow and escort her down the stairs to the waiting carriage. Suddenly, he wished for Kate's calm presence to reassure him. Turning, he made his way to the study, where only her portrait bore him company. He stood before it, his hands clasped behind his back and a frown deeply etched between his brows.

Katherine looked down on her husband from her painted

bench. Her eyes usually laughing, were deep, serious pools. As he gazed on her well-loved face, Charles felt the comfort of her long remembered faith in his judgment.

"Pray for them, my love. You are closer to the angels than I. May you succeed where I cannot."

"I am glad that is over." Deveril leaned back against the cushions with a sigh.

Byrony stared out the window.

Deveril looked over Byrony's stiff figure and saw more than Charles had noticed. "How much did you hear?"

Byrony flashed him a glance filled with hatred. "Enough. Too much."

Deveril grinned. "Hasn't anyone ever taught you that eavesdroppers never hear good of themselves?"

"You should know," she snapped, and was further incensed when he laughed.

"Come, wife, you can do better than that," he invited.

Byrony glared at him. "I did not marry you in order to provide you with sport."

"We shall see about that."

There was no mistaking his meaning. "If you touch me, you will regret it," she hissed.

"A threat? Not wise." The mockery was gone from his voice. Silky menace lurked in the deep tones.

"A promise." No matter what the cost, she would not bow to him. Had she loved him, she would have gladly given her heart, hand, and loyalty. A request from the one she loved and she would have moved heaven itself to grant it. But she would not be forced ever.

Deveril shrugged, the expression on his face changing so quickly Byrony was uncertain if she had imagined the danger she had seen there. After a few moments he broached a more innocuous subject. "Tell me, would you be comfortable in town at present? Would you know how to go on?"

"No, I confess I would not."

"Are you thinking to remedy the situation?"

"Considering how rushed everything has been, I have not thought about it at all," she returned smartly.

He went on inexorably. "Since our futures and our names are now bound together, I have hit on a solution. You need tutoring in all the graces. Until you know how to go on, you will remain at Castleton. It will do neither of us credit for you to go out in company as you are."

While Byrony could not deny the truth of his words, she was incensed at being relegated to the status of a schoolroom chit. "How long will this schooling last, do you think?" One brow raised as she put the question to him.

"That, my dear, depends on you. Kick at the traces and it could be some time. Bend to the yoke and you will be free as quick as may be."

"And what of your own schooling?" she riposted. "It is not I who have alienated the sticklers of the Ton. Who will be your instructor?"

Deveril affected a look of surprise. "But I have you to play propriety, wife. I need no more."

The carriage jolted to a halt before Byrony could retaliate. Which was just as well, she decided as she mounted the steps on Deveril's arm. Even she knew it would not do for her to start her life as a duchess screeching at her husband like a common fish wife. Inside the entrance hall Deveril surrendered their cloaks into the servant's waiting hands. Then he gave orders for his horse to be brought around in an hour.

Byrony was surprised but relieved she would be spared his presence for a time. She had no wish to converse with him and even less to hear more of his plans.

Deveril cast a glance over her. "You will rest until dinner. Tillie is waiting for you with my orders. Dawson will show you to our apartment." Without remaining to see her reaction to his barrage of orders, he mounted the stairs himself.

Byrony fumed silently as she followed Dawson up. What was Deveril about? Fire glowed in her eyes as she stopped the butler with a word,

"Direct me to his grace's dressing chamber."

The man's brows climbed into his hairline as he gaped at her in shock. "His dressing chamber, your grace?" At the look on his new mistress's face he immediately added, "As you wish, your grace."

A precise turn, a few yards down the corridor, and he stopped. "Shall I announce you?" he asked after a brief hesitation.

"That will not be necessary. I shall do it myself."

His bow was flawless but hurried as he departed. If Byrony had been in the mood, she would have appreciated the way he vacated the area. Knocking once, Byrony did not wait for the call to enter. She walked in, temper taking the place of courage. Deveril turned, startled at the sound of his name.

"What the devil!" he ejaculated, glaring at her. He stood, hands on hips with only his smallclothes to cover his body.

"I would speak with you." Byrony faced him, ignoring the bare muscled chest gleaming in the sunlight streaming through the windows.

"How dare you invade my privacy!"

Byrony laughed at the outrage in his voice. "A few hours ago you spoke words that made me mistress here. Or did I mishear that part of the wedding ceremony?"

Deveril waved his valet from the room, more incensed than he had ever been in his life. "What in the name of God is the matter with you?"

"How dare you insult me. A lightskirt may deserve the treatment you meted out to me downstairs but I do not. Whatever you think of me, I am now your wife."

"You have made your point—and in the most improper and annoying way possible, I might add." Deveril turned and walked back to the wash stand. "That door will take you to your chamber." He waved a hand toward the far wall. "I shall see you at dinner."

Byrony reflected darkly as she made her way to her chamber that even when conceding a point, Deveril still managed to get the best of her. It did not bode well for the days ahead.

Chapter Nine

"Oh, Miss Byrony," Tillie said, a pretty wrapper thrown across her arm. "I mean your grace, I never seen such a place in all my born days. I heard tales but never did I think to serve the Castle," she chattered excitedly.

Byrony smiled in genuine amusement for the first time in a long while. She knew just what the woman meant. "Are you happy with your own room?"

Tillie looked surprised for a moment then grinned and nodded enthusiastically. "Yes, your grace. That Dawson has been ever so helpful. He even greeted me when I arrived." Tillie's rosy face reflected her awe at the condescension of the great man of the staff.

Byrony stepped out of the blue satin gown, wishing her own welcome had been as sincere and warm. She slipped her bare arms into the dainty robe Tillie held for her, and lay down on the bed while Tillie pulled the drapes and put away her clothes. The house was silent.

The sun was low on the horizon when Tillie awakened her for a hot cup of tea. As Byrony sat sipping the warm brew, the maid set about lighting the candles until the room was bathed in a soft glow.

Shall I lay out the silver gown, your grace?" she asked, taking the tray from Byrony's lap.

"Do you not think it too formal for the occasion?"

Tillie shook her head. "Oh no, your grace. I asked his grace's man what would be appropriate."

Byrony stared at her. "You did what?"

Tillie nodded, looking shamefaced. "You were asleep. I did not wish to disturb you with my ignorance. This is my first chance to wait upon a lady. I know I am only a country girl but I learn fast, I promise you. I will not tease you to teach me either. I have already sought the duke's valet's help. He took pity on me and said he would teach me how to go on."

Byrony took her time in answering. It had never occurred to her she could not count on Tillie to guide her. To find the one person she thought she could count on to be as unschooled in the ways of society as she was herself was a facer. But she could not ask to have Tillie replaced, she realized. And maybe her plan would serve. If nothing else, at least she knew Tillie wouldn't be forever judging her lacking as she suspected a more well-versed dresser would.

"Please say I can stay with you, your grace," Tillie pleaded.

Byrony smiled slightly. "I would not wish another."

Tillie smiled widely. "Now we must hurry or you will be late downstairs."

She was across the room and diving into the enormous wardrobe before Byrony could blink. Tillie emerged a moment later bearing a glittering creation reverently in her arms. Almost tenderly she laid her burden down on the counterpane then turned to help Byrony into fresh undergarments.

Between them it took little time for Byrony to be arrayed in the soft silver cloth. The muted shade of gray was a perfect foil for her hair and eyes. The unusual sheen changed with every movement, by turns shimmering light and then rich twilight of evening. Matching silver slippers peeped from below the narrow clinging skirt, which hung from a wide band of pearl-encrusted velvet just under the snug-fitting bodice. The dainty puffed sleeves were adorned with narrow banding.

"You are more beautiful than any lady I have ever seen," Tillie breathed as she surveyed the results of their combined efforts. "Now if you will allow me to arrange your hair and add maybe just a touch of color to your cheeks."

With gentle, deft fingers Tillie brushed the glossy black hair until it lay in a silken shower around Byrony's creamy shoulders. Then she contrived a style of rare beauty. The entire length was swept up to the top of Byrony's head and then fastened securely. Taking the resulting thick swathe, Tillie coaxed it into a rippling mass of midnight curls cascading down her back like a waterfall. From the severely smooth sides she pulled two tiny tendrils in front of each ear. The effect was one of stunning simplicity.

"You are a treasure." Byrony was well pleased with her image.

Tillie grinned in delight. "I saw this in one of those fashion plates my lord had brought from London," she confessed.

"My wife does me credit." Unheard, Deveril had entered and stood leaning indolently against the door between their dressing rooms, calmly watching the proceedings.

Tillie jumped back nervously as Byrony rose to confront him. "I am glad my appearance pleases you. Am I late?" she asked quietly, determined to avoid quarreling.

Byrony withstood his scrutiny without betraying her discomfort.

"No. I simply came to give you this." He crossed to her and placed a flat satin-covered box in her hands. He dismissed her maid. "Open it," he commanded when she made no move to look at his gift.

Byrony's uncertainty was reflected in her eyes. Glancing down at the dark box, she lifted the lid. A soft gasp escaped her as she revealed a sparkling necklace of tear-shaped diamonds on a cobweb design of silver wire. Nestled alongside the glittering pool of gems on the crimson lining were two slender earrings of three teardrops each and a fragile bracelet of the same design. Finally, to complete the treasure were three filigree hair clasps.

"They belonged to my grandmother. You are the third bride to wear them." He hesitated then continued when she still did not speak. "It is a tradition." He did not want her to mistake the gift for anything more than it was. Women were a bloody nuisance where jewels were concerned and with this one he wanted no misunderstandings. "Turn around and I shall fasten them on for you."

Byrony turned around in a daze. No one had ever given her anything so beautiful. For so long she had been a waif, an orphan without a family to call her own. The Balmaines had disowned their son in every way but money, and the Ravenslys, because of her mother's pride, had been closed to her.

But her marriage had changed all that. She had a heritage now. A name. A place to belong. She would hold on to it, she decided fiercely as she stared in the mirror watching Deveril work the intricate catch. He didn't really want her, or probably any woman, as his wife. Their marriage would not be an easy one. But many had started with less.

Turning to him, she impulsively laid a hand on his arm. "Could we not try to get along? Neither of us wanted this but must it be war between us?"

Deveril's lips twisted cynically. "I am delighted that a gift of jewelry can work such wonders on your temper."

Byrony gasped with hurt and outrage. Without thinking she raised her hand to slap the ugly look off his face. But before she could strike him, he had her by the shoulders and his lips crushed hers in a kiss that held no gentleness. Byrony fought him, her hands clenched against his chest as she pushed against him. He tightened his arms around her until she could barely breathe. The fight went out of her as he pressed her to his body. The punishment went on and on until Byrony felt darkness closing around her. Before she could escape into its sheltering folds, he released her. She staggered back, her fingers going to her swollen mouth.

"I hate you."

One black brow rose with the arrogance of Satan himself and Deveril headed for the door.

"Where are you going?" Byrony demanded.

"Why, down to dinner of course."

"I shall go with you." She would not be humiliated by him this way again.

"Not like that you will not. Are you so accustomed to your other guise that you do not realize what you look like now?" he said, departing.

Byrony glanced in the mirror, her eyes widening at the disheveled reflection. She looked as if she had come through the bushes backward. Slamming the brush she held down, she swore long and in words even a sailor would blush to repeat.

She felt distinctly uncomfortable walking down the long staircase to the dining room. The eyes of the servants she passed held pity as they looked hurriedly away from her face and she wondered how much they knew or guessed of the circumstances of her marriage.

The meal passed silently, the only sounds being the changing of the many delicious courses. Byrony made sure she sampled each one although she wondered more than once if the food would pass the knot of temper that blocked her throat. Deveril ate little, drinking more than Byrony liked. His dark eyes rested on her from time to time. Occasionally, Byrony could tell what he felt. The brooding gaze held resentment and not a little anger. Bitterness was there too and something else she still hadn't identified when it was time to leave the table.

Deveril was with her as they passed into the hall and she hesitated. "Upstairs," he said loud enough for the footman on duty to hear.

Byrony knew then that the moment of truth had come. He meant to have her without even a pretense of consideration. "I will not—"

His hand closed on her arm before she could finish her denial. "If not willingly, madam, then I shall carry you there myself," he warned, his lips against her ear.

Byrony knew he would carry out his threat. That knowledge propelled her up the stairs with far more strength than the hand beneath her elbow. When they gained her room, Deveril waved Tillie out. Byrony shook off his hold and moved away from him before she turned around.

"I will not be forced."

"Your choice." Deveril shrugged out of his coat and tossed it negligently over the chair. His cravat followed.

Byrony swallowed thickly, backing up as he came toward her. Her pistol. Where had she put it? Trying to think, she kept moving away. The drawer beside her bed! Another step and she would be in front of it. With her body as a shield Deveril would not see her reach inside.

"Come here." Deveril pointed to the place in front of him as he stopped three feet away.

"No," Byrony said with desperate calm. "You will not get your way in this. I will not submit."

Byrony's fingers closed on the pistol. She lifted it without taking her eyes from Deveril's face. His shock, surprise, and then fury were all visible for the fleeting seconds before he halted.

Deveril smiled grimly, his hands clenching. "Another boy's trick?"

"A protection of my honor. For it is certain the man I gave it to shall not protect it for me."

Deveril stared at her, fascinated. Damn her, she would do it. She was actually ready to put a bullet through him rather than give in. The idea astounded him. "My dear wife, I concede defeat—for tonight. Tomorrow I shall have the gun removed from your possession and I shall be most interested to discover what other means you will resort to to protect your, er, honor."

Without another word, he turned on his heel and strode into the adjoining dressing room and slammed the door.

Byrony gazed tiredly at the bed, but passed it by. Instead she chose a large stuffed chair beside the fireplace. Curling her legs beneath her gown, she wearily laid her face on her arm and looked into the flickering flames. Keeping her fingers curled about the butt of the pistol, she tried to listen for any sound coming from the room beyond. All was quiet, for now. Minutes ticked by and slowly her lashes drifted shut.

Deveril stood before her, seeing the weapon in her lap, the way she held it even in sleep. How many times had she guarded her slumber thus? What dangers had she faced to give her such courage.

He lifted her carefully in his arms. He did not bother to remove the pistol from her grasp as he laid her on the bed. She stirred briefly at the touch of cool linen beneath her cheek. Then she was still. Working slowly, he eased the pins from her hair, the slippers from her feet. And still he left her defense in her grasp. His eyes found it almost as often as they traced the shape of her. If she woke now, she would surely shoot him for he had removed her gown and jewelry. Only her undergarments hid her flesh from his view. For a moment he paused and stared down at her. In repose her face was serene, gentle. Her skin was softer and more fragrant than any woman's he had ever known. Silk and lace surrounded her and the deadly weapon in her hand. Lightly touching the ribbons of the shift that covered her breasts, he almost denied his own need to possess that which was his by law. Almost. Just for a moment he remembered a time when he believed that the world was a good place to live in. He shook the thought away. She was a woman. His woman. Bride but not wife. His fingers moved from the ribbons to the pistol and he lifted it from her grasp. She stirred but did not wake.

Stripping quickly, he slipped into bed beside her.

Byrony swam up from the depths of sleep, feeling a breeze brush over her skin. Warm hands touching her, a soft voice whispering strange words in her ears. A fire building within. Her lashes lifted in the darkness as she arched into the hands stroking her body. His lips caught hers, his tongue slipping past her teeth to tease and torment. Byrony had no chance to save herself. Her defenses were gone before she knew she needed them. His hands molded her in ways she had never known. His body pressed down on hers, crushing yet not hurting her. Her breasts were warm and full in his grasp. When he took the taut peaks in his mouth, she gasped aloud.

He wanted everything she had to give. His mouth moved lower, his need curbed by skill. Deveril found the curves of her calves, his fingers massaging in slow, ever widening circles. Her legs shifted farther apart, making room for him between her thighs.

Byrony tried to hold back despite the way he inflamed her senses. Trying to ignore the words he whispered to her in the darkness, she attempted to stiffen against his seduction. She would not enjoy this. She could not enjoy this. But his voice came low, and vibrant with desire.

"Relax, wife, for I mean only delight for us both this night." His hand found the molten core of her as he spoke.

Byrony cried out in shock and pleasure at the caress.

His mouth found hers, his tongue making her understand what he meant to do. She felt his body pushing between her legs, nudging at the fire burning there. Hard, big, and pulsating, it took over the exploration, teasing without possessing her completely. Byrony arched toward him, fiercely wanting him to finish the task he had begun. She burned so. Her skin felt as though it could not stand another touch.

Deveril felt the change from reluctance to passion. He

groaned deep in his throat. He had won. She would soon be his. "Byrony!" Her name was on his lips as he plunged deep into the sheath that waited for his sword.

Her cry of pain was sharp. Deveril's lips torn from the breast he caressed. "You are an innocent," he said. If she had lifted her pistol and put a bullet between his eyes, he could not have been more shocked.

Two tears trembled on her lashes as she nodded.

But what he had begun could not be halted now. For even as he considered the notion, her body adjusted to the invader and tightened around it. Passion, hot and uncontrollable, exploded within him. He tried to gentle his urgency but could not. Byrony rode the storm beneath him, surging and retreating in a battle as old as time itself. She met every thrust with one of her own, striving for a goal she didn't understand. And then suddenly she did. She reached the pinnacle with a keening cry of grief and exultation. The girl was gone and in her place stood a woman, created of man and born in his arms. Deveril's own hoarse shout echoed hers as he, too, found his release from torment.

For a long moment they lay tangled together as survivors from a storm-tossed sea. Then Deveril withdrew with an abruptness that made Byrony dizzy. He was gone, the door slamming behind him before she could say a word.

This time sleep was a long time in coming. Every muscle and sinew ached. She was cold and hot by turns as she remembered the pleasure she had found in his arms. Dawn crept over the sky before she finally slept to dream of darkness without light, halls without doors, and ever present was the face of the dark angel, Lucifer.

Cold! Byrony thought sleepily. She stirred restlessly, seeking the warmth that had been denied her through the night. Before she could wake fully, the emptiness that made her restless was filled. In her half-asleep state she did not notice the softness of the shape she curled against with a sigh of contentment.

To the man watching, Byrony appeared beautiful and too desirable. Unable to resist the temptation, Deveril reached out his hand to touch the alabaster skin of her cheek. His fingertips almost brushed the petal-like curve before he came to his senses. It was more difficult that he believed to leave her. He wanted to be beside her, held in her arms. He wanted to know the feel of her body next to his when he awoke. Already his manhood was alert, hot and ready to savor the sweet tightness of her sheath. He nearly reached for her then. But sanity had won the day. Her seduction was potent even in sleep. And that angered him. She was only a woman. The desire in his eyes died to be replaced with self-disgust and anger.

Deveril turned abruptly away and left without a backward glance. Less than an hour later he returned quietly, taking care not to awaken his slumbering bride. Gone was the rich brocade dressing robe. In its place were a serviceable dark brown coat, riding boots, and a plain sable-hued cloak. He pinned a folded note on top of the pillow beside Byrony. Against his will his eyes lingered on her delicately curved body. Her lips were still rosy and slightly swollen from his last kiss. The surge of longing to kiss her awake, to feel her ardent response once again, angered him afresh. How dare she bewitch him so! His low, harsh oath echoed in the chamber that carried the scent of their mating as he left, this time not intending to return.

Hours later Byrony woke slowly, rubbing her cheek against the softness beneath it. Her fingers crept up, reaching for something or someone. The crisp edges of the paper rustling near her ear startled her, bringing her eyes fully open. The events of the day before and the night flooded her mind. The images were all too real and in the light of morning something she would have rather forgotten. But she could not. Her body remembered the pleasure she had found in Deveril's arms and her muscles ached slightly with every movement.

Sitting up in bed, Byrony pulled the covers around her to shield her nakedness, half expecting Deveril to appear at any moment. When a full minute passed and no sound was heard, she relaxed enough to look around the room. A few seconds later her eyes found the note pinned to her pillow. She stared at it, knowing it would hurt her before she even opened it. Deveril had had what he wished from her and more. She had been a willing prisoner in his arms. No amount of hiding from herself would remove the images she carried in her mind of her wanton responses. Slowly she reached out and unfastened the message.

Madam Wife,

Having fulfilled the terms of our marriage I find I now wish to return to the diversions of my own kind. I am sure you will be as relieved as I. Charles will be delighted to act in my stead as host if you so desire.

Castleton

Byrony crushed the note in her hands, too shocked to feel anything. She wanted to cry but the tears were a hard knot in her throat, denying her even that release. Ravenscourt. Charles. Two lights in the darkness of her life. He would take her in. He would know what to do. Moving without conscious thought, Byrony rose and donned a riding habit and boots. Mindlessly, she chose the severest garments she possessed. Of a dark forest green the outfit was devoid of any and all ornamentation. It was a working habit and made for hard riding. After pinning her hair up snugly to fit under the matching hat, Byrony collected her gloves without looking at her own reflection in the mirror. This morning she neither knew nor cared to know what she looked like. Her whole being was centered on reaching Ravenscourt and refuge.

In the stables, Byrony met with puzzlement when she requested the groom to saddle Sunset and obvious disapproval when she declined the services of a man to accompany her. Being a duchess did have its compensations, she discovered ironically. No one countermanded her orders regardless of what they thought. In moments she was mounted and on her way away from the Castle alone.

Sunset stepped eagerly into the bit, her walk becoming a trot then a canter and finally a gallop. Byrony made no effort to check the mare's flight. She leaned against Sunset's neck, encouraging the horse as they flew over the rough terrain. Slender legs flashed faster as Sunset responded to the urging. The miles wore on and what once had been an easy gallop became a labored push to reach the next hill, to fly over the next obstacle. Normally a careful, sensitive rider, Byrony was so caught up in her own thoughts she did not realize her mount's plight until Sunset stumbled and almost unseated her.

"Oh, Sunset, how stupid of me," Byrony cried in real distress as she eased the mare's pace to a slow walk.

The once sleek sides, now liberally drenched in lathered sweat, heaved under Byrony's legs. The dainty head hung tiredly on a neck wet with the effort she had expended to bring Byrony back to Ravenscourt. Pointed ears flickered slowly in response to her mistress' anguished whispers of encouragement as the stables of Ravenscourt came into view.

Byrony slid out of the saddle without waiting for a groom to assist her and went straight to the mare's head. She was ashamed of herself. She had almost ridden Sunset into the ground because of her own selfishness.

"Byrony, my dear, what is it?" Charles came out of the stable, clearly having just returned from a ride himself. His eyes took in the state of the mare before settling on Byrony's distressed face.

"I must see you." Byrony shook her head, not trusting herself to say any more.

"Of course." Charles signaled his man to take Sunset away. "Come into the house and join me for breakfast."

Byrony inclined her head, never more grateful for his perception and his calm way of dealing with a crisis. No questions, no useless conversation. Just support, freely given.

Charles took her arm and drew her down the path to the house. Once inside he headed for the study, where he urged Byrony into a chair. Kneeling at her side, he chafed her cold hands in his. The pallor of her skin and the agony in her eyes tore at his heart. And what she had done to the mare. He knew Byrony. Only great distress would have made her so careless. What could his godson have done to reduce her to such a state? The possibilities were endless and none of them pretty or honorable.

"I shall pour you a brandy and you must drink it."

Byrony would have done anything, including downing the strong liquor, if it would ease the pain she was feeling. She didn't understand half the emotions churning within but that didn't blunt their sharp claws.

Charles got to his feet and poured them each a glass. He had a feeling he would need something to hear what had driven Byrony to seek his shelter after less than a day as Deveril's duchess.

Byrony drank deeply from the glass Charles handed her. The fiery liquid burned its way through the tight lump of pain lodged in her throat. Charles drew up a chair and sipped his drink as he waited for Byrony to compose herself.

"Deveril left this morning. He left this." She thrust the crumpled bit of paper she had carried in her pocket into Charles' hand. "Why must he humiliate me this way?"

Charles unfolded the note and scanned the wounding words.

"My dear, what can I say?" he asked helplessly. "You

know I would give anything I possess to undo this—this—" Words failed him in his anger. Calming his temper with effort he tried again. "I think perhaps we are both too overwrought to think clearly. Let me ring for a maid to show you to your old room. After you have rested, we shall speak again," he suggested on a quieter note.

Byrony nodded, seeing the sense of what he said. Truth to tell, the ride had stolen her strength. She rose, swaying slightly as she stood. Charles was at her side in an instant. "I shall be all right." She tried to smile at the worry in his eyes.

Charles wasn't fooled by her gallantry. He patted her arm. "It may not be as bad as we both fear. There are so many things you do not know about Deveril. Things I should have, perhaps, told you before you wed."

Her attention caught by the tone of his voice, Byrony waited for him to elaborate.

"Let me think on this for a while. I have failed you both. I must be sure of the course I choose now."

Byrony heard the question he hesitated to ask. Charles wanted her trust one more time. Despite the hurt, the anger, and the loss of freedom in the past, she found she could not deny him another chance. If he could discover a way to salvage the future, she had to help him try.

"I shall rest now. We shall speak later."

To some the small smile and nod that followed would have hardly been adequate recompense for the sacrifice she was making. But Byrony was beginning to understand her dignified uncle. She saw the gratitude and the relief in the precise gestures. If there was a way for them to come about, Charles would do his best to help her find it.

Chapter Ten

Charles sat down in a slump of defeat. How could Deveril have done such a thing? Byrony did not deserve the treatment Deveril had meted out—nor would any woman if it came to that. And Byrony? For all her knowing ways and strange upbringing, she was still a green girl. She had no defense against Deveril's experience.

"It should have worked," he swore again, banging his clenched fist impotently against the surface of the desk.

For no reason, Charles was reminded of a time when he was also unable to give answers to another who had come to him for sanctuary. That was the night Deveril had found out what his mother was. Deveril's face had held the same mixture of lacerated pride, pain, and anger that Byrony's had a few moments ago. They were so alike, the duke and his lady, did they but know it. Both had a capacity for deep emotion. Yet each showed the world a mask of poise and courage that seemed unshakable.

Charles had promised the young Deveril then he would never betray his confidences of that shattering moment. Now he knew he must if he was to help Byrony understand the demons that drove Deveril. If they were to salvage anything of the situation, they would also need a plan of action. They could not just sit and await Deveril's return.

Charles glanced at the portrait of his Kate. Her eyes smiled down at him, giving silent approval of the half-formed strategy in his mind. The challenge of bringing Deveril to heel was an awesome and complicated one. Everything depended on perfect timing and a great deal of luck. Thank god his niece was a gambler, he mused as he rang for a footman to take a message to Byrony.

Byrony came promptly in response to the summons. She had tried to rest but with little success. Instead she had paced her chamber restlessly, occasionally gazing out the window in the direction of Castleton. She couldn't see her new home but she knew it was there. It gave her a strange feeling to realize she actually belonged somewhere. She wanted to go back and yet she did not. She was hopelessly unprepared to be duchess. Even if Deveril had stayed, nothing would have changed that. All those thoughts and more filled her mind as she sat before Charles, waiting for him to speak.

Charles leaned back and steepled his fingers contemplatively. "I have decided to break a confidence. This I do not do lightly, I assure you, but in this case I feel I must." He sighed, hating what he was about to do. "I want to tell you about my godson and his life. If you are to make this marriage work, you will need all the information at your disposal. I cannot count on others to give you the truth."

Byrony said nothing, only waited patiently.

"Corinne St. John is without a doubt one of the most self-centered women on the face of the earth. When Deveril was fourteen years old he came home early from school as a surprise for his mother, who had always made certain she was adored by her only son. Up until then Corinne had played the parent role so well none of us saw what she really was. We knew of her affairs, but like so many, her behavior was discreet enough that no one censored her for it. This time was different. Deveril found her in bed with a boy who had been his friend and companion for years. Worse still, the lad was the son of the coachman. Deveril lashed out at his mother, calling her a whore. She retaliated by telling him he had no right to call her anything for he did not even know who his father was."

Byrony gasped aloud at the cruelty. She had seen Deveril's pride. What a blow such a revelation must have been to a child of his tender years. And from a mother he loved.

"It wasn't true. But Deveril did not find that out for almost a full week. His father was away at the time tending to business and was not aware of Deveril's plight nor did he know Deveril had come to me with the story. When he returned he came straight here and set Deveril right. The duke was his real father and could prove it through the small birthmark all the St. John men carried on their ankle.

"Deveril was never able to forgive his mother, and the love within him turned to hate. Perhaps he would not have become so embittered if the old duke had not died soon after his fifteenth year. Without her husband to curb her excesses, Corinne became even more indiscreet. Deveril saw womanhood at its worst in her parties, outrageous behavior, and total immorality. His attitude hardened further until all of Society knew of the estrangement. Corinne bore the brunt of public opinion and many held her to blame. As a result she lost much of her influence with the high sticklers but no one actually turned her away. One doesn't, you know, not when the person holds such a high rank. Corinne was not one to suffer in silence or without retaliation. She tried everything she knew to hurt Deveril and to make his life as uncomfortable as she felt he was making hers."

Charles sighed deeply, remembering the black time between the death of the duke and Deveril finally coming of age to take over for his father. "His disillusionment with women in general was complete when he came to town. Every mama trotted out her daughter. Every wile was used to entrap not only the title but the wealth of Castleton. And through it all, Corinne did her utmost to make her son's life miserable. She had her revenge in countless ways. Deveril was too young to defend himself from her cold-blooded retaliation. By the time he passed his twentieth birthday the damage was done. Deveril was hardened to all the caps thrown his way and did not care who knew it. Kate always said Deveril was more sensitive than most and saw people too well. At the time I did not believe her, thinking it was only her partiality for Deveril. But I have come to believe she was right. Deveril holds society in complete disdain and makes no secret of his opinion. Often he flaunts his power simply to ignore and poke fun at his peers and the more pompous of them hate his ability to hold a mirror to their flaws. He has many enemies among the sticklers. And they, I suspect urged on by Corinne, have begun to ostracize Deveril from their crowd."

Startled, Byrony glanced at him sharply. "But if she herself is beyond the pale, how can that be?"

Charles laughed mirthlessly. "That is the worst of all. Corinne is not beyond the pale. Far from it. Whom would you wish as a friend? A man who knows your follies and makes no attempt to enjoy them with you, even does everything he can to show you to be a fool? Or a woman who not only participates in every wild rig but turns a blind eye to your activities? You have experience with the dark side of our life. You have seen it at its worst I'll wager."

Byrony nodded slowly, beginning to understand the situation clearly. Her sympathy was stirred at what she had heard.

"This is why I pushed for Deveril's marriage to you. A wife would blunt some of Society's claws. But a milk-and-water miss would never have stood up to Corinne and her crowd. You will be able to. Being my niece guarantees you a place among our kind, and your own courage will see to the rest providing the trappings of your station are there and the conventions are observed."

"This sounds suspiciously like another plan." Byrony did not like the glitter in Charles' eyes nor the way he studied her.

His words had a familiar ring that she could not ignore.

"A plan to call Deveril back from wherever he has gone." It was the simple truth but with a more complex meaning than it seemed on the surface.

"I have just sent a note to the Castle stating that Deveril has been called away on urgent business. Because of your recent long journey he felt it would be cruel to demand you accompany him; hence he travels alone. He left you in my care here at Ravenscourt."

"But why lie? Surely everyone will know it is all hum."

"Perhaps but no one can prove it without asking Deveril and he is not here. And for the why, it is your reputation I seek to protect. And his," he added as an afterthought.

"But what of my ride here? Surely that will look strange."

Charles smiled. "The bereft bride left by her new husband on business? No one would wonder that you would be upset."

Byrony was amazed. Like a benign wizard, Charles had twisted the pieces of their shattered marriage into some semblance of order. How easily he explained everything away. "You are a complete hand, uncle."

"I am a bit rusty but hopefully I will serve. All these years in Parliament should stand me in good stead, I hope."

Byrony surprised them both with a chuckle. "What comes next after we have saved our reputations from total ruin?"

"We are going to mold you into a lady capable of taking London and all its tabbies by storm. You, my dear, shall be the belle of the coming season."

"How?"

Charles held up a handful of notes. "These are to people I can trust in town. In one manner or other each is expert in society. They shall be your tutors. There is a dancing master, a woman for the female arts, a dressmaker, an agency to send down applicants for your personal servants a hairdresser . . . and finally myself to teach you protocol at court."

Byrony stared at him, speechless with amazement.

"If I know anything about my godson I suspect he will hotfoot it to London. It won't suit him to know you are loose in Town."

"Why?" Byrony asked bitterly. "He left me. I did not leave him."

Charles shook his head. "My dear." He rose and came to her side to take her hands in his. "Don't allow Deveril's behavior to scar you as his mother's did him."

Gray eyes met gray. "I shall do my best," she said softly. She got up and on impulse bent to kiss his cheek. "When does this plan commence?"

"As soon as our helpers arrive from London." He released her hands with a smile, clearly pleased by her attitude. "You and I can make a start on the morrow."

The next morning Byrony's training began. Right after breakfast, she met with Charles in the green salon where he subjected her to a probing interrogation revealing her knowledge of languages, books, travel, gambling, and the use of weapons. Byrony was unable to glean a clue to his opinion except when she caught a fleeting glimpse of his surprise at learning she was fluent in German as well as French and could read Greek and Latin.

By the time Charles was done with his questions, Byrony was drained of energy and completely exposed in all her faults and virtues. Like a horse on sale at a fair, she thought, torn between anger and amusement at his ruthlessness. It seemed Charles could be every bit as formidable as Deveril when he chose.

"Well, am I too raw a silk to work with?" Byrony demanded when the silence between them lengthened.

Charles glanced away from his contemplation of the window overlooking the garden. "Hardly. I think our task will not be beyond either of us. And certainly less onerous than I feared it might be."

Byrony laughed. "How kind of you to say so."

"You may not think me kind when we begin. Remember, all eyes shall be on you in Town. We can not afford mistakes. Not only are you the new Duchess but Deveril's absence will make all curious. Add to that Corinne and her penchant for making mischief and the margin for error diminishes." He leaned forward, "Mark me well. You must be very careful. If any word of your past leaks out we shall all be in the suds. The one thing that the sticklers will never forgive is being made fools of. If they embrace you and then find out about your breeches and your gambling, there will be nothing any of us can do to protect you."

Byrony grimaced. "I promise you I shan't disgrace you or myself. As for Deveril, his reputation is his own affair."

Byrony glanced up from the book of peerage she was studying at Charles' command. For the past two days she had been closeted in the study going over the volume, familiarizing herself with England's upper-class families. It was a time-consuming task but one Charles considered necessary as were the stack of newspapers brought from London daily for her perusal. They at least, held her interest.

The sound of a carriage coming up the drive startled her. Charles wasn't due back for more than an hour, and as far as she knew, no one was coming to call. Her tutors. She got to her feet wondering if it could be one of them so soon. Charles had thought it would be a week before anyone arrived. Hurrying to the front door, she saw the butler greeting a tall, handsome man with golden hair and the most beautiful green eyes she had ever seen. His voice was slow with a strange accent she had never heard before. His manner of dress was stylish and complete to a shade, or at least she thought so. He had to be one of her teachers although she had thought he would be a little older.

At that moment the visitor turned and caught sight of her. His smile flashed white against the unusual bronze tone of his skin. "And you are?" he questioned, coming forward.

"Byrony Balmaine, sir. I believe we have been expecting you." Byrony had unconsciously reverted to her maiden name.

One tawny brow rose at her words and the smile grew broader. "Have you indeed? Then I am lucky beyond measure for I had not expected to be here again for some time."

Puzzled at the note of laughter she detected in his answer, Byrony hesitated. "You have been here before?"

"I have. I am John Tarrington, a friend of Charles, or I like to think so in my better moments."

Byrony smiled. "I trust you have many such moments."

He laughed softly. "It depends, my lady."

Byrony led the way to the green salon. "On what?" she asked, beginning to think she would like this teacher very much. If all of London had such free and easy manners perhaps she would even enjoy herself when they removed to town.

"On whether I am in the suds or not." He waited until Byrony took a seat before sitting down herself.

Byrony cocked her head. "And does that happen often?"

"Not as much as it did before Charles came into my life," he admitted readily.

"He does have a way of changing one's life, does he not?"

"The voice of experience?"

"Then you do not know of my situation?"

John spread his hands. "I am afraid I have been a little out of touch."

Byrony wanted to ask why but refrained. "I am not sure it would have done any good if you had been in touch. I do not believe my marriage and sudden elevation to the Duchess of Castleton has reached everyone in London as yet. Because of my mourning, you know," she added when he looked startled.

"You have married Deveril St. John?"

"I have. I'm surprised my uncle did not explain this in his letter."

"What letter?"

The sound of footsteps in the hall drew Byrony's attention. Charles strolled in, hesitated, his eyes focused on John's face. For an instant there was no sign of recognition. Then his smile broke through as he hurried forward. John rose to meet him halfway.

"My boy, when did you return from America? It must be all of ten years since I've laid eyes on you!"

Byrony turned pink as she realized her error.

"And this is my niece, Byrony, Duchess of Castleton," Charles said, turning to formally introduce them.

John smiled and replied. "We have met. Most charmingly, I might add." The twinkle in his eyes invited Byrony to enjoy the situation rather than be disconcerted by it.

"I'm afraid I never gave our visitor time to identify himself, uncle. I assumed he was one of my new teachers," she admitted ruefully. "I must apologize for my error."

John bowed gracefully before her. "Not at all, your grace. I am honored you chose to forget your rank sufficiently to make me so welcome. But surely a lady of such elegance has no need of a teacher."

Byrony dropped her eyes, at a loss as to how to proceed. "How—how kind of you to say so," she managed.

Charles stepped in smoothly. "Will you stay for a while? We would enjoy the company, would we not, my dear?" Byrony agreed and John accepted the invitation. Charles went to the bell pull and tugged on it.

When the butler came to the door, Charles gave the appropriate orders. "Now," he said to his guest, "you may entertain us with stories of how you went on in the Americas."

Luncheon was an enjoyable meal punctuated with incredible tales of Indians, of ladies who fought alongside their husbands by day and graced the homes they helped carve in the wilderness by night, of a complete lack of manners, and of a land where a younger son could make his fortune and prove himself more than just a name in an ancient book of lineage.

After luncheon Byrony returned to her studies with Charles, this time, at her side. John, pleading fatigue from his journey, had retired to rest.

"What do you think of John?" Charles asked while they were taking a break with a cup of afternoon tea.

"I like him. Why?" There was more than cursory interest in his question, Byrony decided, watching him closely.

"I think he will be useful to you while you are here. His family is an old one, and although he has been away from society for a while, he does know it well."

"What are you suggesting?"

"That we enlist his help. He told me he would be going up to town in two weeks. It will be much easier for you if, when you arrive, you have a friend and an escort beyond mine."

"But surely he will have commitments of his own," Byrony objected, not sure she wanted John to know the full scope of her situation.

"It will work well for him, I think. He has confided to me that he has come back to England to find a wife now that he has set up his establishment in the colonies. He is quite wealthy, it seems, and his family name is an old, very prestigious one. He would be a great catch for any matchmaking mama. You know little of London but let me assure you his position will not be a comfortable one. You could provide John a protection of sorts and an opportunity to look about him at leisure."

"You know, Charles, you are altogether too adept at arranging things," Byrony murmured after a moment. Charles' explanation sounded too perfect to be true yet Byrony did not possess enough knowledge of society to refute his arguments. "Are you certain he will go along with such a plan?"

"Why should he not? Most of us need the help of someone. Why should we not share what we can?"

"How much will you tell him of my situation?"

"Basically the story we are putting around. I see no reason why he cannot know of your life on the continent if you wish. He will tell no one. Despite his devil-may-care ways he can be as close as a clam when necessary."

"I shall be guided by you then for you know John far better than I," Byrony said with a sigh. "This plot of your making thickens more with each passing day."

Charles gave her a sharp look. "Do you wish to call a halt?"

Byrony thought about it. One part of her wished they were not forced to such stratagems. Yet she could not deny the challenge of what lay ahead. With John soon to be caught in the coil, the plan offered some diversion to leaven the true purpose of the plot.

She smiled slowly, her eyes lighting. "No. I am a gambler and shall be so until my last breath. We have begun. We shall continue."

The days passed swiftly. The teachers arrived from town bringing with them the means to polish Byrony for the role of duchess of the realm. Tillie, under the expert guidance of a London hairdresser and a retired ladies maid, learned the arts of arranging Byrony in all the glory of her new world. Dresses from the elite dressmaking establishment arrived daily to fill Byrony's closets.

Once John was told what they were trying to do, he also fell into the plan with a will. He undertook to instruct Byrony in the fine art of flirting and dallying. It was he who also partnered Byrony while the dancing master taught her the latest steps to the newest dances. It was his hand that curved about her waist for those first stumbling steps. It was his smile that showered approval on her when she mastered the waltz and the quadrille. And it was his presence she missed when he left for town to set up his establishment in preparation for the Season.

"You liked him." Charles came up behind Byrony as she stood looking out the study window.

"I did. He is a fine friend." She frowned. "I don't understand it. He is so much kinder than Deveril and yet . . ." The lines between her brows deepened in puzzlement. With a shrug she gave up trying to sort through her complex feelings. "So tell me, Uncle, when do you think I shall be ready?"

Charles sat down beside her on the sofa. "I think you are ready now, my dear, and so do your teachers. They will be leaving tomorrow. And next week so shall we."

Byrony was surprised. "So soon?"

"In the past weeks you have learned everything we could teach you. How to dress, to bow to each person of rank, how to walk, how to flirt." He smiled at her look of surprise. "Did you think I would not notice what John was teaching you? He did a good job, did he not?"

Byrony laughed. "He tried. I fear I am more like to box a gentleman's ears than to slap his hand with my fan when he gets too familiar. As for calling a man to my side with my eyes—I was cross-eyed for a whole day learning that trick."

Charles took her hand and raised it to his lips. "My dear, my godson is a fool. You are a delight and there will be many in London to tell you so even if he does not."

"Dutch comfort, Uncle?" Byrony asked with a lifted brow.

"Truth," he denied, releasing her hand. "Now as for your missing spouse. I have not said anything until now for I wished you to ask but it seems you will not."

The light, almost frivolous atmosphere vanished with the mention of Deveril. Tension replaced the smile that had been on Byrony's face only moments before.

"I have been trying to find him. It has taken awhile, for he has not gone to any of the places I thought he would."

"And did you find him?"

"I did. He is at his property in Scotland."

"Scotland!"

"Just so."

"He certainly was anxious to put as much distance between us as he could manage without sailing for India!"

"Will it help to say that except when Deveril walked away from his mother when he was fourteen I have never known him to run from anything or anyone since?"

Byrony studied him. "I don't think I wish to be bracketed with that woman if you please."

"I can scarcely blame you. Nevertheless it is a measure of his deep emotion."

"Yes: he can't stand the sight of me!" Byrony said bitterly.

Charles chuckled and patted his niece's hand. "I hardly think that is the case, my dear. But we shall soon find out."

Chapter Eleven

Four days later Charles found Byrony none the worse for their journey to London. The weather had held for the trip and now that they'd had a day of rest the two of them were met in the sitting room, which was decorated, as was much of the house, in the Adam style and neoclassical in its lines. The chamber was hued in delicate shades of soft blue, and well lighted by numerous candelabra and a large Regency bow window overlooking the streets. Deep blue velvet hangings were drawn back to allow the sun to filter in. The room was nobly furnished with two upholstered Regency sofas facing each other, a stainwood tea table between them. A carpet of Spanish brown "oil floor cloth" covered much of the dark oak floor, and in a far corner reposed an elegant Thomas Hope worktable and matching chair.

Byrony paced to the window then back to the sofa. "When do you suppose John will arrive?" she asked.

"Not much longer, I am sure," replied Charles. "Sit still, child, before you spoil your gown."

Since the dress under discussion was a sleek fall of deep rose and of a style well up to the nines, Charles' concern had merit. Byrony sat and placed her hands carefully in her lap. The sight of her apparently meek posture was the first thing John saw when he entered a moment later.

"Can this be Byrony?" he demanded with a grin, advancing into the room.

Byrony hopped up, her gaze sweeping over her friend. He was looking extremely handsome in a dark brown cutaway coat, pale buff-colored breeches, and a waistcoat of cream silk. His neckcloth was tied with neat precision and his Hessians with the gold tassels gleamed like mirrors.

"No wonder it took you so long to get here," she murmured with a grin.

John preened a little. "Do you like it?"

"Bang up to the mark, I should say!"

"Byrony!" Charles called her to order even as he smiled at the description. "Were all those lessons wasted?"

Byrony laughed, giving a little curtsy. "Oh but how can I resist teasing the peacock."

"Well, play your pranks another time. We have serious business to discuss."

John took a seat beside Byrony. "So the plan is still on? You have not heard from Deveril as yet?"

It was Charles who answered. "We have not, damn him."

Byrony said nothing. Her uncle had the planning of this enterprise.

"Are you engaged tonight?"

"I am but it is nothing I cannot escape."

Charles inclined his head. "Good, for I wish you to accompany Byrony to a ball given at the Earl of Northland's this evening. It is her first appearance in society and everything must be perfect. We shall use my carriage. Please come to dinner with us and we shall leave from here."

John made no demur. "As you wish. And tomorrow?"

"A ride in the park in the afternoon, I think. Do you have your stables set as yet?"

"The first thing I did. I had a feeling you might need it."

The two men exchanged a look that Byrony did not understand. But then that was not a new development between them. She had often thought at Ravenscourt that they were plotting something that she was not aware of. She had even said as much to John but had received most unsatisfactory replies.

"If all goes as I hope, by the end of the week Byrony will have her foot firmly over the threshold of the best houses. None will wonder that she stays with me while Deveril is from home and certainly having a man rich as Croesus as her escort will only add to her consequence."

They laughed together, clearly enjoying a joke Byrony still could not see. She said as much when Charles left them alone to tend to business with his secretary.

"It is no joke. What Charles is trying to do is make sure that Deveril gets wind of what you are up to."

"I know that," she responded impatiently. "But there is more. I can feel it."

John gave her a bland look. "I have no idea what you are talking about," he replied finally.

"Yes you do but you don't mean to tell me. At least you can tell me if it concerns me or is it some plot to help Deveril's reputation?"

John studied her for a long moment. Byrony met his eyes, searching for a clue to what he was thinking. She would not have wished to play cards with him, she realized. This was not a man to betray or bluff.

"You may have confidence that your uncle means to help you."

Byrony spread her hands. "His help has gotten me into this in the first place," she reminded him tartly.

He grinned. "True, and he shall get you out. In the meantime I suggest you enjoy your first season. I remember mine. I don't think any of us ever forget." Taking her hand he pulled her to her feet. "Chin up, your grace. I promise I shall be the envy of half of London tonight and by the end of the week I shall need a hefty stick to beat the men from your door."

Byrony chuckled at his extravagance. "I don't believe a

word of your nonsense," she told him, walking with him to the door.

"Shall we make a wager on the outcome of your debut?"

Byrony's brows lifted at the prospect. She never could resist a bet or a challenge. "Name the stakes."

John frowned. "Now that is a problem. I must think on it." He flicked her chin with his forefinger. "Until tonight, Duchess." With that he was gone.

Byrony stood for a moment in the hall, suddenly realizing that somehow John had managed to divert her from her questions about what he and Charles were up to. Deciding she could not continue unless she knew the whole, she went in search of her uncle only to discover he had gone out for the day and was not expected back until just before they were to leave. Thwarted! Byrony frowned, wondering if her uncle had planned his activities with just this in mind. She would not put it past him. The man had the deviousness of a cat and the cunning of a fox. And most importantly, he loved his godson. She knew he cared for her as well but it was not the same. For a moment Byrony wished she had someone of her own that put her interests first, who would protect her against all comers.

Sighing at the tricks of Fate, she mounted the stairs to go to her room, planning to rest until the ball that night. From all that Charles had told her, these opulent parties could last well into the morning.

Deveril pulled his horse to a stop on the knoll overlooking the sea. The gelding beneath him was a poor substitute for his Orion. The dawn ride that he had thought would blow the cobwebs away had done nothing more than leave him dissatisfied with this place and all that was in it. The breeze from the sea smelled of dead fish and rotting vegetation. The rugged coast line was usually a favorite haunt of his, especially at sunrise. Not so this day. His brow furrowed as he guided his horse down to the beach.

Five weeks he had been gone and still she haunted him. Wife! The word conjured images he preferred to forget. How many wives had he bedded? Too many. Even Olivia, favorite of all his mistresses, had been married when he first met her. What was Byrony up to? Was she behaving as her sisters now that she had a husband's protection? She had been innocent when he had taken her. She was no longer. Did she hate him? Perhaps he deserved it. But Byrony had gotten what she wanted. The memory of her gratitude when he had given her the St. John necklace was clear in his mind. As was the disappointment.

"Damn her!" he muttered, glaring out to sea. "Damn Charles for throwing her in my way!"

Well, he would not be manipulated by his godfather. He would leave all in Charles' hands. The prospect of what Charles would think of that pleased Deveril mightily. A wicked smile chased the furrows from his brow. It would almost be worth it to go back just to see Charles cope with Byrony's temper and her unconventional upbringing.

"Oh, you do look a treat, your grace." Despite Tillie's recent schooling in the fine art of being a lady of the Ton's maid, the girl still retained her country speech.

Byrony smiled at her in the mirror. "I must look a picture for this first night. First impressions, you know."

Tillie tossed her head. "You'll have them all at your feet," she predicted. "You wait and see if you don't." She handed Byrony her reticule and looked her over one last time.

Byrony's hair was dressed in Grecian curls held in place by delicate emerald-tipped pins. Her dress, which was cut low in the bodice as befit a married woman, was of silver tissue gauze over a matching satin underskirt, high-waisted and embroidered all over with branches of leaves made up of small diamonds. Around her neck, Byrony wore a choke necklace of emeralds and diamonds and from her ears dripped matching earrings. The jewels sparkled with every movement yet it was the woman herself who drew the eye. Her carriage was regal, her step was stately, and her eyes held a fire that would soon tantalize all of London. She was the picture of all that a Duchess of the Realm should be.

Byrony descended the stairs, trying to remember all that she had been taught. Tonight was the first of many tests. She had promised herself that the nerves that tied her stomach into knots would be her secret. It wasn't just for herself she had made the vow but for Charles as well. Since she was his niece, his reputation was on display as much as her own and Deveril's.

"My dear!" Charles met her at the bottom of the stairs, his gaze openly admiring. John stood at his side.

"I think I am glad that Deveril is not in town," John murmured, taking Byrony's hand and raising it to his lips. "I am going to enjoy watching the Ton meet you."

Byrony grinned. "Just so that you stay close enough to catch me if I trip."

"Your grace, it will be my pleasure."

Charles placed Byrony's cloak about her shoulders. "Shall we go, my dear?"

Byrony took his arm. "Into battle."

She smiled as she said it but there was nothing humorous about the way she really felt. The challenge of what she was about to attempt had her heart pumping and her mind sharper than it had ever been. The drive to the ball was all too quick as they passed the time discussing possible outings for the next few days.

"Now don't be nervous. Just be yourself. Either John or I will be close by if you get into difficulties." Charles patted her arm as they ascended the stairs to the entrance of Earl of Northland's establishment.

"I shall not disappoint you," she promised just before their names were announced to the assemblage.

Byrony stood for a moment under the staircase chandelier, the lights catching and reflecting the shimmering beauty of her raven hair. The priceless St. John jewels she wore and the unusual gown that set both off to perfection. She counted to four slowly just as Miss Clinton had told her. Then remembering the good lady's commands as though she were standing at her elbow, she began her descent to the floor on her uncle's arm.

The wide carpeted stairway curved toward the east part of the house, which held an enormous ballroom, whose doors were now flung open to recieve the earl's guests. The ballroom was lit with tapers of every size, along every wall. The floor was made of a glossy pink-veined marble. One wall was covered completely in mirrors, lending an illusion of unending space in which to dance. There was a huge fire crackling in the marble-framed fireplace, which seemed to fill the far wall. The Windsor chairs had been pushed back into the corners and against walls to make room for the dancers. There was a five-piece ensemble playing in one corner but the people nearest the entrance had eyes only for the newcomer in their midst. Byrony, the new Duchess of Castleton, had been an on dit since the announcement of her marriage to the wild Devil Duke. All craned their necks to see the woman who had captured the prize so many had sought. Two pairs of eyes followed Byrony's regal progress with something more than avid curiosity in their depths.

Corinne, Dowager Duchess of Castleton, stood beside Lady Olivia Worth. The two could not be called friends for neither woman enjoyed that state with anyone, both being too self-centered to think that anyone could match them in beauty or cunning. What they did share was far more important and, in many ways, far more powerful. Each recognized in the other a like mind and strength. They could have been opponents as easily as cohorts. Fate had put each in debt to the other. The one common interest they shared neither ever discussed. Deveril. Corinne's son and Olivia's lover.

"Lucifer," Olivia hissed as Byrony came their way. "If he

were here I would . . ."

Corinne laid a hand on Olivia's arm. "Careful, you fool. The walls have eyes."

Olivia glared at her across the fan she lifted to cover the lower half of her face. "You cannot be pleased. Look at the jewels she wears. I can remember when I saw them on you."

Corinne's eyes flashed. There were three things she hated being reminded of: the miserly allowance she was paid by her son, her loss of prestige when she became the dowager duchess, and the age her mirror insisted on showing her every morning.

"I did not realize that you were that old."

Olivia's hand clenched so tightly around the fan that it was in danger of breaking. She lowered it to smile into the face of the one woman she both feared and respected. It wasn't a nice gesture and she made no attempt to pretend otherwise.

"He will want an heir. That will mean both of us lose." In a trade of insults she knew she would always give way to Corinne. But even the dowager could not deny the truth of what this marriage meant or how it would hurt them both.

Corinne's face was impassive. She rarely allowed herself to frown. "Then we must make sure the new duchess does not produce the brat."

"How?" Olivia was no fool but despite the weeks since the announcement she had been unable to come up with a plan to put a spoke in Deveril's wheel.

"I do not know as yet but you may depend on it, I shall discover a way."

Byrony felt the rake of eyes as she passed, but as she drew near two women, one dressed in scarlet and the other in black, she was particularly conscious of their stares. Sensing Charles' tension, she glanced at him to find his gaze fixed on the older of the duo. His nod of recognition was the barest courtesy. The flash in the slanted green eyes of the recipient gave Byrony a clue as to her identity. The dowager duchess.

It had to be. But who was that with her?

"Charles, pray make me known to my daughter-in-law," Corinne commanded.

Charles introduced Byrony to the dowager and Olivia. While he had expected to see the former, he had not anticipated the latter. The fact that the two were together disturbed him. Damn Deveril, he swore savagely if silently. If ever there was a coil. There was no chance Corinne would miss an opportunity to acquaint Byrony with the facts of Olivia and Deveril's liaison. With that thought in mind, he drew Byrony away as quickly as possible.

"There are others we must meet," he murmured, sending John a look.

John swiftly took his cue and Byrony's arm. "Let me make you known to my family," he offered, moving deeper into the sea of people.

From that moment on, Byrony scarcely had time to catch her breath. It had been decided between her and Charles that she would not dance since, according to the compromise they had worked out between them, they had put it about that she was in the last weeks of the customary year of mourning. But there could be no fault to find with her attending the various functions that enlivened the Season.

"You are a hit." John handed Byrony a glass of ratafia then took a seat beside her.

"Do you think so?" Byrony sipped her drink and watched the dancers begin a quadrille.

"Can you doubt it? Did not Sally Jersey herself offer you a voucher for Almack's?"

Byrony smiled. "I cannot believe that lady's nickname is Silence."

John raised his own glass to his lips. "Neither can any of those who know the lady," he murmured wickedly.

Byrony refrained from laughing aloud, a practice that would have raised more than one eyebrow. One may enjoy oneself but never wholeheartedly. Such immoderate behavior was only for peasants, or so Miss Clinton had reminded her on many an occasion.

"Be quiet, John, before you make me betray myself," Byrony whispered. She glanced toward the dance floor in time to see Lady Worth looking at her, again. "Who is that rude woman?" she asked on a different note. "I vow every time I turn around she is staring at me as if she would like to run me through."

John followed her eyes and his jaw clenched. A swift perusal of the room showed him that Charles was too far away to be of use.

John would have rather been anywhere than beside Byrony at that moment. To identify Deveril's mistress to his wife was a task no one would want. "She is a friend of Deveril's," he answered finally.

Byrony searched his expression. The words were commonplace enough; the tone was not. "What kind of friend?"

"Please, Byrony, leave it," John pleaded.

She understood then all too well. She turned her head to find the beautiful Olivia. Mistress! Most men had them. In a world of marriages such as her own, many sought their pleasures beyond their wedded partners. She could not condemn him, however, for his liaison with Lady Worth had begun before their marriage. Whether he would continue to see her now was another question.

"I am certain the connection means little." John tried to soften the news in the only way open to him.

Byrony forced a smile. "Then you know more than I, my friend," she said lightly.

At that moment Charles joined them. "Shall we make our good-bye? I think we have been seen enough this night. We should leave everyone time to gossip about the new duchess."

Byrony nodded. It was clear her uncle was in high gig but she could not share his triumph. Until she had discovered the

Lady Olivia's role in their little plot, she had been content with what they had accomplished. Vouchers to Almack's, an introduction to the famous Beau Brummell, and the lengthy, by the Ton's standards, conversation that followed had set the seal on her success, or so John had informed her.

She rose and took her uncle's arm. "I am ready."

It took a few minutes to leave, for every few feet someone stopped them. A few extended invitations, which Byrony either accepted or declined according to the tiny nod from Charles that was her signal of who was acceptable or not. Just for an instant Byrony hated not being able to choose her own amusements but then sanity prevailed. She knew little of those around her. The faces with their polite smiles and compliments often hid more than they revealed. She would be a fool to spurn Charles' help until she knew her way in this new world. At least she had Charles to guide her, for she certainly did not have Deveril's support. His mistress probably had more from him than she did.

"That will be all, Tillie." Byrony turned away from the mirror with a sigh.

Tillie curtsyed, picked up a candle, and headed for the door. "Shall I wait for you to ring in the morning as usual?"

Byrony frowned then shook her head. "No, for I am going to bed so late I might well not awaken with the sun. If I have not sent for you within the hour after that, come to me."

She moved toward the windowseat as soon as Tillie had left. Sleep had never been so distant. So many things had happened. At Ravenscourt it had been easy to forget Deveril for long stretches of time. There had been so much to learn in such a short time she had not had an opportunity or the energy to wonder about him. Now she did. His name had been on everyone's lips at the ball. She had answered countless questions about his whereabouts. The lies she and

Charles had concocted had served everyone but her. And then she had found out about Lady Worth.

Foolishly, it had never occurred to her to wonder about his mistresses. She had been so concerned with her part in this farce of a marriage she had not thought of his. The Lady Worth was certainly suitable for a wife of a duke. Her background was impeccable if impecunious, according to John. So why had Deveril not married her? She was good enough to bed but not wed. And Corinne. She had not expected the woman Charles had described to be quite so beautiful or so blatant in her dislike of her as the new duchess. And then there was the strange friendship of the Lady Olivia and Her Grace Corinne. Two more unlikely cohorts she had yet to see. They did not even look as if they liked each other yet every time she had seen them together they were as thick as thieves.

Byrony sighed and leaned her head against the windowpane. The evening had been little more than a play acted on a stage it seemed only she saw. All of them had lines and parts to perform. Was this what had turned Deveril so against Society? she wondered, staring out into the night. She could not fault him for his attitude. To live like this year after year would sour anyone. She had never known such dishonesty. She had seen gamblers cheat and men steal, it was true. But none of these acts had the hypocrisy of what she had witnessed tonight.

She thought of Scotland, where Deveril was. She had never been there. Was it as rugged as she had heard? Did he ride beside the sea? Was he free to race the clouds across the dune at sunrise? The questions drifted in, filling her with yearning. Deveril could roam at will with no one to say him nay. Putting her hand to the window, she thought for a moment of his freedom. She would gladly have suffered his presence just for that.

"Deveril, I wish you had taken me with you," she whispered, with all her heart.

Chapter Twelve

Hyde Park. Rotten Row. The fashionable place to be on a fine spring day. Society in all its glory on parade. Cattle milling in the center green, ladies in elegant dresses strolling down narrow paths with their faithful maids a few paces behind to play propriety. Open carriages resplendent with velvet squabs, liveried drivers, and handsome horses. The road that wound through the lush countrylike area in the heart of London was crowded. Byrony marveled at the sight. Charles and John had not done it justice when they had described the Park to her.

"What do you think?" John asked, edging his horse closer to Byrony's mare. "Is it not a sight to behold?"

Byrony laughed softly. "Do look at that man over there. The one in the bilious green raiment. I vow his mount is straight from the fair."

John cast a glance over the gentleman in question. "Man has no cattle sense. Wager he didn't buy that creature at Tat's."

Byrony sighed as she slowed her horse yet again. The sedate walk that was the normal pace of the Row was definitely not to her liking. "I fear we are both being unkind," she murmured, searching for a break in the crowd.

John reached out and caught her hands. "Something

wrong, Byrony?" he asked quietly. He released her almost as soon as he touched her. It would not do for them to appear too familiar with each other in full view of the Ton.

Byrony turned her head, her eyes troubled. "Is there not some place we can go to really ride? We have been here almost a full hour. Is it not enough?"

John's brows rose. "Do you dislike this so?"

She hesitated, almost tempted to lie. John had given up his morning to accompany her. It would be ill mannered if not unkind to tell him how little she cared for the outing. "Not dislike," she replied finally, hoping a half truth would do. "I would just prefer a little freedom. Don't these people ever long for a run? How can they be content with so tame an exercise on such a fine day?"

Now he understood. "You are simply feeling the pinch of the change in your circumstances. I felt the same way when I came down from Ravenscourt. In America the rules are much simpler and freer. I felt bound hand and foot by all of this after being away for so long." He urged his horse on with Byrony following suit.

"And now?"

"Oh, I obey the rules but only the ones I wish. The others I bend."

"Like Deveril?"

He shook his head. "No. Deveril flaunts his dislike and it is foolish beyond permission. His attitude only sets up people's backs. Even when we were in school together, he was the same way."

Byrony stared at him, forgetting for a moment where they were. "I did not know that you were in school together. You never mentioned it."

John looked faintly uncomfortable. "I started to once or twice," he admitted finally.

Byrony opened her lips to probe further but at that moment they were hailed from a passing carriage.

John swung his horse out of the flow of riders. "This is

someone I think you will enjoy," he said, a smile lighting his face.

Byrony followed more slowly, wondering at the delight he displayed for the slender woman in the carriage. She was no beauty and certainly no young miss. But her smile had the radiance of the sun.

"This is Lady Arabella Winston. Her Grace Byrony St. John, Duchess of Castleton." John produced the introductions with a laughing flair that invited the women to join him. "My two favorite ladies in all of London," he added, giving Lady Arabella a wicked look.

She returned it with interest and a rap of her fan across his knuckles. "Your manners ever were deplorable, you scamp. I see that the colonies have only made you worse."

John tipped his head, entering into the spirit of flirtation with a will. "I see our London air has not dimmed your beauty."

Lady Arabella laughed, clearly enjoying herself hugely. Byrony said little. She was too fascinated by the naturalness of the exchange. For the first time since coming to London she was seeing someone being herself. Her spirits lifted with every word. She had not wanted to believe that no one was to be trusted, that every word had to be guarded and weighed. The chains that bound her eased a little with the knowledge and she smiled.

Arabella glanced at her just at that moment. "I think we scandalize her grace," she murmured to John. "Perhaps we should be more circumspect."

"Oh, no," Byrony protested.

Arabella laughed aloud. John joined her with a deep chuckle. "You must come around to visit me," she invited. "Have John bring you if Deveril is not in Town as I collect he is not. He always was one to please only himself. The Devil." She frowned, suddenly recollecting herself. "It is not a love match, is it?"

Byrony inhaled sharply at the question no one had dared

to ask. Arabella waved away her reply before she could make it. "Forget that I said that. It is none of my business. And certainly too rude to deserve an answer." She tipped her head, her dark eyes, soft where there had been only amusement seconds before. "I am not always so rag-mannered. John will vouch for me."

Byrony heard the plea within the apology and knew she would not deny this lady her forgiveness. She badly needed a female friend. Charles and John were wonderful to her but she always had the feeling there was more to both than she saw. Even had she been completely comfortable with one or both, she still would feel the lack of a woman to confide in.

"I suspect all of London would like to know what keeps Deveril in Scotland instead of here," she admitted at length. There was no sense in wrapping Deveril's behavior in clean linen for this woman. Instinctively, Byrony felt she could be trusted. And she had learned long ago to go with her instincts.

Arabella looked surprised at her candor. "Not necessarily, your grace. Deveril ever has the reputation for uniqueness. As far as I know, he has never done as he ought."

"Please call me Byrony."

Arabella inclined her head. "I am Bella to my friends."

"If a mere man may venture to interrupt this conversation," John teased with a grin, "I must suggest that we be moving on. We have held up traffic long enough."

"Do you go to the Southmore soiree tonight?" Bella asked quickly.

Byrony nodded. "Shall you be there?"

"In my best gown." Bella gurgled softly. "I suspect you will outshine me but I promise not to be jealous."

Byrony was still smiling as she and John pulled away so Arabella's carriage could move on. Now she had two friends in London.

The next week passed in a round of parties, rides, or drives in the Park with either John or Charles. Getting to sleep before the wee hours of the morning and rising just before noon became a habit that Byrony still found restricting. Knowing Arabella and her circle of friends made Byrony's days less of a task but still she could not shake the feeling of being weighed and tried by the Ton. She heard whispers of her reputation. The Devil's Duchess. The name should have been no surprise. Part of Deveril's reputation had become hers. Byrony wondered sometimes late at night when she waited for sleep to come if all of Society was watching just to see if she was as wild as her husband. At times like that she felt the ties of her life even more strongly. She wanted to break out but could not. All around she was hedged in by propriety. And Deveril? He was free, enjoying himself in Scotland.

Deveril was not enjoying himself, although had he been asked, he would have denied the charge. In truth, he was hardily bored. He had met with his steward, looked over his property, ridden countless miles on a barely adequate mount, and visited with his tenants. He had played the part of landlord to the hilt. His London cronies would have laughed to see his diligence and he knew it. But he did not care. His holdings were a responsibility he took very seriously. His people were more than just so many bodies to provide coins for his overflowing coffers. But more than that he enjoyed the chance to exercise his mind in the planning of his business. Or at least he had done until his marriage.

"Damn her," he muttered, refilling his brandy glass.

His thoughts had become his enemy. Her image was in his mind too frequently. His sleep was disturbed. His mood annoyed even him. Getting to his feet, Deveril stalked to the window and glared out at the stormy sky. What was she doing now? He could picture her even now with that pistol in her hand. Courage. Was there ever a woman in his life with her courage? Beauty. The memory of her in his arms when he had taken her innocence still lingered. The satin feel of her skin against his. The gasp she gave when he claimed her. Her cry of satisfaction when she had reached fulfillment. Dreams. Nightmares with no relief for him.

"Damn her! Damn Charles and his meddling!"

He turned from the window. He would not be ruled by a chit of a woman. Let her exist without him. She had his title, his wealth, his name. Even Charles was her ally. Deveril scowled as he poured himself another brandy. One sip then two. He glared at the glass he held. The fine liquor had lost its power to dull his mind, a sure sign he was drinking too much. And it was all that ill-bred wench's fault. The spirit sloshed in the crystal as he slammed the glass down on the table and strode from the room. Tonight he would sleep undisturbed if he had to ride that damn gelding into the ground to exhaust himself enough to do it.

But he didn't sleep. Not that night and precious little the following three evenings. The gelding had been exchanged for a rough-gaited mare and finally another hard-mouthed gelding when the second went lame after one wild ride. Deveril's temper deteriorated with each successive poor mount. Finally, he could stand the miserable beasts no more. Commanding his man to pack, Deveril vowed to return to Castleton to obtain a whole new stable if he had to go all the way to London to do it. It was disgraceful he had allowed the Scottish property to fall in such a state, he assured himself as he began the long journey back to Castleton.

"What do you mean she is not here?"

Deveril stared at his steward, ignoring the shiver his harsh tone had provoked in the man. He had just come in. He hadn't even changed out of his dirt before he had inquired of his wife. And what did he find? She was galloping about the countryside. Had she no breeding? She was in mourning, damn her.

"Where is she?"

"She was at Ravenscourt, I believe, your grace."

Deveril inhaled deeply, feeling his temper uncurl its wicked tail. "And what is she . . ." He stopped and pierced the servant with a dagger look. "Was?" he drawled dangerously.

The steward gulped like a hooked trout. Taking a nervous and totally involuntary step backward he stammered, "She is not there now, your grace. I believe she has removed to London in the company of Lord Ravensly."

"Charles!" No curse could have been uttered with such feeling. No man had been so sorely tried. Deveril wanted to hit something or at the very least relieve his spleen on both his godfather and his inconsiderate wife. How dare she descend on the London scene without him. And Charles. He would deal with him posthaste. His meddling had gone on too long.

"Give the order to have my horses put to at dawn tomorrow. I shall rest the night here."

"Very good, your grace." Dawson backed hurriedly out the door, relieved to escape Deveril's wrath. For a moment there, he had feared for his safety.

Deveril had no thought for the fright he had given his servant. Nor did he remember the ostensible reason he had left Scotland to come to Castleton. All that filled his mind was his missing wife and Charles' perfidy in taking her to London. He had no doubt his esteemed relative was even now hatching another one of his infamous plots. And, the Devil take him, he would not be caught yet again. This time he would escape the coil and bring Byrony back to the Castle, where she belonged.

Dawn was an ungodly hour, especially on as little sleep as Deveril had had. Despite an excellent dinner, a number of glasses of fine wine, and a soft bed far superior to the finest inns that had been his resting places on the journey from

Scotland, Deveril felt as if he had been pulled on a rack. His head throbbed with a vengeance. Tooling a couch in his condition was not a pleasant task for man or beast. The mail couch that blocked the road just outside London for over an hour was the final spur to Deveril's temper. At last he was striding into his townhouse and found the dust covers still in place.

"Where is her grace?" He demanded awfully of the butler.

Very few men could cow Smithington at his most dignified. Deveril succeeded with just one look from his blazing eyes.

"I believe she is staying with Lord Ravensly."

Deveril's hands clenched into fists. Both of them would regret this, he promised himself. "Get this place open before the day is out," he commanded, glaring at the shrouded furniture.

Smithington goggled at him. "But it is almost evening, your grace," he objected. Thirty years of training in the art of being up to anything his master could toss his way was lost to the shock of Deveril's orders.

"I don't care if it is the middle of the night. Do you?"

Smithington swallowed hard. "No, your grace," he stammered. "It will be as you wish."

Deveril inclined his head before mounting the stairs to his chamber. He would have a wash and a change then be on his way. Byrony wanted schooling for this day's work and he meant to see that she had it before the night was over. Charles, he would handle when it suited him.

"Are you certain you will not accompany us to the theatre?" Byrony asked for the third time in as many hours.

Charles glanced up from the squab he had just cut into. "No, my dear. I am worn to the bone with all the racketing about that you and John do. I have need of a quiet evening." He smiled slightly at the worried frown she directed his way.

"There is nothing wrong, I assure you."

"I could stay home," she offered, not really making a sacrifice with the suggestion. While the play was bound to be amusing, especially in the company of John, Bella, and her friends, she still would gladly give it a miss for a quiet night herself. Or, if she were truly honest, an evening that was not a repeat of so many others. Meeting the same people, hearing the same on dits and the same music that she could not dance to had long since palled.

"I would not hear of it. The Ton would boil me in oil for depriving them of their Devil's Duchess."

Byrony wrinkled her nose at the description. "The Devil's Duchess. Do you think I will ever escape his name? Or the need to be careful in every word I say lest someone tar me with the same brush as they do him."

Charles sobered at the question. "Is it so bad?"

"Sometimes. Especially when Corinne and Olivia are about. Both seem to go out of their way to cut up my peace."

Charles gave her a sharp look. "As long as that is all they do."

Byrony looked at him, her fork poised halfway to her mouth. "What do you mean?"

Charles laid down his utensil and leaned back in his chair. "I do not like things I do not understand. This alliance between Corinne and Olivia disturbs me greatly. What can they have in common? Corinne is no one to suffer another woman's beauty without cause. And Olivia has never had a companion of her kind. One thinks she loves Deveril and the other is known to hate his very name. How can they be cohorts?"

Byrony had no answer although she had asked the same question of herself many times. She shrugged and tried to look unconcerned. "Perhaps it means nothing."

Charles shook his head. "That I do not believe and if you are wise you will not either."

"All they do is watch me," she murmured after a moment.

"So I have noticed. The question is why."

"Perhaps they hope to catch me in some embarrassing indiscretion."

Charles turned the idea over in his mind. It had merit but he could not see how it would be accomplished while Byrony was in his care. His precautions were too well thought out. John was always at her side if he was not. And Byrony herself was wise in ways that most females were not. She would be no easy pigeon to pluck.

"Just be careful," he warned her as the butler entered to announce that John had arrived.

Byrony rose. "I had not realized it was so late. Do you mind if I leave you, uncle?"

"Enjoy yourself," he commanded gruffly, accepting the kiss she touched to his cheek.

Byrony was not a woman to bestow her affection lightly. Yet she honored him with caring and he hoped love. The aching loss of Kate was not so great as it had once been since Byrony had come to his house. For a moment his eyes softened as he watched her walk from the room. Her grace and dignity grew with each day. If only his Kate could have known her. How proud she would have been of her niece.

Byrony entered the salon to find John standing at the window looking out. His back was to her and not for the first time she wondered that such a handsome man would be content to squire her about instead of finding a lady of his own to pay court to. She had thought Bella and he were important to each other. But time and close observation had made her doubt her instincts. Or had it? She frowned suddenly, recalling the way Bella's voice softened on his name.

John turned in time to catch her expression. "Am I in your black books for being ten minutes early?" he asked with a teasing grin. He came to her, hands outstretched.

Byrony touched his fingers briefly then pulled back with a

smile. Her concerns about Bella and John slipped from her mind. "Are you early? No wonder you caught me at the table."

John affected a horrified pose. Byrony laughed as she knew he wished. He played the clown so often she had learned to be the audience.

"You wound me dreadfully. To be second to a piece of cow."

"It was a squab, actually. And quite good in the bargain."

They moved into the hall, where the butler waited with their coats.

"I do not wish to hear." John grimaced, this time meaning the gesture with all his heart. "My chef is not worth the coin I pay him. Tonight's offering would have served to shoe my cattle. I don't suppose you would consider allowing me to finish your squab while you take yourself to the play?"

Byrony shook her head as he handed her into his carriage. "No, my friend. I have no doubt my nemesis will be about. You are my protector or have you forgotten?"

John settled into the seat across from Byrony, suddenly sober. "I had not. Those two harpies worry me exceedingly."

"And Charles," Byrony admitted with a sigh.

John's interest sharpened. "What has he said?"

Byrony shrugged before looking out at the passing streets. "Nothing to the point. He simply is concerned at the unlikely friendship. I think he wishes Deveril were here to handle them."

"And you. Do you wish it?"

Byrony would have preferred not to answer. In truth she had no reply. She still did not know how she felt about Deveril. Since coming to London her view of him and his life had broadened. From Tillie she discovered that the servants thought highly of him. From society, she learned firsthand how his attitude had created such a gulf between him and his contemporaries. It appeared everyone had been more than eager to enlighten her as to his crimes or his virtues.

"Does it really matter?" she returned at length. "He is not here."

John accepted her answer. Her loyalty was to the man who deserted her and left her to the mercies of the London cats. There was much in her to admire but this one trait above all others had touched him. He had seen her cut by the gossip of the Devil. He knew she hated her nickname. Her smile and dignity never faltered despite the unfamiliarity of the world her marriage had pulled her into, despite those who would see her humbled. Charles and he tried to shield her but they were unable to protect her completely. Her eyes sometimes looked out on the horizon as though she longed to be free yet she never complained. For that he loved her and would never tell her. She belonged to his friend though Deveril valued her not.

"He cannot stay immured in Scotland forever," he said finally and as evenly as he could manage.

Byrony's soft lips tightened in the darkness. "Do you really believe that?"

"Deveril is not a stupid man."

Byrony wanted to ask what he meant but some force stayed her tongue. Instead she turned the conversation to easier channels. "That is one thing on which all of London can agree, I think," she drawled cynically. "His wisdom can be questioned but never his intelligence."

Deveril's carriage pulled to a stop in front of Charles' townhouse. Lights blazed a welcome but he scarcely noted their warm glow. He entered, a scowl on his handsome face, and pinned the butler with a steely look.

"Where is my godfather?" he demanded tightly.

At that moment Charles came out of the dining room on his way to the study and his nightly brandy while seated before his wife's portrait. He halted in midstride, an expression of surprise crossing his aquiline features.

"Oh there you are, Dev," he said mildly coming toward him.

Deveril met him halfway. "Where is she?"

"Shall we go into the study?" Charles asked blandly. Deveril went, not because he cared if half the servants in the house heard him but because he knew Charles wouldn't answer him otherwise.

"Well?" he demanded when the older man was silent.

Charles took a seat, watching Deveril pace about the room. "Why do you wish to know? As I recall, you left Castleton without a word," he murmured at length.

Deveril halted to glare at him. "My privilege, I believe."

"And it is mine to choose not to tell you anything about my niece."

"My wife," Deveril corrected harshly.

"So you do remember it, after all," Charles remarked dryly.

"I am losing my temper," Deveril warned.

"The rest of your acquaintances may quake at such a threat but I do not."

"You have no right to interfere."

Charles laughed shortly. "If I had not, Byrony would have been left at the Castle, alone and friendless for all these weeks. Was the lure of Scotland so strong that you needs must leave her in so humiliating a way?"

"Why I went is none of your affair."

"It is when it affects Byrony. I will not have her hurt. Not even by you." Charles rose to face him. "I shall not hand her over to you again until I am confident you will treat her as the lady she is and not like one of your lightskirts. She is your wife and deserving of your consideration."

Deveril's hands clenched against his sides. "How dare you tell me how to treat my wife," he bit out.

"Someone must tell you to your head what you are about. You seem incapable of seeing your behavior for what it is. Do you know what they call Byrony here? The Devil's

Duchess. How do you think she feels about that?"

"You should have thought of that before you tricked me into this marriage."

Charles ran his fingers through his hair in a distracted gesture. This scene was more difficult than he had expected it to be. Deveril was angrier than he had ever seen him. "Perhaps, but what is done cannot be undone now."

Deveril flung himself into a chair. "I shall not beat her, you know, but she will behave herself. After all, that was the whole purpose for me in this marriage or had you forgotten?" One black brow rose to punctuate the question.

"I have forgotten nothing."

"Now where is she?"

"Out."

Deveril waited but no more information was forthcoming. "The rest, Charles." The command was soft but unmistakable.

Charles sat down with a sigh. "She is attending the theatre."

Deveril studied him closely, hearing more than the words he spoke. "Who is she with?" His voice was softer this time, a sure sign his anger was increasing.

"John Tarrington."

Surprise silenced Deveril for a moment. "The last I heard he was in the Americas."

"He is back now and on the lookout for a wife."

"If that is true, what is he doing with mine?"

Charles glanced at him quickly, then away again. The idea of planting the seeds of jealousy in Deveril's heart to awaken him to Byrony's attractions died a swift death. In Deveril's present mood, Charles could foresee danger in such a course.

"Byrony needed an escort with you gone from town. For all her knowing ways, she is still unschooled in society. John and she hit it off and I asked him to act as her companion when I could not. His family and mine have been close for years and all know of my special feeling for him so there could be no question in his actions in regards to my niece."

There was a rebuke in his words but Deveril chose to ignore it. "Tell her maid to ready her things while I go to the theatre to get her." Deveril rose and started for the door.

"No."

Deveril halted at the quiet refusal. He turned, his eyes kindling.

Charles got to his feet. "You will not embarrass her this way. You deserted her. Everyone in this town knows it. You will not now compound that folly by publicly dragging her back to your side. She will remove to your home in an orderly fashion and in broad daylight."

"She will remove to my side any way I say," Deveril shot back.

"Do this and I promise you our friendship is at an end."

For a moment neither man spoke.

"You take advantage of my esteem for you," Deveril said bitterly. He hated weakness, especially his own. Yet he could not deny this man. "I shall be here at ten tomorrow. See that she is ready," he capitulated with ill grace.

Deveril departed lost in his thoughts. His anger was dulled by the confusion of his emotions. What had he almost done? It had taken Charles' ultimatum to bring him to his senses. Byrony. His wife. The wife he had not wanted. Yet here he was fighting Charles to return her to his side. He had deserted her. He frowned, remembering what had driven him to Scotland. For an instant he recalled how easy it would have been to slide between those sheets that morning and lose himself again in her softness. As he had stood beside her bed at dawn, he had wanted to feel her silken warmth enfolding him, to hear her gasp of fulfillment. Instead he had quit the field, blocking out the memory of her passion and his own.

Now he was back and fool that he was he was trying to put temptation in his own way. He had even risked his relationship with Charles to do so. What would he do with

Byrony when she returned to him, for god's sake? He did not even want a wife!

"Damn her!" he muttered, trying to banish her image from his mind.

That was why he rode at night instead of sleeping. That was why he wanted her and hated himself for wanting her at one and the same time. She was the fire in his blood. To gain his freedom he would have to give himself to the fire until it burned itself out. Satisfied at last with his reasoning, Deveril relaxed against the cushions. Weariness overtook him, reminding him that he had been traveling for many days. Suddenly his bed held more appeal than it had in weeks. Tomorrow was soon enough to test the fire.

Chapter Thirteen

"Uncle?" Byrony paused, one foot on the bottom stair as Charles came out of the study. "Is there something amiss?"

Although she had enjoyed the theatre with John, she was tired and wished nothing more than her bed. Perhaps she should have been too excited to sleep since she had been introduced to the Prince Regent when he had made one of his rare visits to the theatre, but even that had failed to spark her interest. Every day, London was losing some more of its glitter. She was in danger of becoming as jaded as its inhabitants, or so she feared. Hoping Charles would not want to indulge in one of their late-night chats, she waited for him to speak.

"Could you spare me a moment, my dear? There is something I wish to talk to you about."

Byrony inclined her head before following him into his favorite room. Dropping her reticule on the chair, she took a seat next to his in front of the fire. It wasn't the first time they had sat thus, but it was certainly the first time it had been this late when they had done so.

"Deveril was here earlier looking for you," Charles said abruptly.

Byrony stared at him.

"He wants you to return to him tomorrow." Charles

turned to her. He had come to a decision while he had waited for her to come home. Now he meant to keep the promise he had made to himself and to Kate. "Do you wish to go back to him?"

Byrony blinked. "Do I have a choice?" she asked.

"Yes, you do." Charles took her hands in his. "I will not deceive you. Deveril is in a black mood. One that even I worry about. I forced this marriage with the best possible motives but I will not see either of you hurt with it."

"Tell me what he said."

Charles shook his head. "There is no need to repeat every word. I want you to know that I care about you and that I shall back you regardless of what you decide."

The ramifications of his offer sank in slowly. Byrony stared at him, realizing that he had in essence promised to support her despite the very real possibility of a scandal if she chose to live apart from Deveril. The price this proud man would pay would be overwhelming. The scandal would rock them all. Deveril was accustomed to setting the town on its ear but Charles was not. And she? She had no one but this kind, generous man to please and to care about.

"I made my promise," she murmured at last, her eyes steady on his. "I will not deny that I have been hurt by Deveril's attitude and humiliated as well. But I am no quitter. He is my husband." She paused then added on a stronger, more determined note. "But this time he will not make all the rules. I will not be deserted again. Nor will he humiliate me with another woman."

Charles stared at her warily "Byrony, what do you mean to do?" he asked, fearing the worst. He could not help remembering that this was the woman who lived in a man's world and made it her own. This was the woman who had gambled and won enough money to bring Julia home. And this was the woman who had held a pistol pointed at his chest and had been prepared to use it if necessary.

"When is Deveril coming for me? Or does he just intend to

send a carriage as though I were a servant in need of conveyance?"

"He will come himself at ten."

Charles watched her absorb the information. As well as he had come to know her in the past months, he could not tell what she was thinking. Her silver eyes were dark with shadows and plans that did not include him. Fear settled in the pit of his stomach. The situation was no longer in his control. Both Deveril and Byrony were now their own masters and even he did not know which was stronger.

"What are you planning?"

Byrony patted his hand before releasing it. "I have not decided as yet. One thing I can tell you is that I shall not sit tamely by and wait for him to collect me. I have a date to ride with John tomorrow. I think that I shall keep it."

Charles was shaking his head before she finished speaking. "I would not," he said hurriedly. "Choose something else besides another man, for your own sake, my dear. I beg of you."

Byrony rose, her expression as determined as her voice. "I am not so foolish as to try to make him jealous. After all, he would have to care for me for that."

"Believe me, there will be little difference in the real thing and this where Deveril is concerned. You do not know him."

"And he does not know me." She smiled as she said it but there was no humor in the curve of her lips. Picking up her reticule, she headed for the door.

Charles watched Byrony go, unable to think how to persuade her to choose another method of teaching Deveril a lesson. He foresaw many storms ahead for his two favorites and there was nothing he could do to help either of them any longer. He, like the rest of London, appeared set to view a struggle of Herculean proportions.

Byrony mounted the stairs lost in thought. How dare Deveril come back expecting her to simply pick up as though nothing had occurred between them. Did he not know the blow he had dealt her? Of course he did. He must have meant it. She frowned, shaking her head when she realized she did not want to believe that of him. The weeks in London and her exposure to Corinne, Olivia, and those like them had given her more of an understanding of her husband and the demons that drove him. For the first time she wondered if he had truly meant to humiliate her. What if he had had another reason for leaving? Had he wanted to hurt her, he certainly had a far superior weapon at hand than desertion.

Their wedding night. Deveril could have made her pay then in ways she would never have forgotten. What it must have meant to him to be faced with her and a pistol aimed at a prized part of his anatomy. His pride should have demanded retribution, and yet when he had found her asleep and at his mercy, he had not hurt her. He could have but he had not. Instead he had taught her the wonder of a man's passion. The things he had shown her that night still lived in her memories and haunted her dreams. That was the real hurt. That he could leave her when her body had still trembled in the aftermath of his possession.

Byrony undressed and dismissed Tillie absently. Finally, she could admit the truth. Damn his aristocratic hide. He had made her want him and then left her. This stranger had called up responses she barely understood. Emotions that shocked her senseless. He had no right. This was a marriage of convenience. There was no love on either side. Only a mutual benefit.

Sliding between the sheets, Byrony stared at the darkened ceiling. "You changed the rules, Devil, my husband," she whispered. "I am no biddable wife to countenance your peccadillos. At least not unless I can partake of their joy. We are joined in this game. Now we shall see who deals the cards."

"The Duchess of Castleton attended the theatre escorted by John Tarrington. Her grace, the hit of the season, was seen in conversation with His Majesty and later Beau Brummell. As always the Devil's Duchess charmed all with her beauty, poise, and grace."

Deveril slammed the newspaper down on the breakfast table, his eyes dark with temper. Devil's Duchess! How dare they print that trash about one of the highest titles in the land. They made her sound like some damn puppy on a leash. Hit of the Season! Why wouldn't she be, backed by his title and wealth and Charles' sponsorship. He glared at the words, wishing he had the stupid reporter's neck between his hands. Then the fool would know respect. Pushing away from the table, Deveril got to his feet. It was a good thing he had come to London when he had. What was Charles thinking of to allow Byrony's name to be bandied about in this rag? He completely ignored the fact that the newspaper in question was one of the biggest and most influential in London.

Calling for his hat, he left the house, scarcely noticing that Smithington had managed to prepare his residence for him and his bride in an amazingly short time. There wasn't a dust cover in evidence, and the gold knocker on the front door gleamed with polish, shining brilliantly in the early morning sun. His carriage stood at the curb, the horses restive at the short wait. Normally, Deveril would have taken the edge off their paces but this morning he had more to think about than their high spirits.

Byrony! Her image had been with him once again when he awoke. He could hardly wait to feel her skin against his once more and that angered him almost as much as it enflamed him. Bending her to his will would be no easy task. That knowledge, too, held him imprisoned. There would be no more pistols in his bedroom or in her hands. She was his wife and she would remember that.

With that fine idea foremost in his mind, Deveril mounted the steps to Charles' townhouse. The butler took his hat just as his godfather came out of the study to greet him.

"Where is she?" Deveril drawled ominously.

"She is out. She had an engagement she could not break."

"You mean would not, I think." Deveril glared at his host. "Are her trunks packed?"

Charles inclined his head. "Her maid is ready as well."

That surprised him. What was the chit playing at? "Does she think to keep me cooling my heels awaiting her pleasure?" He stared out the window. "Have her things and her maid loaded into the coach waiting outside," he said at length. "And tell Byrony when she returns that Castleton awaits her."

"You will not wait for her?" Charles asked, a bit taken aback.

"I have other business to attend. My wife is not my only consideration. I have been away from town too long." He strolled toward the door. It wasn't difficult to imagine Byrony's temper when she found out her little plan had backfired. If he had learned one thing about his hot-blooded wife in the short time he had known her, it was that she hated losing.

Charles watched him go, mistrusting the expression on his face. It was almost identical to the one Byrony had worn earlier when she had tripped down the stairs to keep her date to ride with John. How could two people be so much alike and too blind to see it, he wondered as he sat down in the chair before Kate's portrait. Both of them were bent on getting the upper hand.

"Where did I go wrong?" Charles stared at Kate's portrait, his fingers steepled in front of him.

"Byrony, is it not time we were leaving?"

John slowed his horse from a gentle trot to a sedate walk. He and Byrony had left the crowded Row a few moments before in order to find a place to let the horses out a bit. The secluded walks were not the choice of most of the Ton but they were an excellent slow ride through country-like surroundings.

"Are you not enjoying my company?" Byrony asked with a smile as she brought her mare alongside John's gelding.

Just for an instant John almost gave in to the need to tell Byrony how much he enjoyed her company. His love was growing daily and there wasn't a thing he seemed to be able to do about it. Byrony saw him as nothing more than a friend, and even had that not been true, he could not take advantage of his friendship with Deveril.

"I always find pleasure in your company," he answered finally if a bit formally.

Byrony glanced at him, surprised at the intensity in his voice. The strange gravity of his expression surprised her. Pulling her mount to a stop, she asked, "Is something wrong?"

"I might ask you the same thing," he countered, watching her closely. His reply was partially a diversion but it was also the truth. "So far this morning I have been treated to a fine display of a Society grand dame or a coquette, depending on your whim. You are neither."

Byrony glanced away, caught without a defense. She had not considered John's perception and his deeper knowledge of her behavior. She had thought she hid her nervousness better. "I don't know what you mean."

"There's no need to lie," he said gently. "You would not be the first to tell me to mind my own affair."

Byrony regarded him ruefully. "I would not treat you so. You are my dearest friend."

John just barely contained the wince at her blind acceptance of his role in her life. "Then as your friend, let me help," he pleaded, reaching across to touch her hand lightly, just once. Damn Deveril for not being here to guide and support her. If he had been lucky enough to have her for his wife, he would have wrapped her in silks and laces and she would never want or hurt again.

"There is nothing you can do." This was between her and Deveril and no other now that Charles was out of it. "Truly it is nothing more than boredom."

John searched her face. He knew how she chafed at the restrictions on her freedom. Her eyes held his without a blink. His suspicions faded. "How would you like a picnic in the country?" he suggested impulsively. "I will even roust out Bella to join us."

Byrony could just picture the madcap with such an expedition in the offing. The idea brought the first real smile of the day to her lips. Then she remembered Deveril and she sobered. "I cannot promise," she said slowly.

"Why?"

Byrony sighed. There was no help for it now. She would have to tell him. "Deveril is in town. I return to him today."

John froze, for a moment too stunned to speak. This was the one thing he had not expected. "When today?" he asked finally.

"At ten."

"Ten?" John stared at her. "It's gone that already."

"I know."

The calm of her answer silenced him for an instant before understanding dawned. "You meant for him to find you gone?" He was shocked.

She nodded. "I did."

"But why?" he asked blankly.

"That is between the two of us, surely."

"Not when you bring me into it, it is not," he denied, suddenly angry. "I will not be used."

Byrony touched his hand. "I did not mean to use you, truly. I just could not let him dictate to me. Cannot you understand?"

"But he is your husband."

"So everyone keeps telling me."

John sighed, half angry at himself. He knew how Deveril must have hurt her with his indifference. How could he be so insensitive as to suggest she tolerate his behavior? She deserved better than Deveril's treatment.

"I am sorry. I had no right."

Byrony stopped him with a small smile. "My actions are not pure, I am afraid. I would run him through if I could."

John grinned, not believing her for a moment. "Commission me instead. We are more evenly matched."

Byrony bit her tongue to hold back the flow of words. In that moment she realized John did not know her, not really. He saw her as a lady in distress, a helpless woman who needed a man to protect her. At least Deveril had never made that mistake, she thought as she turned her horse to head back the way they had come. He was more like to take her to task for her unladylike behavior than to try and wrap her in cotton. He met her temper with one every bit as hot as her own. John would think she didn't mean the rash words she spoke.

At home she found Charles waiting for her and Deveril gone.

"Where is he?" she asked.

"Gone."

"Where?"

"He did not say."

"And what about me? What am I to do?"

This was the moment he dreaded. "I am afraid you will have to make your way to Castleton alone. All your trunks and Tillie are already there."

Byrony stared out the window, contemplating her predicament. All she had was her riding habit unless Tillie had thought to leave her a gown. When she had ordered everything packed this morning, she had not considered Deveril's options.

"You still have a choice," Charles said. "I meant what I said."

Byrony shook her head. "My answer is the same."

Charles rose and came to her. His hands on her shoulders,

he kissed her lightly on the forehead. "Then go, but remember if you need me, I shall be here."

When Byrony arrived at Deveril's house, Smithington greeted her with the intelligence that her things had arrived and his grace was out and was not expected until late.

"Coward!" Byrony swore, climbing the stairs with more energy than ladies should display. Tillie was waiting for her with a hot bath drawn before the fire. A relaxing soak should have been just the thing after her morning ride. The luxury surrounding her should have delighted her eye. Neither rated more than cursory notice. Byrony had more important things on her mind.

Byrony sat up with a jerk that sloshed water onto the floor. "Perfect," she murmured, with a smile that hinted at things better not known by anyone with a faint heart. The boredom that had haunted her footsteps for so many days was gone as she turned over in her mind how best to carry out her idea. The first thing was to send around a note to John. She would need an escort for the Alvaney Ball.

"You may tell her grace I am at home." Deveril handed his hat to the butler.

"I am sorry, your grace, but her grace is not at home at present." Smithington stared off into space, not one muscle betraying his private thoughts concerning the events occurring in his household.

"Damn her," Deveril swore, glaring at the hapless Smithington. "You let her leave."

Smithington goggled at him. "I, your grace," he stammered. "I could not stop her."

"Are you telling me you were not a match for the chit?"

"Lay hands upon her grace!" He stepped back, shocked to the very core of his correct soul.

Deveril raked his fingers through his hair. Reining in his temper was never easy but he made the effort. It wasn't Smithington's fault. It was Byrony's. He headed for the stairs before he remembered to ask where exactly his wife was. This time he would collect the rebel himself. No more of this soft footing around for him. Tonight he would lay down the law. It would be a wonder if half of London had not been entertained by their antics this day.

"What was her destination?" he asked on a calmer note.

"The Alvaney Ball," Smithington replied faintly.

"Was she alone?"

Smithington shook his head.

"Her escort?" Deveril took two steps toward him.

Smithington swallowed. "John Tarrington," he croaked.

"I'll kill her."

Smithington gaped after him as he took the stairs two at a time. In his room he stripped the clothes from his body. A warm bath did nothing to calm his temper.

"I want the black this evening," he said to his valet.

Meade paused, eyeing him dubiously. Deveril favored black above all the colors in his wardrobe but there was only one outfit that was completely ebony. Seldom worn, but nonetheless striking, it had only one touch of color and that was the white shirt that went with it. Deveril never wore any jewelry with it except the St. John signet ring.

It was on the tip of Meade's tongue to inquire as to his destination. The black was formal attire that scarcely fit the at home he had been told to prepare for this, the first night the duchess was in residence. Only his training and the knowledge that Deveril was in one of his moods kept him silent as he carried the clothes to the duke.

Deveril dressed swiftly. Byrony was a fool if she thought to make him jealous. More experienced women than she had tried such tactics and failed. What was Charles thinking of when he allowed her to make a byword of herself and his name? That had been the whole purpose of this charade of a marriage. Where was the benefit to the Castleton name if Byrony continued to carry on like the veriest courtesan? He would not have it, and after tonight, John Tarrington would know his feelings on the matter, as would Byrony. He would not stand by to be cockolded.

These thoughts and more filled his mind on the drive to the Alvaney establishment. Carriages lined the streets and the lanes, testifying to the huge attendance of London's finest. Liveried servants of all shapes and sizes scurried about helping the guests alight in all their glory. Deveril's men handled the chaos with aplomb, bringing him to the entrance in good order. He stepped down, unaware of the whispers of shock and awe at his attendance. All eyes followed him as he mounted the stairs ahead of those still waiting to be announced. His high rank entitled him to the privilege, though he rarely used it thus. Tonight, however, he was in no mood to cool his heels outside. He had come for one reason and he would not waste a second in setting about his purpose.

When Deveril reached the top of the stairs and stood looking down on the ballroom floor, his name was announced. The musicians were playing for the dancers but not one person present failed to note his appearance. In the stark, unrelieved black, Deveril stood out like a raven in a flock of parakeets. The light from the chandelier overhead shone on his ebony hair, casting shadows over his face that were both menacing and irresistibly attractive.

Deveril descended the steps and moved through the crowd with the lithe and regal grace of an athlete, acknowledging greetings with bored indifference. His eyes slid over the females of the assemblage. He neither noticed nor cared that for all their disapproval the prim and proper recipients of even his most cursory gaze had sudden fantasies of ravishment between the silken sheets, candles gutted to the holder, and hot passionate words pouring in their ears.

Where was she? Deveril stared at the circling dancers. She

had not been among the spectators so she had to be there. Then he saw her. A swirl of crimson, an ebony mane tossed back, a pair of laughing lips. Byrony! His eyes narrowed as he watched her, seeing the changes that had been wrought in his absence. Only the midnight hair seemed the same. The woman he had bedded had had the potential to be a great beauty—even then he had known that. Since then she had blossomed, and he had not been around to see it.

For a moment their eyes locked.

Byrony lifted her head, giving it a tiny toss. No one looking on would have recognized the gesture. Deveril did. It was a challenge. It dared him to do his damndest.

Turning his head, Deveril scanned the other guests. He did not have far to look. Olivia. Perfect.

Chapter Fourteen

Byrony whirled around the floor on John's arm. This was the first ball where she had been able to dance. Her supposed period of mourning was at an end and she was now in colors and could enjoy all the entertainments that the socially prescribed period of grief had denied her. Not that it mattered. True, she was finding the evening pleasing enough. John was an escort any woman would delight in having to herself. But nothing could occupy Byrony's mind for long, not when every second she was searching the room for a glimpse of Deveril.

Then she saw him. Deveril stood there watching her, those blue eyes gleaming with memories that found a matching image within her. Shivers traced down her spine. He had no right to look at her like that. Not after the way he had deserted her. Then the lashes dropped and lifted once again. This time there was searing anger in the sapphire depths. His gaze slid to John then back to her face. Byrony felt its touch as a slap. That angered her. She lifted her head, tilting her chin.

Damn him, she swore silently, stiffening as Deveril strolled into the crowd—straight for Olivia! The sight of his former mistress in a low-cut gown that clung to every lush curve made Byrony wish for her pistol. Which one she would have shot was, fortunately, an academic question.

Turning her head, she gazed into John's eyes.

"How much of a friend are you?" she asked softly.

John looked in her eyes and saw a stranger. The clear determination in the silver depths was new and vaguely uncomfortable.

"What's wrong?"

"Deveril is here?"

"Where?"

The sight of Deveril with Olivia on his arm made him falter for a split second. Now he understood Byrony's look.

"Shall I take you home?"

"No," she murmured, thinking quickly. "What I would really like is to get out of this crowd. A walk in the gardens, perhaps?"

"But you know what the tabbies will make of us alone together with Deveril in attendance."

"Do you think that it will really matter in the end? We are an on dit now. The four of us. This way at least two of us will have some privacy."

There was no arguing with that logic but John could still not be easy in himself. He looked again at Deveril, catching him staring their way. The glitter in those ice blue eyes sliced through to the bone and reminded John, for a fleeting moment, of the look in Byrony's eyes only seconds before.

"I don't like this," he muttered as the music drew to a close. He offered Byrony his arm.

Byrony laid her hand on his with a smile. "I promise you this will be the last time I ask you to help me."

Her words made him feel guilty. She asked so little, this gallant creature. He patted her hand and smiled. "You may command me always. I promise you. I am not really so hen-hearted."

The return of the teasing companion she had come to rely on relieved Byrony. "You may regret your generosity," she said softly, only half in jest.

"Never."

The two of them were so caught up in their conversation that they were unaware of Deveril and Olivia's approach. Byrony glanced up to find her husband looking at her with that detestable haughty lift to his black brows.

"John was the first to speak. "It is good to see you back in Town. I have looked for you."

"Have you?" said Deveril silkily.

Olivia tittered. "It would seem you were hoping for his continued absence."

Before Byrony could retort, Deveril had extended his arm. "My dance, I believe, madam wife."

Byrony had two choices. She could create a scene or she could submit graciously—for the time being. Withdrawing her hand from John's arm, she placed it on Deveril's. Whether by accident or design the band chose that moment to begin a waltz. Without a word, Deveril swung her onto the floor in perfect time to the music.

Deveril's eyes traveled slowly over his elegantly clad wife as she swayed with him. She was attired in a crimson satin gown with a daringly low-cut V-neckline. Her breasts rose tantalizingly above snowy French lace. From the top of her elegantly coiffed head to the tips of her dainty feet, she looked every inch a duchess—a far cry from the chit he had married.

"Well, madam wife, you are certainly altered in looks since last I saw you."

Byrony kept a bland smile on her face which did credit to her training. "Did you expect to find me here in my breeches?"

"I did not think to find you here at all," he returned, swinging her past a more sedate couple. "I expected you to remain where I had left you—at my Castle."

"Unfortunately you departed so quickly you forgot to leave your orders for my disposal behind," Byrony remarked sweetly.

Deveril was rather taken aback by this new Byrony he held

in his arms. She managed to throw her barbed comments at him without losing her poise. He wanted to shake her. Where was the temper he had enjoyed provoking—and the passion?

If Deveril only knew how difficult Byrony found it to think straight with memories of his body against hers evoked at every moment of this infernal dance. His hand was warm on her bare back, his words soft despite their cutting edge. The candles on the wall cast faint shadows on the edge of the floor where they danced, reminding her of the darkness of her chamber when he had taken her to wife. Heat pooled in her blood. Her limbs felt heavy and the quickness of her breathing had little to do with the exertion of the dance. Her only defense against the memories was to hold herself distant from them. But it was difficult. Far more so than she would have imagined.

"When this dance ends, we shall depart," Deveril said firmly.

Byrony looked calmly at him. "I came with John."

"You will leave with your husband."

"And if I do not?"

"You will regret it."

The music slowed, bringing the dance to an end. Neither spoke as he released her. Immediately Byrony turned and walked in John's direction.

When she reached him, she turned back to see that Deveril had wasted no time in claiming Olivia as his dance partner.

"Let me take you home," John offered, following her eyes to the pair.

"Not yet."

Byrony allowed him to lead her from the floor. Weariness seeped into her bones with every step. Now that she did not have Deveril to spar with, she felt drained of life. The boredom that was fast becoming her constant companion settled over her. The sight of Bella approaching without her usual escort trailing at her heels was welcome.

"So he is back," Lady Bella remarked cheerfully. "I had

not heard."

Byrony could not help smiling at her irreverent way of putting it. No one else of her acquaintance would have been so bold in noting Deveril's arrival. "I believe he returned yesterday."

"So now your freedom is at an end. A pity. The kind of a marriage that you and Deveril seem to have has always appealed to me. A woman has so little freedom. From her father's house to her husband, with both having the ordering of her life. You men have had it all your own way for far too long." She glanced at John, giving him a roguish look. "It makes me glad I have not found a mate as yet. Perhaps I should consider visiting the colonies. From what you tell me, the ladies there are far better off than we."

John shook his head amused. "Bella, you are no rebel and you know it. Think of what we men must endure at the hands of your fair sisters. And besides, you are too tender for such a life. You are meant for this."

"Do you think so? I recall blackening your eye one year. And beating you to the fox the next. I may never have shot a gun to drive off an Indian attack but I'll wager I could learn just as easily as a man. I wish sometimes I could ride about in breeches. Do you have any idea how confining these skirts are?" Bella demanded, warming to her point. She had been in love with John for years, at least two before he left to seek his fortune in the Americas. But great hulking fool that he was, he did not see it. He only seemed to have eyes for Byrony. When she had first met Byrony, she had been jealous until she realized the duchess was more interested in besting her husband than snaring John.

John grinned. "But surely more beautiful than leathers."

While John and Bella bantered, Byrony watched the dancers, unable to keep her eyes from the distinctive figure of her husband as he led Olivia through the steps of the quadrille. The smile he gave to Olivia was more than Byrony could bear. She averted her eyes and forced herself to enter the fray with John and Bella. By the time the music stopped, she was enjoying the lively argument.

"Oh no." Bella's sudden look of horror stopped John in midsentence.

"What's wrong?"

"The dowager just arrived. Look."

Byrony turned to see Corinne as she stood poised on the steps to be announced to the assemblage. Byrony glanced at Deveril. She saw him note his mother's presence but try as she might she could detect no change in his demeanor. The dowager could have been a stranger for all the interest he showed.

"Oh god, she is coming toward us," Bella whispered.

Byrony waited, trying to look calm. Thus far she and Corinne had exchanged as few words as possible. She could not imagine why the dowager would force a meeting now.

"I had heard Deveril was back," she began abruptly. "And I understand that you are still residing with Charles."

"You are mistaken. I am with Deveril and in our home."

"And yet he dances attendance on Olivia," she drawled, glancing at the pair across the room. "I wonder that he does not fly to your side to protect you from me."

"You overestimate your importance, your grace. Deveril knows I am perfectly capable of taking care of myself. I need no one's protection."

Byrony was glad that she, Bella, and John had drifted close to the terrace doors to take advantage of the cooling breeze from the garden. They were somewhat isolated from the rest of the guests by their position and therefore had a measure of privacy to talk while still remaining in full view of the assemblage.

Corinne stiffened at the insult. "That was not wise," she hissed, her expression twisted with anger. "He will not be a husband to you. There will always be such as Olivia to occupy him."

"I think you have said enough," John interrupted in a

hard voice.

Corinne barely acknowledged him with a glance. "You have pride. I have seen it. How long will you be satisfied with crumbs?"

Corinne turned without another word and left. John's hand on Byrony's arm offered comfort.

"That woman is poison," Bella muttered. "I swear I don't know how Deveril could have her for a mother."

"Many would think he deserved her," John added, glancing across to his friend. The fact that Deveril had not come to support Byrony against the dowager rankled.

"No one deserves her." Bella shivered. "I cannot think why she is invited anywhere."

Byrony shook her head. "Perhaps her power is so great that it is fear that prompts others to seek her good office."

Against her will she looked to the place she had last seen Deveril. The sight of him, with Olivia on his arm, hurt. It took a second for her to realize he was slowly working his way to his mother. Corinne had not seen him yet. Byrony watched Deveril speak, saw Corinne stiffen and turn slowly to face him. The shock on the faces of those around them was clear even across the distance separating Byrony from the tableau. Even Olivia looked ready to sink through the floor.

"I don't believe it," John murmured, his eyes also on the scene unfolding. "I thought he never spoke to her in public."

"He does not," Bella confirmed. "I have never known him to seek a meeting. Why do you suppose he has done so now?"

John frowned thoughtfully, before glancing at Byrony. "I think I have misjudged your husband. I do believe he is taking her to task on your account."

Byrony inclined her head without saying a word. Somehow she knew John had the right of it. Corinne's face was dark with suppressed anger, her eyes stabbing at Byrony as the dowager looked beyond Deveril to where she stood.

"Look, he is leaving and he is taking that cat Olivia with him," Bella whispered, her disapproval plain.

Any softer feelings budding within Byrony faded. It was true that many married couples came and left with partners other than each other. But considering the circumstances, Byrony felt hurt.

John offered her his arm.

"I think I, too, would seek my bed. I am suddenly very tired," Bella said. "I am in no mood to be entertained any more tonight."

Byrony could not but be grateful for Bella's support. If the three of them were seen leaving together, there would be less talk than if she and John departed alone. While she wouldn't have asked for Bella's help, she was not strong enough to refuse it. She was weary of the stratagems that had become a way of life. Briefly she wished for the simplicity of her former existence. But Charles and the weeks of education at his hands had taught her the folly of her past. If nothing else she knew she could never return to what had been.

The three of them gained the door and stood on the steps awaiting the arrival of their carriages. John's arrived first.

"I wonder what is keeping my coachman?" Bella asked, peering into the darkness.

"We'll wait with you until he comes," Byrony offered.

Bella hardly heard her. "There he is but where is my coach?"

John moved toward the man. "I'll see what's amiss," he said over his shoulder.

Bella frowned. "I knew I should have stayed at home. I was promised to friends for tonight's escort but one had to go out of town and the other caught a chill."

"This is one time when I wager you would enjoy the offices of a man," Byrony couldn't help pointing out.

"Wretch!" Bella gave her a look. "I never said they did not have their uses." She brightened as John rejoined them. "Is there a problem?"

"One of your horses has gone lame. Your coachman has

sent home for a replacement."

"Fiddle!"

"We can take you up with us." Byrony's suggestion scarcely proceeded John's.

"Would you?"

"Don't be a pea goose," John chided, urging both women down the stairs. "My horses are waiting."

Bella giggled as she followed Byrony into the carriage. "Such a gentleman," she remarked.

John settled back. "And such a lady. No vapors and no whining. What is the world coming to?"

Byrony stared out at the passing scenery. She tried not to think of Deveril but it was an impossible task. His image intruded too vividly for her peace of mind. She could not forget that he had left with Olivia in tow. Equally, she could not forget he had met his mother for her sake. How could one man pull so many feelings from her, she wondered in something approaching despair. All of her life she had exercised a measure of control and that now was at an end. Deveril made her do things—feel things—she never would have thought possible. She had used John shamefully and known she was doing it. She had attempted to make Deveril jealous simply to satisfy her own vanity. The knowledge was almost more than she could bear. She wanted an end to this war but she had no idea how to bring about peace without surrender.

Preoccupied, Byrony made her goodnight to Bella without knowing she did so. She only roused when John called her name in a stern voice.

"You are home," he said, studying her in the soft light of the carriage lamp. "Shall I come in with you?"

Byrony shook her head. "No, not tonight. I need to be alone." The irony of her statement did not escape her.

"Are you sure?"

She touched his hand. "Yes. Do not worry about me."

John forced himself to stay in his seat. She would not have his help. He had to respect her wishes and truth to tell he was relieved. To have seen and perhaps heard Deveril turn his temper on her was more than he could bear. Yet he had no right to interfere. Byrony would not allow him to protect her.

"Do we still ride tomorrow?"

"Perhaps. I shall send a note round."

Neither of them added *if Deveril allowed it.* With a small smile of gratitude, Byrony descended the steps and tripped into the house. Smithington was waiting at the door to receive her. A few moments later she entered her bedroom to find it empty. Puzzled, for Tillie had never been absent before, Byrony glanced around. The sight of Deveril reclining on the chaise in front of the windows made her heart pound.

"You startled me."

Deveril rose in one graceful movement and came toward her. Stroking her cheek with his forefinger, he stared into her silver eyes.

Byrony jerked back her head, pushing his hand away. "Don't touch me. It is a lie and we both know it."

Reaching out, he caught her shoulders, gripping them painfully.

"And I suppose your 'friendship' with John is less of a lie."

Byrony inhaled sharply. "He is your friend. How dare you think such a thing of either of us?"

"He was my friend many years ago, I'll grant you," he said. "But he has proved himself otherwise by taking what belongs to me."

"Only when you made it quite evident you didn't want me—leaving with your mistress on your arm! What happened, did she not want you?"

"If I had wanted her I would not be here now." He shook her hard. The force of his hold tumbled Byrony's hair down her back in a shower of pins and jewels.

"Damn you! Release me!" She raised her hand and dealt him a stinging slap.

Anger turned to icy rage. Deveril dropped his shoulder and tossed her over it. Outraged and humiliated, Byrony fought and wiggled but was helpless in her ignominious position. Three steps brought Deveril to the bed. He dropped Byrony in the center following her down before she had a chance to scramble away.

Byrony saw the smoldering desire in his eyes. She heaved upward, trying futilely to catch him by surprise.

Deveril rode her as he would a wild horse. His knees pressed to her sides, he caught her wrists in one hand and pulled them high above her head. Byrony fought the hold with all her might. Skirts flying as she kicked and squirmed, she was insensible to the vulnerable position she held. She learned fast when Deveril's free hand ripped her bodice clear to her waist. Her cry of outrage was lost as his mouth covered hers.

His chest pressed her deep in the mattress, stealing the power from her struggles as effectively as his lips stole her breath. His heat surrounded her. She could not breathe. She could not move as he took his pleasure of her tender mouth. His hand traced the full contours of her breasts and she shivered despite herself.

"I hate you," she gasped.

Her answer was a kiss that made the one before seem loverlike.

What came next was beyond Byrony's understanding, either of herself or Deveril. Yet even as she struggled, she could not stop her body's response. One moment she was clawing his back as he tried to mount her and the next she was pulling him to her in desperate need. His cry of satisfaction was no louder than her own when he thrust into her body and completed the union both strained for.

Her eyes gleamed with molten fire as she matched his erotic rhythm. If he would mark her as his, so would she make him hers.

"You belong to me," he breathed, lifting her hips high to accept him more fully.

As they reached as one to the peak of fulfillment, their cries of exultation were triumphant.

Chapter Fifteen

Byrony rolled over onto her back, groaning faintly as her body protested the movement. She ached in places a lady was supposed to have no knowledge of. Drowsily opening her eyes, she found herself staring into Deveril's face. She froze. Every memory of the long, passion-filled night flooded her. The knowledge of the passion she had shared with him in the darkness stirred heat in her blood. And she saw the same remembrance in Deveril's eyes as he lay without moving and watched her.

Neither spoke. No touch was exchanged to soften the harsh reality of the morning sun pouring in the windows. Byrony could not look away. His face. So different yet the same.

"Byrony, I . . ." Deveril began then hesitated. His gaze dropped as he tried to think of what to say. The sight of the three marks of his fingers against the satin smoothness of one shoulder drove every other thought from his mind. He stared in horror at what he had done, for there was a matching set on the other shoulder as well. Never had he touched a woman without remembering his strength. To have forgotten himself with Byrony made him sick to his soul. Drawing back, he slid from the bed and almost stumbled on the untidy pile of his clothes. The evidence of his haste was in the torn fasteners and rumpled linen.

Byrony watched, bewildered at his actions. She had seen his face change, seen the horror in his eyes. Had she disgusted him with her unbridled display of desire, she wondered. Reaching out to him, she started to ask. But at that moment Deveril turned his back to her and she got a look at the bronze contours. The twin scratches she found there stayed her hand. Her eyes widened as she realized that she had done that to him. Shamed, embarrassed and completely at a loss for words, she lay in silence.

She heard the click of the connecting door shutting between them as Deveril left and the sound of the bolt shooting home on his side. Weary beyond measure, she rose and stared around the room, seeing it clearly for the first time. The bed linen was twisted as though caught in a storm. Her gown lay in a tattered heap at her feet. The pins and jewels from her hair were scattered all over the rug. If Tillie saw the room in this condition she would know what had occurred, Byrony realized slowly.

Somehow she managed to set the room to rights, concealing the evidence. Then she went to the closet for a robe. The mirror hanging there caught her reflection and she observed the faint bruises on her shoulders. She wished she could forget her wantonness, the way she had responded, no, in the end invited Deveril's possession.

Tillie's knock at the outer door roused her from the study of her reflection. Pulling a wrapper at random from the closet, she bid her enter.

Tillie was smiling as she carried the tea tray into the room. "Good morning."

Byrony wanted to sink through the floor at the knowing look on the maid's face. Obviously Tillie had come in at the regular time and found Deveril in her bed.

"Shall I run your bath while you have your tea?" she asked, setting the tray on the table beside the chaise.

"Please and then I would like you to leave me. I will dress

myself this morning."

Tillie was certain to see the marks on her body if she stayed, and to find the torn bedding and gown.

"As you wish," Tillie agreed with a grin. Silently moving about the room, she prepared the toilet. "Which dress shall I lay out for you, your grace?"

Byrony thought a moment. "My habit. I am engaged to John Tarrington for this morning. I also shall need you to see that a note reaches him as to the time. I shall write it presently."

Tillie's cheerful mood dimmed at that bit of news. "And his grace . . ." She stopped and bobbed an awkward curtsy, awkward from the embarrassment of her blunder. "I meant no disrespect," she apologized quickly.

Byrony waved her words away. "You may bring the paper now if you like."

Eager to pass the moment, Tillie brought the writing supplies and stood patiently by while Byrony wrote the short note. Message in hand, she left Byrony to her privacy.

Byrony breathed a sigh of relief when the door closed behind Tillie. Maybe she should not have sent for John but the idea of staying in the house where, at any moment, she might run into Deveril was insupportable. Later in the day when she had a chance to relax and hopefully forget what had happened would be far better. Maybe by then she would have a plan of action on how she should behave in this strange marriage.

John was punctual, a characteristic Byrony blessed as she walked down the stairs to meet him. Thus far she had not seen Deveril since he had left her room.

"How beautiful you look this morning," John complimented her when she reached him.

His eyes glowed with admiration at the picture she made in the deep blue velvet habit. The simple cut Byrony favored fit every curve and presented her sleek figure to its best advantage. Only a woman with Byrony's innate grace and willow slimness could wear such a plain garment without losing a bit of her femininity. The hat perched atop the smooth plait of ebony hair sported one feather that touched saucily against her cheek and tickled the corner of her lips.

Byrony managed a smile. "I hope the horses are ready for I own I am, though I wish it was not the Row that was our destination."

John escorted her out the door. "The Season will be over soon enough. Then you may retire to the country and ride any way that pleases you."

John tossed her up on the mare. "Now, no more blue moods. Today is a beautiful day and deserves to be enjoyed." Vaulting into his saddle, he flicked the reins and started his gelding down the lane.

Byrony followed, determined to follow his sane if dull advice. The need for a wild gallop was stuffed into the dark corners of her mind beside the wild night she had shared with Deveril. Just for one insane moment she wished it was Deveril whom she followed instead of John. He would know where to go. He would race the wind with her and laugh as he did it.

The next hour passed slowly for Byrony. She suffered John's careful probing about Deveril's mood with as much good grace as she could muster. She greeted friends, Bella included, and pretended to enjoy herself in a crowd. And when she returned to the house, she had one dull head and need of her bed. The idea of going out to the party that she was engaged for that night was almost more than she could contemplate. But to cry off was to invite gossip. She and Deveril between them had given the Tabbies quite enough to mull over and titter about.

"Is your head better?" Tillie asked, coming in to light the candles.

Byrony rose from her bed and stretched. "A little," she replied honestly.

Tillie hesitated, then plunged in. "Perhaps an early night would set you to rights."

Byrony noted the careful way she put her suggestion. "I daresay but I cannot. It can be no secret to you why."

Tillie's glance swung to the connecting door then back but she said nothing. "Shall I bring a tray up to you or would you prefer going downstairs to dine?"

Byrony, too, glanced at the closed door. She did not want to ask but she had to. "Is his grace dining in this evening?"

"I believe so."

Byrony sighed. If he would be at the table, she had best be there as well. "Do I own a simple gown? Something that will not require me to have my hair up? I do not think I could stand the pins or the weight."

Tillie went to the closet and withdrew a clear rose muslin with a low-cut bodice edged with a deep ruffle. Small roses were sprinkled along a wide flounce at the hem but beyond that the dress was plain. Holding it up, she spread the skirt for Byrony's inspection.

"Will this do?"

"Perfectly. Let's leave my hair completely down."

Deveril stared into his glass of brandy wondering what to say to her. That he could not spend another day avoiding his own wife was clear. At the very least she deserved an apology for his unbridled behavior. The fact that Byrony had chosen to escape his house at the earliest possible moment after he had left her showed how deeply he had wounded her with his treatment. But would she believe him when he told her that he had not meant to hurt her. That he had been driven by a need to possess her unlike any that he had ever known. How could she when he did not understand the forces governing his actions himself. No woman had ever driven him to such savagery before.

"Your grace?"

Deveril looked up to find Smithington standing in the doorway. "What is it?"

"Her grace awaits you in the dining room."

Deveril stared at the man. He would not have been surprised to learn that Byrony had returned to her uncle's house. But this—this astonished him.

Dinner was a subdued affair. Somehow they managed to speak civilly—if somewhat stiffly—to each other.

Finally, Deveril could stand it no more.

"I want to apologize for my behavior last night," he announced abruptly.

Byrony blinked. It was her turn to be astonished.

"I have never used a woman the way I used you last night," Deveril continued. "There can be no excuse for what I did. I give you my word as a peer and a gentleman that you have nothing more to fear from me in that regard. I shall not trouble you further with my attentions."

"I don't know what to say," Byrony replied. How could she tell him that she wanted his attentions—enjoyed them perhaps more than she should.

"We have struck a bargain, you and I," Deveril said, choosing his words carefully. "I wish to strike another one. Be my wife in public, run my home, and stand at my side. In return I give you my name and my protection such as it is." His lips twisted cynically. "And I promise that there will be no more bruises in this marriage."

Deveril watched her mulling his offer over, wondering if she would trust his word.

"If that is what you wish," Byrony murmured faintly. Her heart was heavy. So Deveril wished for a marriage in name only. No doubt he missed the embraces of his mistresses. So be it, then. "Do we go together to the Edgemonts tonight? I am promised there and it is too late to send my regrets."

Despite his good intentions, Deveril was annoyed that Byrony had accepted his apology and bargain with such seeming equanimity. However, he swallowed his annoyance, reflecting that he deserved no better.

"Certainly," he replied curtly.

When dinner was at an end, Deveril offered Byrony his arm. Byrony took it, trying not to lean on its strength on the way up the stairs. For the first time in her life she prayed Tillie knew some home remedy to kill the ache in her head.

Despite her migraine, Byrony was ready within an hour. Deveril was waiting for her in the blue salon, looking extraordinarily handsome in claret and dove gray. Light shone on his raven hair as he held her cloak out. Byrony stepped close, wishing that she dare ask to remain at home, wishing that matters stood better between them, that he was her husband in more than name. The need to have someone to care for her, if just for a moment, was almost overwhelming. But she must continue to be strong.

Deveril handed her into the coach. The drive to the Edgemonts was accomplished in silence. Yet it was not a completely uncomfortable one. Deveril was unusually solicitous about her comfort. The band of pain around her head loosened somewhat, bringing a measure of relief. By the time they were announced she felt more her usual self. Deveril was at her side as they greeted their hosts. She was conscious of the stares of the other guests, for this was the first time that she and Deveril had appeared in public together. Byrony sensed their avid anticipation of some kind of a scene, and she tensed, wondering if her head or her temper could stand the strain. Feeling rather than seeing Deveril's quick look, she kept her smile in place with effort.

"Nerves?" Deveril said as they strolled into the ballroom. "I had thought you were used to all this by now."

"I did not know it would be this bad," she murmured. "The way everyone is staring at us I begin to think I arrived in my petticoats."

Deveril smiled appreciatively. Involuntarily, he glanced over her figure. Byrony had chosen a deep blue velvet gown that set off her hair and skin to perfection. The daring creation was simple to the point of plainness until the wearer danced or walked. Cunningly concealed in a wide panel of the skirt was an intricate design worked in diamonds and silver threads. The entire effect was as startling as it was beautiful. Around her throat lay the magnificent St. John diamonds. Byrony was a regal and exquisite duchess and to her husband infinitely beautiful.

"Believe me, you are not in your petticoats," he drawled before swinging her into his arms for the first waltz. "Now let us enjoy ourselves and pretend our audience is in Jericho."

Byrony laughed and at the sound of it Deveril impulsively pulled her close, wanting to feel her body move against his once more. Byrony leaned into him, content to be held in his arms, to float across the floor under his guidance, the music flowing around them. All too soon it was over, the enchantment ended as swiftly as it had come.

Deveril released Byrony, stopping just short of shaking his head to clear it. She was as potent as fine wine and just as intoxicating. He would have to be careful or he would lose what little control he possessed where she was concerned. Abruptly he bowed and strode away, leaving Byrony to stare after him in dismay.

"May I bring you some punch?"

Byrony turned to smile at a nice man whose name she could not remember. "Yes, thank you." The faint red that crept under his skin told her she had made another conquest. She watched him thread his way through the crowd with detached interest. She missed John's approach with Bella on his arm.

"I must say you two were the surprise of the evening," Bella said gaily.

Byrony swung around, this time with a real smile curving her lips. "Bella. I saw you across the room earlier but you were surrounded by your admirers."

Lady Arabella laughed cheerfully. "And I fear I have lost one more to you," she returned, inclining her head in the direction of Byrony's partner. "But where is Deveril? I saw him with you a few moments ago."

Byrony waved a hand toward the doors leading to the room where the gentlemen played cards. "He has deserted me again," she admitted. Though the words were teasing, her meaning was not. John gave her a sharp look, making her regret her outspokenness. Bella missed the subtle nuance completely.

"Men!" She patted Byrony's arm in consolation. "Shall I find you another partner? I know Cornelius can be so prosy."

Her description was given in the kindest way but Byrony could not help but agree to the assessment. She might not remember the man's name but she could not forget his ability to ramble on endlessly.

"I don't suppose you could manage to think of a reason for me to leave early. I have the most dreadful head," she confessed, opting for the truth.

Immediately, Bella was all concern. "Why did you not say so? Did you not tell Deveril? Surely he did not insist you remain?"

"Did he refuse to take you home?" John asked, his voice edging toward anger.

"No, of course not. I did not tell him."

Byrony's head pounded fiercely with each sharp word. Having her friends badgering her was more than she could bear. Glancing around for a rescue, she was surprised to see Deveril winding his way through the crowd, clearly on his way back to her side.

"Deveril!" Bella exclaimed. "We were just talking about you. Byrony's not feeling quite the thing."

One black brow rose in Byrony's direction. "Indeed?"

"Yes," she murmured, "I do have a devilish headache. I fear it's a touch of the migraine. I'm sorry to be such a ninny—"

"You're only a ninny for not having said something in the first place. We'll go home directly."

Byrony hardly had time to make her good-byes. The astonishment on Bella's and John's faces would have been amusing if she had felt well enough to appreciate it.

In the carriage, Deveril wasted no time on proprieties. Slipping his arms behind her, he lifted her into his lap and tucked her head on his shoulder. "Sometimes your courage is more folly than bravery," he said gruffly.

Byrony heard the words through a haze of pain. At another time she would have hotly disputed his assessment but for now she was content to be held and cosseted. The memory of another time when his touch and voice had been gentle, even though his words had not, flickered in her mind. A dark night. A ride where every movement brought a surge of pain through her body. His hands had held her steady then. His body had cushioned her from the worst of the jolts. His heat had warmed her. She had felt safe, secure, and very dear.

Byrony closed her eyes and tried not to think beyond the moment.

Chapter Sixteen

Deveril shielded her body as best he could. Every movement of the swaying carriage brought new torture to his own. The feel of her pressed against him brought memories he had to forget for the sake of his own sanity. The warmth of her soft breath against his neck made him ache to taste her lips once more. That she needed him and had let him hold her filled him with the desire to protect and care for her.

When the coach finally pulled to a stop in front of his townhouse, he eased her from his lap. "Stay still. I shall carry you. You are too weak to walk," he ordered.

"No I—"

He stopped her protest with a finger pressed to her lips. "And just now you are not strong enough to fight me. Wait until you are better." He lingered only long enough to be sure she would not move while he got out.

Byrony peered through her half-closed lashes, dazed by the pain yet aware of the voices outside, the orders being given in a sharp tone. Now that his arms had left her, she felt the coolness of the night air against her skin. She shivered, wishing for his warmth to embrace her once more. Then his arms were enfolding her once more, lifting her from the cushions as though she weighed little more than a child. The light from the lamps beside the door hurt her eyes and she turned her head snugly into his chest. His scent immediately surrounded her, bringing a strange kind of peace as they made their way through the house.

When he laid her down, she protested instinctively, fearing he would leave her.

"Rest easy. I will have Tillie fetch you some laudanum for your head."

"No thank you," Byrony managed.

"Then keep your eyes shut. The light only makes the pain worse," Deveril commanded gently, easing her gown from her shoulders.

The sight of her body as he lifted it from the velvet wrappings stirred his desire. The creamy fullness of her bare breasts made his hands ache to touch them. He tried to ignore the heat pooling in his blood. She was almost unconscious with pain and he was eyeing her like a starving dog stalking a tender morsel. Moving swiftly but still carefully, he stripped the rest of her garments and slipped her beneath the sheets.

"Sleep," he commanded, bending over her. "Your head will be better in the morning."

Deveril stroked the hair back from her forehead, hating the lines of tension that marred her brow. They lightened beneath his fingers, filling him with satisfaction that he could give her ease. Sitting down, he continued to brush his fingertips gently over her, waiting for her to sleep. Her breathing slowed and deepened and still he remained, keeping watch in case she woke.

Dawn arrived in a soft blaze of colors yet Byrony did not stir. Rising, Deveril stretched then went to the window to close the heavy drapes to block the light. A faint knock at the door startled him. Glancing at Byrony, he was relieved to see she slept on unaware of the summons.

Tillie waited outside, her broad face anxious. "How is her grace, your grace?" she asked softly.

"Still sleeping." Drawing his fingers through his disheveled hair, he tried to think. "I will leave you to watch over her this morning. I have an appointment I cannot break. Do not allow anyone to disturb her while I am gone. If you can, keep her in bed until I return."

Tillie nodded. "She will not set one foot outside this door," she promised. "I shall see to it."

Deveril had to smile at her confidence. If he knew his Byrony, she would do exactly as she pleased when she pleased and no one would say her nay. Not if they were wise.

"Just do your best," he murmured before turning back to check on Byrony one more time before he retired to his own chamber and a much-needed bath.

The interview with Olivia had been put off once. It was not one that he relished but he really had no choice. If he meant to share a life with Byrony, he knew without her telling him that she would not countenance a blatant relationship with any other woman. If he intended to take a lover, he would have to be far more discreet than he had been in the past. Yet, at the moment, the idea of having another woman in his bed or on his arm was curiously displeasing. He knew eventually he would succumb to some pretty face, for since his promise to leave Byrony alone he must have someone. But not now. And certainly not Olivia.

"You can not mean this, Dev," Olivia said in horror when Deveril told her of his decision a few hours later. Even the exquisite diamond necklace and earrings that lay in a bed of pink velvet on the table next to her did nothing to soften the blow he dealt her. "After all we have meant to each other over these last two years."

Deveril stared at her lovely, hurt face, feeling nothing but pity for her. "It was never meant to be permanent. You knew that," he pointed out candidly. "I never made you any promises." He rose and went to her side. "Come, let us have done with these delusions. We enjoyed each other and that is as it should be. Now it is over." For the first time in a long while it mattered what another felt. Not because he had any special feeling for this woman but because he had begun to care what he did to others.

Olivia peered up at him for a moment, a puzzled expression in her blue eyes. "I do believe you mean that." Shaking her head, she tried to reconcile the man who stood before her with the one who flaunted almost every one of Society's conventions. "Are you feeling well?"

Deveril's brows lifted and he nearly smiled. "Perfectly. I just find it difficult to wish you misery because of me," he murmured, staring down at her. "Is that so impossible to swallow?"

"From you it is," Olivia returned, still suspicious. "You have changed and I'm not sure I don't prefer the old you."

That did bring a smile but there was little humor in it. "I think it is time I took my leave."

Olivia rose, bringing her body against his with an ease born of long familiarity. "You will regret leaving me, you know. In all your wanderings you still came back to me. Next time, perhaps, I shall not be waiting." She would not lose him so easily. That country upstart, that half-French flirt, would regret this piece of work.

Deveril caught her arms, holding her away from him. "I shall not return," he said firmly.

"It's that child," Olivia burst out, unable to control herself. "I knew she was trouble the moment I clapped my eyes on her. But she will not make you happy. She will not give you your freedom to seek your pleasure as I have done." The last was added in a tone that just barely escaped being a screech.

Deveril was no stranger to women and their tantrums. Ignoring the delivery and concentrating on the words, he shook Olivia once, hard. "That woman is my wife and my duchess. You will not speak of her so."

Olivia glared at him, furious that he would defend Byrony. Jealousy rose in a wave to swamp her good sense and manners. "You defend marriage! Ha! The only reason you married the chit was to provide the gossips with a sop!"

"By god, you go too far," Deveril said in a dangerously soft voice. "I have tried to be fair to you. I came here to make an end that would leave you some pride. But you would have none of that. Now mark me well. Our liaison is at an end. Whatever indiscreet remarks that you are foolish enough to make about my duchess, I shall hear. My displeasure is not something to be taken lightly, as you should know."

Olivia felt a fissure of fear touch her.

"Forgive me," she pleaded, coming toward him with tears in her eyes.

"You cry beautifully but it is a talent wasted on me. I know you too well."

Olivia began to cry in earnest. Deveril would not come to her again. She was a woman who had not only enjoyed his lovemaking but the prestige of catching and holding the attention of one of the most elusive bachelors in all of England. The thought of what the gossips would have to say about her made her ill. They would laugh at her behind her back. And who would have her now? She'd had no time to look about her for a replacement for Deveril. She had truly thought he would stay with her despite his marriage.

"Good-bye, Olivia." Deveril headed for the door.

Once outside, he sent the coachman away, preferring to walk back home. Olivia's reaction had been a surprise. He had not thought she was so foolish as to believe that he would marry her. Woman were such strange creatures, he mused. All except Byrony. She was a woman of honor, too much so sometimes for his peace of mind. She never would have behaved as Olivia had done. Angry she might have been but he could not see her resorting to tears to sway a man's mind. She was more likely to threaten to run him through for playing her false.

He frowned as he reflected how little he cared for the man he had become in the last few years. At first it had been anger and hurt that had made him wish to show his peers in all their follies. As a youth who was more boy than man perhaps that had been understandable and even forgivable. Kate had certainly thought so although his father had not. Yet time had not lessened his need to puncture the hypocrisy that was rife in his world, if only to provide himself with amusement. In that he was no better than his mother. And until Charles had thrust Byrony into his life, he had been too blind to see what he had become.

Now his eyes were open and he was realizing that he cared about not only what Byrony thought of him but what Charles thought as well.

When he entered his house, his first thought was for Byrony. Was she up? Smithington thought not. Worried, Deveril mounted the stairs, pausing only long enough to knock once, lightly, at her door. Tillie opened it a crack until she saw who it was.

"She is still asleep, your grace."

"Summon me when she awakes," he commanded. "I shall be in the study."

Feeling at loose ends, Deveril went back downstairs and asked his secretary to join him. Since he had been away from London for months, there was much that required his attention. The morning passed into noon without any word from upstairs. Deveril found himself listening for a knock at the closed study door. It finally came shortly after lunch.

But it was only Smithington, announcing the arrival of Lord Ravensly. Deveril dismissed his secretary while rising to greet his godfather.

"What brings you to see me?" Deveril asked, smiling a little.

Charles paused then came toward him, hand outstretched. "Deveril, you are in good form this day," he greeted him with a clap on his shoulder as he clasped Deveril's hand in his.

"As are you," Deveril returned, gesturing him to take a seat. "Do you come to see Byrony?"

Charles' silver brows rose at the ease with which Deveril referred to his niece. "Is she about?" he asked.

Deveril frowned, looking more the duke of old for a moment. "She is abed as yet. She had a migraine last night. I had to bring her home from the Edgemonts."

It was Charles' turn to frown. "She told me about those headaches of hers. But I thought they had ceased when she had reached maturity."

"Do you know what causes them?"

Charles thought for an instant. "She was never sure but I think it is worry or unhappiness."

Both of which Byrony had had in full measure for many months, Deveril knew. Steepling his fingers, he leaned back in his chair. "How has she really done in London?" he asked after a moment.

Charles, too, leaned back although every sense was alert to Deveril and the questions he could see in his eyes. "The papers do not lie. Byrony was a hit and I can tell you that neither Olivia nor Corinne liked it one little bit though for different reasons. They have tried to scratch her at every opportunity but Byrony has ignored most of it. At first I was not even certain she knew what they were up to."

"How did you find out?"

"John told me that Byrony had asked him to explain Olivia's place in your life."

"The devil!"

Charles smiled at the outrage in his voice. "You must know what she's like," he murmured, enjoying his godson's shock. Seldom had he seen him so open, his expression so easy to read.

"I have never known such a woman in all my born days. Is nothing sacred to her?"

"Better you should ask is nothing sacred to you or to me? If we wish to know something do we not ask, each in our own way? Kate was one such as Byrony. She, too, asked the questions the devil himself would blush to hear." He smiled, remembering his wife and her penchant for carrying him into mischief at every turn. When she died, the light and the excitement had gone out of his life until Byrony had joined him.

"What a creature you saddled me with," Deveril said.

Charles noticed the almost affectionate tone with a lift of his brow. "You know I had decided to repair to Ravenscourt but I think I shall stay in Town awhile longer. Things grow interesting of late."

Deveril looked ruefully at him, seeing the laughter in the wise eyes that had seen too much of human folly.

Knowing when it was best to retreat, Charles rose. "Please tell Byrony that I stopped. And convey my wishes for her speedy recovery."

"And mine," Deveril murmured wickedly.

Charles inclined his head. "And yours," he agreed blandly. "I hear that you saw Olivia this morning. I take it that liaison is at an end."

"News travels fast in this town," Deveril remarked.

"I shall await the next installment with bated breath."

"Let us hope it does not disappoint you." He opened the door for Charles.

Deveril, once set on a course, was not easily detoured. Having decided that he would cease to kick at the traces like a green colt, he set about becoming a staid member of Society. Once Byrony was recovered from her infirmity, he escorted her to any number of entertainments, never leaving her side until he was certain her dance card was full and her enjoyment ensured. Even then he did not desert her, coming in from the various card rooms where he usually took refuge to dance a waltz or two with his duchess.

The Ton was agog at his unprecedented behavior. Byrony was at first puzzled then just plain unhappy. The excitement of pitting her will against Deveril's was gone. Nothing she wanted was denied her. When she expressed a wish for a phaeton and two costly prime bits of blood to draw it, Deveril got the carriage and horses for her. When she decided she wanted to learn to drive the phaeton herself, he taught her and without once raising his voice. A tiger dressed in scarlet-and-gold silk to ride with her on her tours of the Park? And it too was done. No discussions, no objections, not even a raised eyebrow marred her home life. She rode or drove in the Park, passed the evenings entertained by London's finest, and shopped until she began to hate the sight of new gowns. In short her life became a reflection of all that Deveril had fought against so long and all that she found more boring and useless by the second. The unceasing need to be seen and to enjoy one's self without thought for the morrow held no appeal.

"Damnation!" Byrony swore, snatching off her riding habit and flinging it into the corner.

Byrony dismissed Tillie, her temper too uncertain to tolerate any of the maid's fussing. She had just returned from a ride with John in the Park and even he was against going to the masquerade at Vauxhall, arguing that it was a romp unsuited for her station. John was fast becoming as staid as Deveril of late. Neither of them could seem to understand that she was bored beyond recall. If she did not do something soon to put a little life into her humdrum existence, she would go mad. She was not used to this idle schedule. Her gender denied her the freedom of concerning herself with business as Deveril did. She had no club where she could meet and go a few rounds with a boxing champ or have a match with a noted swordsman. All she had was this interminable visiting and dressing to be seen.

"I'm sick to my back teeth of it," she muttered, pacing the chamber.

It made no difference to her that she was as naked as the day she was born. The restrictions of her skirts were not to be tolerated at that moment. Her strides lengthened as her temper shortened. Never had she felt so ill used or betrayed. The one thing she had come to prize in Deveril was his spirit. She disliked what he had become. She wanted his temper, the excitement he brought to her life. Even when they fought, there had been exhilaration in the meeting. Freedom too.

A knock at the door disturbed her train of thought. Frowning she called out for the person to leave her. "But Lady Arabella has called," Tillie protested through the closed panel.

Byrony started to deny the visit then thought better of it. Maybe Bella would have some ideas. Had she not often spoken of her own need for more freedom? "Tell her I shall be down in a flash," Byrony replied, hurrying to her wardrobe. Pulling a gown at random from the overflowing rack, she dressed then quickly coiled her hair atop her head. Not as neat as Tillie would have it but it would do, she decided with a quick glance in the mirror.

Bella jumped to her feet, laughing gaily when Byrony entered the room a few moments later. "Finally, I have someone to talk to," she teased, giving Byrony both her hands.

Byrony started at the greeting. Bella sounded almost as exasperated as she herself felt. "Something amiss?" she asked, taking a seat.

Bella shook her head. "Nothing new. It's just that time of the Season again. I come to Town every year, ready and eager to renew old friendships and to make new ones. The shopkeepers beguile me and the parties are a welcome change from winter in the country. But after I am here awhile it begins to pall." She shrugged, the laughter dying in her eyes. "Foolish, is it not?"

"No, not to me," Byrony replied. "I, too, have felt as though something is missing."

The two women exchanged glances, both understanding the other a little better.

"Is there nothing we can do?"

"Nothing respectable, I fear. Believe me, I have thought of all the possibilities," Bella murmured dejectedly. "I wish I was one for polite gambling. Some of the ladies of my acquaintance indulge themselves that way in the afternoon. But, alas, I have no skill with the cards."

Byrony brightened at the mention of a familiar pastime. A try at the tables would offer far better sport than an attendance at a questionable Vauxhall masquerade. "Are you saying that if you did have the skill you would consider going?" she asked, hardly daring to hope.

Bella glanced at her curiously. "There would be no harm in it. Many ladies of our station enjoy gaming. There is one house in particular that is rumored to be partially owned by a person of quality, as it happens. It is a favorite of all who wile away the afternoon with the cards."

Byrony knew such things existed, of course, but she had not been sure Bella or others like her would not still hold such pursuits in a bad light. To find out this was not so was an unlooked-for gift. "Then let's go," she said eagerly, getting to her feet.

Bella's eyes rounded. "Do you know how to play?"

Byrony nodded, a smile of anticipation curving her lips. There was money enough in her reticule for a small stake, and in her hurry to see Bella, she had chosen a gown suitable for going out. With only the addition of a shawl, she would be ready for the expedition. More than ready, eager to try her skill once again.

"I do and I shall teach you as well. That is, if you wish to learn?" One brow rose as she ended with the query.

Bella nodded enthusiastically. "I would like it above all things. So many of my friends go there." She frowned, suddenly remembering something. "But usually they lose. I do not think that I would like that."

Byrony urged her to the door. "We shall not lose. I promise."

Chapter Seventeen

"Quickly, close the door," Bella commanded as soon as she and Byrony were in her bedchamber.

Byrony laughed softly while she complied. "I swear you are enjoying this"—she hesitated, searching for the proper word—"conspiracy more than I would have thought possible."

Bella dumped the contents of her reticule on the bed and plopped down beside the pile of money. "This is the most fun I have had in ages. I felt so decadent going to that gaming place with you. And when you won!" She rolled her eyes wickedly. "I could scarce contain myself."

Byrony came across the room to take a seat on the bed with Bella. "For a moment there I thought you would shriek," she admitted with a grin. "It was fun, was it not?"

Bella nodded enthusiastically. "I cannot wait for tomorrow when we shall go again."

Startled, Byrony stared at her. "Tomorrow?"

"Why not?" Bella sifted her hands through the tumble of paper and coin before her. "Look at the money we made today. I had no idea one could do so well at the tables." She frowned suddenly. "I did not know you had such skill. How came you by it?" she asked, her head tilted to one side.

Byrony had been expecting this question since they had

left the discreet house that catered to the higher-ranking members of the Ton and their vices. It had not escaped her notice that Bella had been as curious about the games of chance as she was about the players. Her friend had watched her like a hungry cat at a mouse hole, delighting in every round she had won. And Byrony had won. The weight of Bella's purse and her own was ample proof of her luck and skill.

"From here and there," Byrony replied vaguely. "I am just sorry you did not try your luck longer. I am sure that you would get the knack of it in no time."

Bella laughed. "Never in a hundred years. I like our plan much better. I put up half . . ." She paused, groping for the cant term that she and Byrony had laughed over. ". . . the stake," she produced finally, triumphantly. "And you do the work. I get to watch and rake in the profits. An excellent plan all around. So when will we meet tomorrow and where? I cannot wait to try again."

"Do you think that is wise? After all, it was your idea to keep our going a secret."

"Do you not think it amusing and exciting to outwit Deveril and John?"

"I don't see the necessity. That house was perfectly respectable. Half the ladies we know were there today. Even if we are careful, there is no way someone will not tell Deveril or John. Or Charles," she added after a second.

"But that is half the fun," Bella objected. "It's harmless, after all. Deveril certainly won't cavil at your going. John is sure to read us both a scold for he does not hold with gambling at all." She scowled suddenly. "I cannot think why, for he was a great gun before he went off to America."

"He still is. I think you judge him too harshly," Byrony commented, coming to the defense of her friend.

"Maybe with you but certainly not with me," Bella returned darkly. "Do you know he had the nerve to tell me that hat I bought last week made me look like a member of the muslin company. I was never so mortified in my life, I can tell you."

Since the confection in question did indeed lend Bella a racy air, Byrony could not defend the milliner's creation. "I hope he apologized for his words in the end," she murmured, eyeing Bella's face. The strange expression she saw there once again made her wonder if Bella might not be interested in John. The thought slipped into her mind and would not be dislodged.

"He did not," she muttered indignantly. Her eyes flashed with temper. "I wore the thing the next day when we walked with him in the Park. Do you remember?"

Byrony did, well. The scowl on John's face had been a sharp contrast to the mischief on Bella's. "Is this why you are so set on pursuing the gaming tables?"

Bella didn't answer for a moment. A sheepish smile flitted across her mobile mouth. "I own that is part of the reason. There is nothing that sets up my back more than for someone to tell me that I ought not to do something. Especially when that someone has done far worse in his past. Besides, I am bored. Just as you are. Why should we not enjoy ourselves?"

There was no arguing with her logic. Bella had the right of it. "I still think I should tell Deveril," she said at length. The idea of keeping her activity a secret seemed both foolish and unnecessary in her circumstances. And she could not think that Deveril would object too strongly to her pastime if she were careful.

"Fiddle!" Bella flounced off the bed. "I thought you braver than this. I am disappointed."

"It is not a question of courage," Byrony shot back. No one had ever questioned her nerve. She found that she did not like it that Bella had. "We'll keep the secret for as long as possible. The best we will get is a few days, anyway."

Bella was all smiles now that she had won her way. "You will enjoy it. You will see." She returned to the bed. "Now let us count our profits and divvy up the shares."

Byrony could not suppress a chuckle at her friend's eager eyeing of the pile of money. "It is a good thing you realize you are no gambler, I think. You would make a first class pigeon for plucking otherwise." The moment the words left her mouth Byrony knew she had made a mistake. The cant terms had slipped too easily off her tongue.

"Then it is a good thing I have you to win for us," she mumbled, between counts.

Breathing a silent sigh of relief, Byrony promised herself to be more careful in the future. While the pleasure she had derived from the afternoon's outing had been more than she had had in a long time, it was not worth revealing her checkered past. Suddenly she wondered whether Deveril or Charles would be quite so complacent about her activities as she first supposed.

With that in mind Byrony found that the second expedition to the gaming house the next day was both more exciting than the one before and more worrying. Watching her tongue around Bella was almost amusing, winning at the various games even more so. But every time someone greeted her, every familiar face brought home the risk she was taking. For the first time in her life, she feared the outcome. It would not just be she who lost if her past came to light, but Charles and Deveril as well. The thought was a sobering one. Especially when she and Bella chanced to see the one woman that neither had even a pretense of a fondness for.

"What is she doing here," Bella hissed, directing Byrony's attention to the stairs leading to the private rooms on the second floor.

Byrony glanced around to see Corinne on the landing, staring down at her. "Perhaps the same thing that we are," Byrony replied slowly, watching her mother-in-law. It didn't surprise her that Corinne would frequent an establishment of this nature.

The expression on Corinne's face was not difficult to read. The woman was clearly displeased to find them there. But what had put the brief glimpse of fear that Byrony had seen in her expression? Corinne was not a person to give way to that particular emotion without good cause. Whatever it was, it was none of her affair Byrony decided, turning her attention back to Bella.

Pulling her shawl closer about her shoulders, Bella glanced at the door. "Let us leave."

Byrony nodded, following her out. "Are you pleased with this day's take?" she asked as they entered the carriage.

"Indeed. You are truly a marvel," Bella said with a grin. She folded her hands in her lap and tried to look as if butter would not melt in her mouth. "I wish you would tell me how you do it."

"A little luck and a bit of skill," she murmured.

Bella gave her a curious look before changing the subject. "What's on the second floor?"

Startled at the seemingly irrelevant question, Byrony hesitated before answering. "You mean of the gaming house?" At Bella's nod she added. "Private rooms, usually where the stakes are much higher than those at the tables."

Bella's eyes widened at the information. "Then it is true, what I have heard."

"What are you talking about?"

"Corinne," Bella said impatiently. "I have heard rumors that she has a foot in Dun territory but I had not thought it possible. Perhaps it is if she is gambling upstairs and it is as you say."

"Are you sure about this rumor?" Byrony asked, wondering if Deveril knew.

"As sure as I can be without checking with the source." Bella studied her for a moment. "Would you like me to find out for certain?"

Byrony did not answer immediately. As soon as she had spoken, she wished the question unasked. What had prompted her to ask such a thing of Bella? Instinct. That sense of something not being right, that sense that had kept her safe in the past and which had lain dormant since coming to London had returned full force. It would not be denied.

"Yes, I believe I would," she decided at last.

Bella, friend that she was, did not demand an explanation for her curiosity. "I may be able to find out tonight. The person who told me should be at the ball."

Byrony leaned back against the cushions with a sigh. Suddenly she wished she had not heard of the gaming house or of cards, gambling, and Corinne. There was so much she still did not know about the society in which she moved. Perhaps her instincts were playing her false. But she had not imagined that expression on Corinne's face. And if what Bella said was true, then the St. John name could be in danger. And she knew how Deveril valued that. Had he not married her in an attempt to retrieve his creditability? What would he do if he found out about his mother's deep playing? She could not even begin to guess. For that matter, she could not imagine how he had not heard of it before now. If Bella knew surely he would too.

Knowing she could not solve the puzzle without more information, Byrony chose to change the subject. "What about tomorrow? Do you still wish to go back?"

Bella was more than happy to leave the subject of Corinne. She had never liked the woman. As far as she was concerned the crown could lock her up in debtor's prison and throw away the key with her blessings.

"I don't know." Bella lifted the full reticule, jingling with coins. "I was having such fun. There is something exciting about winning money this way. I hate to give it up. Don't you?"

Byrony hesitated. She could not deny that for the most part she had enjoyed her contact with the past she had left behind. The challenge of beating the odds, even the silly, secretive way Bella insisted on their visits being had given her relief from the increasing boredom. But her winning had attracted a great deal of notice and probably curiosity as well. Deveril would not be pleased and neither would Charles.

"Let's give tomorrow a miss. It will allow us time to decide if we wish to continue," she suggested slowly.

"A good plan," Bella declared. The carriage pulled to a stop in front of Bella's house. "Will you come up?"

"Not today. It is later than we usually get back and we both need to prepare for the ball tonight, don't forget."

Bella clapped a hand over her mouth. "I had forgotten. Fiddle!" She hopped out of the carriage. "I shall see you there." With a wave, she skipped up the stairs and into the house.

In a short time Byrony, too, entered her house. Finding Deveril in the hall was a surprise she could well have done without. The state of quiet courtesy between them had continued unabated for too long for her to know how to bring about a change. All she could do was greet him with a pleasant expression and a short question on the passing of his day. His answer should have been equally unsatisfying. It was not.

"You are home late. Had you forgotten we have an engagement tonight?"

Byrony stopped, one foot poised over the first rung of the stairs. She glanced over her shoulder to see him watching her intently. "I am sorry," she responded carefully. "Did you require my presence?"

Deveril frowned.

"No. I wondered where you were."

It had not escaped his notice that Byrony had changed in the last few days. Her step was jauntier, her eyes were bright, and her afternoons were mysteriously full. Why two outings would make such a difference he could not think and that worried him. That streak of independence was still strong, as was the high mettle that he so admired. The combination was a potent one, especially when Byrony was clearly chafing at the bit for more excitement than the Season provided.

Byrony blinked, not expecting the carefully voiced query. "Bella and I spent the afternoon together."

He studied her dispassionately. "Do you intend being home tomorrow? I had thought we would drive out in the country."

Byrony's eyes lit at the offer. It was the first time Deveril had invited her anywhere. All thoughts of Bella and the gaming house flew from her mind.

"For the day?"

"If you like."

Byrony came to him, stopping only a foot away. "Will we be alone together?"

The question raised his eyebrows. He had forgotten how blunt she could be. "Do you wish it to be so?" he asked, oddly afraid to commit himself.

He wanted her to say yes. The need he felt to lessen the distance between them surprised him with its strength. He was tired of fighting his attraction to her. Tired of trying to sleep in a cold bed. Tired of watching other men dance attendance on his wife. Byrony. Her name haunted his dreams and destroyed his peace. He wanted her in his arms. He had to have her. Not out of honor but out of love.

Love! How long had he loved her? He did not know. But here in this semidark hall, the least romantic setting possible, he knew that he did. Byrony was watching him with those great silver eyes filled with wariness and hope. The simplest question had stolen her speech. And he loved her.

"Just the two of us," he replied, his voice huskier than it had been a moment before.

Byrony searched his face. He meant it. Joy filled her at the thought. "When?" It took every ounce of willpower she possessed to remain calm and seemingly unaffected.

"Early."

Deveril clasped his hands behind his back. He had almost pulled her to him. The fragile communication was too new, too precious to risk a mistake like that. But he had almost succumbed to the temptation when he had seen the spark of delight in her eyes before that gambler's control had taken over. She was wary, afraid to believe in him, and he could not blame her. He deserved her suspicion. His treatment to date had been anything but gentle or kind. It would be different in the future.

"But the ball. We shall be late getting back. Will you really wish to leave early?"

Deveril laughed softly. For this he would walk through hell itself but he could not tell her that. She would not believe him. Not yet. "I can manage it. I am not in my dotage yet," he drawled.

Byrony laughed. "No. So I see."

Deveril inhaled sharply. When she laughed like that, he was hard pressed to control himself. He wanted her in his arms. Tomorrow could not come fast enough to suit him. Byrony might not know it but she was soon to be courted as she had never been.

"We had better hurry or we shall be late," Byrony murmured.

"I shall meet you downstairs when you are ready."

Nodding, Byrony went upstairs. With Tillie's help she bathed and dressed in something of a daze. Never in her life had she felt so at odds with herself. It was as if she had been waiting for this to happen since she had married Deveril. Yet what this was she could not say. All she knew for certain was that she wanted to be with him without feeling as if he were only doing his duty. She wanted to talk to him, really get to know the man he was. So much of his personality was hidden from her. There was so much she did not understand. And she wanted to understand, more with each passing day.

"How is that, your grace?"

Byrony glanced in the mirror to see a stranger staring back

at her. The delicate emerald gown she wore was beautiful but it was the expression in her eyes that held her attention. When had she ever looked so dreamy-eyed, so lost in a world of her own? When had her skin ever bloomed with such color, or her hair shone with such black fire? What was it about Deveril that touched her as she had never been touched before?

"You have done a splendid job," she murmured.

Tillie beamed. "You are easy to work for," she admitted. "I am the envy of all the maids in London," she added with pride. "And his grace is deemed most fortunate in having you for his duchess."

"Prompt I see," Deveril commented as she entered the blue salon. "And beautiful too."

Byrony paused in midstride. Another first. A compliment and one truly meant. "Thank you," she stammered, losing a bit of her poise.

Deveril smiled at the slight stutter. He had never known Byrony to be unsettled by anything.

"Shall we be off?"

He took her arm.

Byrony inhaled carefully, unwilling to betray just how much Deveril's about-face unnerved her. Her body remembered his touch with embarrassing frankness. Already she felt the heat of desire licking at her senses. The thin gown she wore was poor protection against his gaze. She thanked whatever Fates still had an eye on her that the semidarkness of the coach provided her with some cover until she could discover what game Deveril was playing now.

At the ball the music swirled around them as he guided her through the waltz, his mind only on her. She smiled at him and he felt bathed in sunlight. Her breath rushed between parted lips that he longed to taste. He drew her nearer, wishing they were alone so he could tell her how beautiful she was. How much he ached to have her beside him. The open terrace door beckoned. A dark garden. The scent of flowers carried on an evening breeze. Before the thought could take shape, Deveril was urging Byrony closer to the privacy he craved.

A moment later they were alone. He stopped in the kind shadows that shielded them from sight, still holding her in his arms. "Byrony." Only her name had the power to pass his lips.

Byrony stared up at him, reading more in his face than she ever thought to see. "Why now?" she demanded just as he bent his head until his lips hovered above hers.

Deveril was so near he could hear her breath as she gasped a little. But more importantly, what he heard was the doubt in her voice. "Can you not accept that I have changed?"

Byrony searched his face. "Have you? Or will I wake up and find that you have left me again?"

"I will not leave. You must trust me enough to believe that."

"I am afraid." In the darkness it was easier to admit the truth.

"Do you think I am not?" The words slipped out before he could stop them. Seeing her eyes widened in amazement at his admission, he could not regret his confession.

Deveril's lips crushed hers. He was past control, past caring if anyone should chance upon them.

Byrony was swept into passion before she could draw a breath. His tongue was a sword that thrust into her mouth with such hungry insistence that she had no defense, wanted no defense. The taste of him, the feel of his hard body against hers called forth her deepest instincts. She responded with all the feelings roiling within. For a long moment she was held suspended between heaven and hell, held in the Devil's arms.

"Byrony, are you out here?"

Bella's gay call brought them down to earth with a jarring thump. Deveril was the first to react. Lifting his head, he stared down on Byrony's flushed face and cloudy eyes. "I'm sorry," he whispered.

"For the kiss?" Byrony whispered back, pain beginning to unfurl within her.

"No!" His fingers outlined her red lips. "For losing our privacy."

Byrony touched his cheek, stroking the lean contours.

Chapter Eighteen

"Finally!" Bella exclaimed, ferreting Byrony out. Her eyes widened on seeing Deveril at Byrony's side. "I did not realize . . . John did not say that you were out here with anyone . . ." She stumbled to a halt, clearly nonplussed.

"Shall I procure us some refreshment?" Deveril asked, giving Bella a smile that Byrony could only think of as kind.

Bella all but goggled at him. Byrony would have laughed if she had not been prey to a similar feeling. "Please," she murmured.

"Well, I never," Bella muttered, watching the duke walk away. "What is going on?"

Since Byrony had no idea, she wasn't about to try to answer such a question. "I might ask you the same thing," she said instead.

Recalled to the reason she had been so eager to find Byrony, Bella explained in a rush, "I just found out about Corinne. It is worse than I thought. She is definitely under the hatches and has gotten in with the money lenders as well. Can you imagine?"

The last thing on Byrony's mind was her mother-in-law. But she could not deny the startling nature of Bella's information. "Surely not the percent people! No one in their right senses gets involved with those men. I had thought

Corinne would be more up to snuff on that head."

"Well, I think she deserves exactly what she gets," Bella muttered, having been the recipient of more than one of Corinne's barbed comments.

Byrony could not help but agree although she did not say so. "Maybe she has the gambling fever and can't stop. There are many like her."

"You can defend her?" Bella stared at her in surprise.

Byrony shook her head. "No. Though you cannot but understand how she would get hooked. Look at us. We go for amusement."

"But we win."

"Perhaps she did in the beginning. Gaming houses are tricky places," she added, thinking back on the number she had known intimately. The games were not always as much an arena of skill as the innocent would assume.

Deveril could not have chosen a more inopportune moment to return. "What gaming houses?" he asked with a frown.

Byrony turned and accepted the glass of punch he handed her before answering. "None in particular," she said, giving Bella a look. "We were discussing something that Bella overheard."

Deveril stared at her suspiciously. There was something in her voice, a shade of meaning he did not understand. "May I know?"

It was Bella who stepped into the breach this time. "It is not really important. Just some girl talk. You would not find it amusing."

"That's what brought you haring after Byrony?" His brows winged upward in unconcealed skepticism.

"Well no," Bella mumbled, thinking fast. "I came to find out if she and John had plans for tomorrow."

Byrony just managed not to betray her surprise with an unthinking response. Deveril wasn't so quiet. "Just why would you think that she had?"

"They usually ride together on Wednesdays."

"They won't tomorrow." He glanced at Byrony, daring her to disagree.

"No, I won't be," she supplied quietly, shocked at the sudden notion that Deveril was jealous of John. Why it occurred to her now was beyond her. Deveril had certainly given no indication that he found anything amiss in her continued outings with the other man. Or had he, she mused, remembering a day last week when he had invited her to drive in the park and she had declined because John had already been on his way to pick her up for the same purpose.

Bella studied first one then the other. Then slowly she smiled. "I am so happy for you." She took Byrony's hands in hers, pressing them tightly. "You do not know how much this means to me." With a kiss on Byrony's cheek and a flurry of pink taffeta skirts she was gone, leaving Byrony and Deveril staring after her in confusion.

"Do you know what that was about?"

"I haven't a clue," Byrony admitted, thinking hard. Suddenly the light dawned.

Deveril caught the change of expression immediately. "You do know," he accused without heat.

"I think I do," she corrected with a grin. "I think my friend is interested in John. He has come to England to look about for a wife, you know."

"You cannot be serious. They have known each other since they were in prams together." Deveril turned to glance into the ballroom, where the band was striking another number. The sight of John twirling Bella onto the floor silenced him. But not for long. "I don't believe it!"

Byrony laughed, watching the couple. "Do you think your eyes lie?"

"I think Bella is a scheming minx," he stated flatly, with conviction. He glanced at her, searching her expression intently.

Byrony looked back at him, wondering why he watched

her so.

"I thought John was dangling after you," he admitted after a moment.

Byrony gaped at him. "Me? Good God, what ever gave you such an idea. I am a married woman."

"That is not always an obstacle."

"To me it is. I do not break my word."

"Is that the only reason?"

"Is it not enough?" she shot back.

Deveril shook his head, damning himself for a fool. Turning, he set his glass aside and took hers to place it alongside. "The music beckons. Shall we?" He held out his arms.

Byrony did not hesitate. She wanted to be held by him. The kiss he had given her still lingered in the gentle throbbing of her lips and the taste of him on her tongue. When he pulled her close, his heat and his strength surrounded her, blotting out the ballroom into which he guided her. They could have been alone for all the attention either of them paid to the assemblage.

Many eyes followed their progress, most with curiosity, a few with envy. But two pairs marked the smiles on their faces with hatred. One pair, the lover scorned. The other, the dark force that had bred the Devil.

"It would seem you now possess a cold bed," Corinne remarked, without taking her eyes from the circling pair.

Olivia drew in her breath in a hiss of rage. Her eyes flashed. "At least I can afford to pay for mine," she shot back.

Corinne gave her a glare that would have cut glass. "I shall come about."

Olivia laughed mercilessly. "When? Before or after they haul you away. I was there today, remember? All of what you lost was my money, if you will recall."

"You shall be repaid."

"I doubt it."

Corinne drew herself up and stared at the younger woman. "Be careful how you speak."

Olivia waved her hand around the tiny alcove in which they stood. "I am safe enough. No one can hear us unless I scream." She nodded toward Byrony and Deveril as they passed close by. "It is too bad you did not have the duchess' luck. I hear she is quite a card sharp. She has yet to lose."

Corinne turned her head to trace her rival's progress. Byrony had beat her on every suit and the stupid chit did not even realize it. Byrony had the position and the wealth she had lost when her husband died. She was also the darling of Society. Byrony even, it seemed, had Deveril's good opinion. Not that she cared for that except that Deveril's open disdain of her had cost her much in prestige and in friends among the Ton. That she hated. And now the chit had the gall to play in her favorite house and win every time. Byrony did not need the money. It was only an amusement for her.

Corinne gritted her teeth, wishing she did indeed have half the skill that was Byrony's. Suddenly, she was struck by the oddity of such a run of luck. She knew well that those games downstairs could be fixed when anyone began to win too much from the house. Was that not the reason she had decided the higher-stake games upstairs held more of a chance for her to get even?

So how had Byrony beat the house? Surely luck could not have played a part in that. "You know most of the gossip in this town. What do you know about the Devil's Duchess?" Corinne demanded on impulse.

Olivia hesitated, clearly searching her memory. "Not much. Her mother died a little over a year ago. She was still in the last stages of mourning when she came to town. She came from the continent by way of Dover, I think. She stayed at Ravenscourt until she married Deveril."

"What about her father? Who was he?"

"A younger son of an old French family. Nothing unusual,

as far as I know." Olivia frowned. "Why? Do you know something that I do not?"

Corinne shook her head. "No, but I may shortly."

Olivia perked up at the tone. She knew it well. Whatever Corinne was playing, it was definitely meant to be to her benefit. And anything that profited Corinne would benefit her as well.

"Tell me," she pleaded eagerly.

Corinne glanced at her without really seeing her. Her agile mind was already deciding where to start her search. Bribery was always an efficient tool. "You will know soon enough, believe me."

Across the room, Deveril and Byrony had just finished their dance. As one they returned to the privacy of the terrace. Neither spoke as darkness closed in around them. Deveril took her hand in his.

"Are you tired?"

Byrony started to reply truthfully then thought better of it. Suddenly she knew she wanted to be with Deveril tonight. Whatever the reasons, whatever the problems that lay between them, she did not wish to sleep alone and awake in a cold bed yet again.

"Yes," she whispered.

Deveril lifted her hand to his lips. "Then let us go home."

Home! The word seemed foreign on his tongue. She could not remember the last time, if ever, she had had a home. She had lived many places but never had one been truly a home. Although she had wished for one when she was a child, as she had grown older she had ceased to dream. Yet this one statement, which probably meant little to the man who made it, had the power to shake the very foundations of her beliefs. Suddenly she wanted what she had never known.

"Yes, let us go home," she murmured softly.

His eyes gleamed darkly in the faint light from the candles in the ballroom. For a moment Byrony was sure he would take her in his arms but instead he used the hand he still held to pull her through the doors into the light. Tucking her fingers into the crook of his arm, he guided her through the throng to the front entrance. No one stopped them yet it seemed to Byrony that a way was cleared for their passage.

The carriage appeared in moments after they reached the front steps. The ride to their townhouse was accomplished in silence such as Byrony had yet to know. There was a sense of expectation in the air. Deveril still held her hand and she loathed to remove it. The warmth of his fingers on hers was curiously pleasing. The way his side brushed hers with every sway of the coach heightened her awareness of him. Her breathing quickened. She felt hot then cold by turns. Beside her, she could feel the tension drawing Deveril's body taut as a bow string.

At last the carriage came to a halt. Deveril walked with her up the stairs and stopped before her door. Turning to face him, she searched his face. The light of the hall candles cast shadows over the rugged planes, keeping secrets she desperately needed to know. His eyes gleamed with blue fire as he stood looking down at her.

"I am done with this." His head lifted for an instant so that his gaze slipped over the closed door then back to her face. "We are married."

At another time Byrony would have fought the way he spoke with all her power. Yet this night, the husky throb in his deep voice told a different story than the words themselves. He wanted her, really wanted her. It was in the blaze of his eyes, and in the way his hands held hers so tightly.

Her lips beckoned, parted for his kiss. The taste of her was sweet on his tongue, yet tart for she was no gentle miss. When she gave she also took, took more than any woman he had ever known. Experienced she still was not. But the fire in her made up for all the expertise she lacked. Her hands on his chest kneaded like a cat, flexing through his shirt so that he was aware of every stroke of her nails. He groaned, lifting his head.

"Send Tillie to bed."

Byrony opened passion-glazed eyes. "Give me three minutes," she whispered.

Deveril released her with marked reluctance. "Only three."

Byrony slipped through the door. Tillie was waiting in her customary place in a chair beside the bed. She rose at Byrony's entrance. "You are home early."

"Help me," Byrony commanded, already tugging at her gown.

Puzzled at the haste, Tillie nonetheless rushed to her side and began undoing the delicate creation. "Is something wrong?"

"Something is right, I think," Byrony corrected, her voice muffled by the soft fabric as Tillie drew the dress over her head. Byrony emerged, disheveled but determined. "Get these pins out of my hair and be quick."

"Like that, is it?" Tillie mumbled, trying not to grin.

Byrony shot her a look, before smiling herself. She had to admit she did look a bit odd rushing about. "Wait until you get married," she muttered, defending herself.

Tillie giggled and hopped to with a will. "Just so's I find a man to have me," she replied.

With thirty seconds to spare the two women had Byrony ready. Tillie whisked herself from the room a bare instant before Deveril walked in. Byrony was breathing rapidly from her exertions as she stared at him across the room. The chamber was lit by only two sconces, one on each side of the bed and by the fire that burned in the hearth. The soft lighting flickered with the opening of the door. Deveril stood on the threshold drinking in the sight of Byrony as she waited for him before the fireplace.

With the illumination behind her she might as well have been naked. Every ripe curve and contour was outlined for his delectation. Rosy nipples rippled in erotic abandon beneath the fine silk of her nightgown. The dusky hair at the apex of her thighs was made even more dark by the shadowed lighting.

Whatever control he had left deserted him at the picture she made. Deveril was across the room in four strides, his arms molding her to him.

"God!" he groaned, kissing her hard.

Byrony flowed against his strength, absorbing and demanding at the same time. His roughness did not frighten her for she knew instinctively it was only a product of the need driving her to the edge of madness. When his arms held her so tightly she could scarcely breathe, she simply pulled him closer. When he lifted her in his arms, his lips still locked with hers, she looped her hands around his neck and bound him to her all the more. The softness of the bed beneath her back made no impression, for it was his hardness pressing into her belly that held all her attention.

She ached to feel him within her once more. Her fingers closed on the shaft that had stroked her with such delight in the past. To know him again, to feel him deep inside drove her to explore the rigid flesh. His groan was lost in her mouth as his body jerked in pleasure at her touch. Her gown melted away beneath his own questing fingers.

Lifting his head, he had to see her eyes, to know she truly wanted him and it was not just the passion he could arouse in her that made her accept him into her bed.

Deveril caught her face in his hands. "Say my name, Byrony. My name."

She would give him anything he wanted to have him douse the flames licking at her body. "Deveril," she whispered, pulling his head down to hers. She took his mouth in a rush. She wanted no more words, just sensation.

It was all Deveril needed, for he was a kindled torch. He made his entrance, pushing his hard muscle between her thighs in an agony of need. He tried to be gentle but she would not have it so. She thrust toward him, completing the union. She was eager, hot, and wild. Her fingers raked his back but he felt no pain, only an exhilarating freedom in her abandon. She matched him stroke for stroke. She fit his pulsing body like a glove of fire. Together, they rode toward the summit of fulfillment. In the last second, Byrony pushed him hard over onto his back. The position startled them both. The rhythm broke then reformed in a new more complex pattern. Throwing back her head, Byrony gave herself but to the passion his hands and lips created as he fondled her breasts. Never had she known such pleasure as she thrust against him again and again. Suddenly it was too much. She tried to draw back. His hands held her firm as he lifted her hips to receive one final exploding thrust. Her cry was a woman's call of deep satisfaction. His answering shout a man's triumph. Two had come to join as one.

Sleep came as swiftly as desire, catching them both still tangled in each other's arms. Night crept slowly into day before Deveril stirred. His arms tightened on the soft body cuddled against his side as he opened his eyes. Byrony lay half on top of him, her hands holding him even in slumber. He wanted to wake her, to assure himself the night before was no dream. His hand lifted to touch her cheek then he stopped. He could not bear it if she regretted giving so freely to him. Did she but know it, she had told him more in that generosity of her body and the demand of her passion than all the words she had spoken or not given voice to.

No honor on earth compelled a man or a woman to such lengths. No duty made her take more than he had known he had to give. No marriage lines made her silver eyes gleam like polished metal as she rode him like a wild stallion who had never known a bit or saddle.

So he stayed his hand and resolved to bide his time. Easing away from her warmth, he slipped from the bed. Today was theirs. He meant to do his best to see that Byrony enjoyed herself. She had to see him as something more than a husband. And he? He wanted to know what she thought.

What went on behind those beautiful eyes. What kind of woman had a man's logical mind and the seductive wiles of an enchantress. In short he meant to become acquainted with his wife, with Byrony.

Byrony awoke at the first touch of cool air against her skin. All night she had been warm and now she was cold. Frowning before she even opened her eyes, she felt his absence. Her hand moved on the rumpled sheets, closing over empty space. Once more he had left her alone. A strange fragrance tickled her nose as she buried it in the pillow. More than Deveril's scent lingered in the silk. A rose. Her lashes lifted and she found herself staring at the crimson petals of a half-opened bud. For a long moment she didn't move as warmth flowed into her body. Warmth from within, not from the feel of Deveril pressed against her in sleep.

A smile touched her lips as she lifted her hand to lightly stroke the red velvet rose. "The devil," she whispered. No one listening could have been certain whether the name was a curse or an endearment.

Byrony glanced at her reflection one last time. The new habit was all she could wish for. Black velvet, snow white shirt beneath, simple lines that clung to every curve. She had never looked better and she knew it. She was gladder than ever that she had convinced Deveril to allow them to ride out to the country instead of drive. This way it would truly be just the two of them. No servants, nothing but time to escape the confines of the city and explore each other and the countryside.

A smile curved her lips as she left her room. Deveril was waiting for her when she reached the bottom of the stairs. She wanted to reach out to touch him but did not. The servants were there.

Taking her hand, Deveril slipped it into the crook of his arm. He walked her to the horse then threw her up into the saddle himself. This day she would be his alone. No man would touch her but himself. The journey out of the city was broken by only snatches of conversation. Byrony for her part was content to follow in Deveril's wake. He knew the area far better than she. Besides it gave her time to study her husband away from the trappings of his position. He sat his horse with enviable grace, moving easily with the animal. He neither betrayed impatience when they were delayed nor pushed hard when the road was clear. Instead he set an even pace that took them out of the city with deceptive speed.

Finally they reached a road that was light of traffic, where they could ride abreast. Byrony brought her mare up beside his stallion. "Are you enjoying yourself?" Deveril asked, turning to her with a smile.

Byrony nodded. "How far are we going?"

"Maybe an hour or more. There is a place I know not far from a pleasant inn. I think you will like it."

And like it she did. The place was a small pond complete with a family of ducks. Willows dripped slender tendrils over the water from their places on the gently rolling bank. Deveril had spread a blanket beneath the oldest of the trees, a huge willow with branches that formed a lacy green canopy over them. The air was heavy with the scent of flowers and sweet grass. Byrony lay back on the blanket, watching the clouds float by between the branches overhead.

Deveril looked at her, his eyes tracing the slender shape of her through the velvet habit. Leaning down, he braced an elbow on one side of her. Her eyes swung to his, trapped by the compelling sapphire gaze.

"What happened in the hall?" he asked quietly.

Byrony blinked, caught unaware by his question. "Nothing," she replied too quickly.

Deveril frowned. "Can you not trust me?" The words escaped without thought. He had not meant to challenge her. He wanted her compliance today, gentleness. They had never had that and he suddenly knew he needed it as he never had before.

"I am trying," Byrony said slowly. "It is difficult to trust someone you do not truly know."

"I trust you." He touched her cheek lightly, his fingers tracing the bones of her face. "I heard you and Bella last night."

Byrony stared at him, again lost in the conversation. "What about Bella?"

"You spoke of a gaming house. At first I thought to forbid you to go. It was clear you wanted to. I could see it in your face." His hand slipped to her throat, where the pulse beat steadily beneath his touch. "But I changed my mind. Suddenly I wondered how I would feel if you told me what to do and then expected me to obey you. I would hate it and fight you."

Astounded, Byrony could only listen in silence.

"You are a woman of rare good sense and understanding. You have a courage I admire and an honor I have never known. It is not in you to do something foolhardy like risking your reputation with an ill-conceived display of skill at the tables. Too many people would question your luck or skill. Women of your station play for amusement, winning infrequently. You would win as often as you chose, I suspect. Therefore you would not play."

Byrony could not doubt his sincerity or the truth of his words. She had been a fool. She should have known better. Her need for diversion never should have overpowered her good sense but it had. And she compounded her stupidity by trying to keep her activities a secret from Deveril and Charles. And why? Because of Bella and a need to prove to Deveril he could not rule her. She had needed to feel as if she were in control of her life once more. All she had really done was place herself in jeopardy.

She had to tell him. She opened her lips to do just that. Deveril took it as invitation. His head lowered, his lips brushing hers with a tenderness he had never shown her. The gentle touch drove every thought from Byrony's mind. The unexpectedness of the delicate way his hands traced over her body was deeply seductive. Before she could gather her wits, her body was responding, arching against his caresses with leashed eagerness. She would tell him later, she promised herself just before she slipped completely under his spell.

Chapter Nineteen

Byrony lay against Deveril's side, content to be silent. Their world was equally soundless, here beneath the concealing branches of the willow. Sun filtered through the limbs, casting soft shadows on their nakedness. She and Deveril could have been Adam and Eve alone in the garden for the first time.

Deveril stroked her hair, enjoying the feel of her against him. One day, he promised himself, he would tell her. One day when she looked at him and did not have that wary, careful look in her extraordinary eyes. He studied her head as it rested on his chest. Her eyes were open, he realized. She had been so quiet that he thought she slept.

"I have a confession to make," Byrony murmured finally, gathering her nerve. She could not forget what Deveril had said about the gaming houses. She had to tell him despite her promise to Bella. For once her honor must bend, for she had given her word to two but one had greater claim.

Deveril's hand paused and then continued its soothing motion. "You have?" he prompted when she made no effort to elaborate.

"Bella and I were not just talking about the gaming establishment. We had already been there. Twice." Byrony lifted her head to look him in the eye. She would not have him think she did not have the courage to face him directly. "Corinne saw us there as well."

Deveril frowned as he stared back at her.

"I knew you would not like it," Byrony hurried to explain. "Charles has made it clear how careful I should be lest someone find out about my past." Byrony hesitated then decided to make a clean breast of the whole. "I could not tolerate the boredom. I knew even as I did it that I should not. That I was taking an unnecessary risk with all our reputations. I knew, too, that I could not hope to keep my activities a secret from either of you."

Byrony waited, not knowing what to expect. Deveril was capable of understanding but he was equally capable of feeling just as Charles did. And with justification since he had ceased to cut a dash through Society and now trod the straight and narrow like a judge.

"I deserve your censure. I knew how important your name was to you in the end. You married me to retrieve it."

Deveril froze for one long moment. Still she did not see what stood before her face. Pain shot through him at the knowledge. Sitting up, he eased her away from him.

"I think it is time we returned home."

"Now?" Byrony blinked in surprise, searching his expression for a clue to his intentions. She found nothing. No anger. No disappointment. Nothing. Uneasy at the blank face he gave her, she asked, "Why?" Something was wrong, terribly wrong.

Deveril turned away from her to pull on his shirt. "It grows late and we have an engagement tonight."

Byrony stared at his back, caught by the strange tone in his voice. "Are you angry with me?" she asked.

"No."

Still he did not turn his head to look at her. "You must be, else you would face me." The challenge slipped out without thought.

Deveril swung around. "Why must I be angry? Why do

you expect it? Do you think I could not understand your need to kick at the traces? Do you think me so inhuman not to know how the London cage stifles?"

Now she saw emotion, hot fiery feelings spilling past control. "But I put us all in jeopardy."

Deveril stood up, glaring down at her as though he hated her. "Did it not occur to you that there is very little a duke or any member of his family can do that will ostracize him from Society. Witness my mother. She has been doing her possible for years and has not succeeded." Turning away he gathered the rest of his clothes and snatched them on.

Deep in thought Byrony helped Deveril collect their things before they mounted up for the ride back to Town. The day had begun so well, with both of them in such accord. Now there was only silence between them. She glanced at Deveril. The lines on his face seemed deeper than they had that morning. He looked weary beyond measure. He still sat straight in the saddle but he appeared to have withdrawn from her and his surroundings. The impression stayed with her even as they reached Town and Deveril guided them through the crowded streets.

She was glad to see the townhouse appear out of the late afternoon fading light. She needed time to think, time to discover an answer out of the feelings tugging at her. The sight of two carriages, the coachman walking the horses in the street before their door, made her draw rein. The last thing she wanted was visitors.

"What the devil!" Deveril swore as he, too, identified the equipage. His godfather and his mother. Of all the times. He was not in the mood for either of them.

Byrony seconded his opinion if only in her mind. They dismounted without speaking and started up the stairs. The door swung open before they got a third of the way up. Smithington hurried out, looking anything but dignified. His hair stood on end, his eyes were nearly wild.

"I could not stop either of them, your grace. I could not."

He wrung his hands, clearly too distraught to make sense.

Deveril mounted the steps in a stalking stride. "Where are they?" he demanded.

Byrony hurried after him. The raised voices filling the hall answered Deveril's question before Smithington could.

"Get these footmen out of here," Deveril ordered. "Take everyone to the kitchen until I settle this." He leveled a glare at Smithington that made the older man blanch. "And warn them all if I hear one word . . . *one* . . . about this from anyone outside this house I shall personally see that the culprit never works anywhere again. Do I make myself clear?"

Smithington's head bobbed as he swallowed hard. "Of course, your grace. It shall be as you say." Hurriedly, he signaled to the men on duty to follow him.

Deveril glanced at Byrony. "You need not get involved in this."

"I am coming with you," Byrony said, determined to be present. She had a feeling that whatever had brought Charles and Corinne to Deveril's home had to do with her.

"Can you not trust me in this either?" Deveril asked bitterly. "I am your husband."

"It is not a question of trust," Byrony began, only to find she was talking to Deveril's back. Hurrying to catch up before he went into the salon without her, she tried to stop him long enough to explain.

Deveril shook off her hand. He was disgusted with himself. He should not have lost his temper with her. "Come, let us get over this ground as soon as may be before the whole of London hears them."

Now that they were within a few feet of the closed salon door, Byrony could make out some of the words Charles and Corinne were hurling at each other. Her name figured largely in the argument.

"And you are a meddling witch with nothing better to do than ruin people. You cannot tolerate anyone else being happy. I watched you destroy Deveril's father and I saw you try to ruin him. But I beat you, you harridan." Charles' face was mottled with rage as he glared at the dowager. "How dare you bribe my servants."

Corinne laughed, a high sound that seemed to split the thick air with a knife-like precision. "I found out about that precious niece of yours. And soon all of London and my son will know how they have been hoodwinked by the pompous Lord Ravensly."

Deveril slammed the door with a thud that brought both combatants' heads around with a snap. "I already know, mother dear," he drawled, taking a step toward her.

Byrony watched them all, sick to her soul to know that she had brought them to this with one ill-conceived start.

"I knew what Byrony was and had been before I married her. To my cost I did not value her as she deserved, and fool that I am, I left her in Charles' hands. He loved her but he did not understand her. So he tried to make her fit this damnable mold we all live in called Society.

Byrony could not have moved if her life depended on it. Warmth filled her as she watched him face her relatives. Love such as she had never known flooded her being. No one—not family, not Charles—had ever defended her. No one had stood for her when she needed help.

"I should have been by her side instead of nursing my pride like a fool. I have no more use for this hypocrisy than she does. Yet I left her to fend for herself, left her prey to all the slurs and insults my behavior drew down on her head."

Corinne pulled herself together with effort. She was losing the only lever she had to get the money she needed. "That's all very fine but what do you suppose those narrow-minded people will do when they find out what she is. Your sneers won't protect her or yourself from them."

Deveril's hands clenched. "No one will find out."

"I shall see that they do," Corinne said.

"Damn you, woman," Charles burst out.

Deveril silenced him with a sharp wave of his hand. "That you will not do." He stalked to his desk and snatched open a drawer to withdraw a bundle of papers. "I have half your markers. Some of these are years old. Some are more recent." He pinned his mother with a look. "At a guess, I would say you are one step ahead of imprisonment. It is your choice."

Corinne stared at the notes as if hypnotized. "The bargain," she whispered hoarsely.

Deveril smiled and it wasn't a pleasant gesture. Retribution had come at last. For one sweet moment, he savored the thought of the power he held. Corinne had destroyed so many, himself, until Byrony, among the victims. Now he could even the scales.

"Don't!" Byrony commanded, suddenly realizing what Deveril intended to do. Moving forward without thought to the others, she grasped the hand that held Corinne's future. "To do what you are planning makes you no better than she is."

Deveril stared at her, searching her face. "She would destroy you without a qualm."

"It does not matter. It never has, not to me."

"You thought it did to me," he could not help but point out.

"I know and I am sorry."

"Very touching," Corinne snarled. "The bargain. What do I have to do?"

Deveril did not take his eyes from Byrony's face as he spoke. "I will pay these and the rest. Your allowance will stay as it is but you will leave this country and never return." Now he did lift his head to give her a long look. "I have more power than my father ever had. I have been on both sides of Society. If you set foot in England, if you say one word about Byrony, I will know. And not even she will save you from me. I give you my word on that."

Corinne tried to hold his gaze and failed. She was beaten.

She knew it. "I hate you," she hissed as she headed for the door. "She will never make you happy."

Deveril said nothing as he slipped his arm around Byrony's waist and drew her to his side. "You have three days. I advise you to use them well." His only answer was the door slamming sharply behind Corinne as she left.

"Good show," Charles muttered, coming to their side. "Damnable woman." He fixed Byrony with a glare. "Now, young lady, what could you have been thinking about? When I found out that Corinne had bribed my coachman to betray where and when you had arrived, I knew there had to be a reason for her to suspect something was amiss. I did not expect to hear that you had been gambling and were not sharp enough to at least pretend to lose once in a while. Where were your wits? If you must take chances, at least hedge your wagers."

"Are you done?" Deveril said without giving Byrony a chance to answer the charges.

Charles glanced at him, startled at the tone he had never heard Deveril use with him. "You cannot mean to condone what she did?" His brows rose in astonishment.

Deveril matched his look with one of his own. "I mean to tell you nothing. Byrony is my wife and it is my right to comment on her behavior. You forfeited yours when you gave her in marriage."

Charles studied first one then the other. "Do you wish it this way?" he asked of Byrony.

Byrony stared back at him, seeing the love he had for her in his faded eyes. "I do."

Charles was silent for a moment then he started to grin. "Then my plan succeeded after all," he murmured, his anger forgotten. "I wish Kate could see this." He all but rubbed his hands together. He had almost given up hope his matchmaking would take.

Deveril's lips twitched as Byrony's eyes widened. "My godfather and Kate were ever matchmakers in my youth," he explained.

"You mean he planned this, really planned this? Did you know?"

"I suspected. As you would have if you had known more about my world. There were many families who would have favored my suit just for a portion of my money," he said, some of his old cynicism coming back. "As a redeemer of reputations, you are not the safest wager in Town, my love."

Indignant at what both of the men in her life had put her through, Byrony started to draw away. Then the last of Deveril's words sank in. "Am I your love?"

Deveril pulled her close, dropping the bundle of notes he still held without a thought. "My love. The one and only woman in the world who could match me. No other could hold me at bay with a pistol aimed at a very important part of my anatomy on my wedding night. No other woman I know could take a shot in the arm like a man and still have the courage to trust herself to a stranger to see her safely free." At the word *trust*, his face clouded. Neither of them noticed Charles slipping quietly from the room. "I had your trust then. If I had not left you that morning . . ."

Byrony covered his lips with her finger before he could finish. "I no longer remember that morning," she whispered softly, the bitterness and anger sliding away as though it had never been. "All I remember is waking up last night and finding a rose on my pillow. A rose put there by the man I love."

Deveril stared at her with eyes that displayed all the love he held for her. For the first time in his life he did not try to conceal his feelings.

"I trust you with my life, my husband."

"Enough to leave this existence behind?" he asked, seeing the answer in her eyes. "I have a need to see the world with you at my side. I want to ride in the desert and race the wind with you."

"Float down the Nile on a barge."

"See the Americas and maybe hunt buffalo with the Indians."

"See Venice and St. Petersburg."

Deveril laughed aloud at the sheer joy of having a mate who understood. A mate who would share his life, not just tolerate it. But most of all having a woman who had the courage to love the devil in a man.

GOTHICS A LA MOOR—FROM ZEBRA

ISLAND OF LOST RUBIES
by Patricia Werner (2603, $3.95)
Heartbroken by her father's death and the loss of her great love, Eileen returns to her island home to claim her inheritance. But eerie things begin happening the minute she steps off the boat, and it isn't long before Eileen realizes that there's no escape from *THE ISLAND OF LOST RUBIES.*

DARK CRIES OF GRAY OAKS
by Lee Karr (2736, $3.95)
When orphaned Brianna Anderson was offered a job as companion to the mentally ill seventeen-year-old girl, Cassie, she was grateful for the non-troublesome employment. Soon she began to wonder why the girl's family insisted that Cassie be given hydro-electrical therapy and increased doses of laudanum. What was the shocking secret that Cassie held in her dark tormented mind? And was she herself in danger?

CRYSTAL SHADOWS
by Michele Y. Thomas (2819, $3.95)
When Teresa Hawthorne accepted a post as tutor to the wealthy Curtis family, she didn't believe the scandal surrounding them would be any concern of hers. However, it soon began to seem as if someone was trying to ruin the Curtises and Theresa was becoming the unwitting target of a deadly conspiracy . . .

CASTLE OF CRUSHED SHAMROCKS
by Lee Karr (2843, $3.95)
Penniless and alone, eighteen-year-old Aileen O'Conner traveled to the coast of Ireland to be recognized as daughter and heir to Lord Edwin Lynhurst. Upon her arrival, she was horrified to find her long lost father had been murdered. And slowly, the extent of the danger dawned upon her: her father's killer was still at large. And her name was next on the list.

BRIDE OF HATFIELD CASTLE
by Beverly G. Warren (2517, $3.95)
Left a widow on her wedding night and the sole inheritor of Hatfield's fortune, Eden Lane was convinced that someone wanted her out of the castle, preferably dead. Her failing health, the whispering voices of death, and the phantoms who roamed the keep were driving her mad. And although she came to the castle as a bride, she needed to discover who was trying to kill her, or leave as a corpse!

Available wherever paperbacks are sold, or order direct from the Publisher. Send cover price plus 50¢ per copy for mailing and handling to Zebra Books, Dept. 3279, 475 Park Avenue South, New York, N.Y. 10016. Residents of New York, New Jersey and Pennsylvania must include sales tax. DO NOT SEND CASH.